# Almost Worthy

## CAT MORGAN

ISBN: 978-1-0696480-0-6

To Devin, for all your endless love and support.

# Content Warning

This story contains sexually explicit content, strong language, and topics that may be sensitive to some readers.

# *Prologue*

## Six Months Earlier - Los Angeles

Connor Fitzgerald lifted the glass to his lips just as someone bumped into him from behind. Liquid flew out of the glass, and Connor moved his leg, narrowly saving his dress pants from the liquid as it sploshed onto the floor.

"Ah! *Désolé! 'Scuse-moi.*" Abel, the local town veterinarian and handyman, grabbed on to the back of Connor's chair. His cheeks were red. As he looked at Connor, recognition spread across his face, and he broke out into a wide, familiar smile. "Connor! *Ça va?*"

"Yes, I'm good," Connor smiled easily, reaching out a hand to steady the older man, who swayed a little bit on his feet.

"Abel! What are you doing over there? Come back!" yelled Arielle from the diner, pulling Abel back onto the dance floor. She noticed Connor sitting at the table, her blue eyes widening with excitement. "Connor, come join us!"

Before Connor could respond, the DJ's voice boomed through the speakers. "Ladies and gentlemen, it's time for...the cha-cha slide!"

"Yes, yes, come dance with us!" cried Abel, still in his native French, unable to make the switch back to English in his current state of inebriation. "We must dance the cha-cha!"

Connor got up from the table, giving them both a quick smile. "I think I need another drink first."

"Oh, come on now!" said Arielle with an exaggerated frown, not buying his excuse for a minute, but then the song started to play, and someone pulled her arm.

Connor took advantage of the opportunity, and he slipped away towards the bar, where his mother and brother were talking, both of them holding glasses of champagne, mirrored expressions of amusement on their faces. While he and his brother were both half-Asian through their Taiwanese mother, Michael had always looked a little more like their French Canadian father, Sebastien. It was only then, watching them sipping champagne in identical movements, that he realized how much Michael resembled their mother.

"Oh, hey," said Michael, noticing Connor and grinning. "What, no cha-cha slide for you?"

Connor rolled his eyes at his brother, then turned to the bartender. "Can I get a double espresso, please?"

"You've got it." The bartender moved toward the large espresso machine that had been largely untouched for the evening.

"This late? How are you going to sleep tonight?" His mother frowned at him, the gold of her pearl earrings shimmering in the ballroom's light.

"I have a high tolerance," smiled Connor.

Her frown melted into a wistful smile as she grabbed onto his arm. "Are you having fun?"

"Of course. I should be asking you that. It's your night."

"Oh, I'm having a great time," Cecelia Lin smiled, looking quite pleased as she surveyed the ballroom at the strange assortment of characters she had dragged halfway across the world for this event.

Connor suspected that his mother had been a little ashamed when she'd gotten remarried so quickly after her divorce twenty years ago. She had given up a prestigious career as a translator for the CEO of a massive media conglomerate in East Asia to move to Sebastien's sleepy little hometown of Fleurmont, Quebec.

When her marriage to Sebastien had imploded just a few years later, she had gotten remarried to another Fleurmont man - Owen Robitaille, Connor's stepfather. Now, twenty years later, she was finally celebrating their marriage in a way that was fitting for Cecelia Lin - at the Sphinx Hotel in Los Angeles, where Cecelia and Owen had first met.

The setting was perfect, and so was the guest list. Cecelia had invited everyone from her past life and her current life. The result was a handful of prim ladies from Taiwan and Singapore looking slightly out of place next to the warm, boisterous townspeople of Fleurmont.

Connor looked at the table closest to them, where a group of middle-aged Asian women decked out in perfume and expensive jewelry were looking out at the dance floor, appearing a little shell-shocked by the performance they were seeing by the townspeople of Fleurmont.

Half the town had flown to Los Angeles for the wedding anniversary, and it was the townspeople who had definitively conquered both the open bar and the dance floor.

Owen emerged from the dance floor, his blue eyes twinkling as the song ended, shooting Connor a massive grin before taking his wife's hands.

"Will you dance with me?"

"I would love to," she beamed, setting down her glass of champagne. Giving her boys a final wave, she let Owen lead her onto the dance floor.

Connor and Michael watched them dance in silence for a few minutes.

"They look happy, don't they?" said Michael.

"Yeah, they look happy," Connor agreed.

"Twenty years," said Michael, shaking his head. "I can't imagine being committed to anyone for that long."

"Can you imagine being committed to anyone at all?" Connor snorted.

Michael was a notorious ladies' man. He'd had girls throwing themselves at him since high school, and nothing had changed now that he was thirty-one and had found career success in Toronto.

"I guess not," grinned Michael, and he looked away towards a woman in a red dress that Connor didn't recognize, who had been eyeing Michael from the next table over.

Michael finished his champagne.

"See you later," he said, and walked over to the woman in the red dress.

Connor watched Michael lead her to the dance floor. Michael whispered something in her ear, and the woman let out a laugh.

Next to them, Cecelia and Owen were still dancing. Cecelia smiled, putting her arms around Owen's neck, and they swayed gently to the beat of the music. Connor smiled.

He took his coffee and stepped out onto the outdoor terrace connected to the ballroom. It was only six in the evening, and the sun was still high in the sky. The ballroom was on the fifth floor of the hotel, and from the outdoor terrace, he had a clear view of the set of pools on the third floor of the hotel. Seagulls flew overhead, their cries muffled by the sounds of the waves in the ocean.

Suddenly, a shriek of laughter came from below, and Connor looked down to see a group of young women standing on a pool deck. This wouldn't have been unusual, except all four of them were dressed in extravagant, floor length dresses. They were young, maybe in their early twenties, and one woman clearly stood out. She was wearing a hot pink dress that was so bright you couldn't miss her from a mile away.

Even two floors away, Connor noticed how blue her eyes were, how they were an exact match for the colour of the ocean. She was beautiful.

Without warning, she shoved the woman closest to her into the pool. The woman shrieked, and the other women around them gasped.

"What do you think you're doing?" one of them yelled.

"Oh, my God."

"Don't you dare talk to my friend like that!" the woman in the pink dress yelled as her friend resurfaced from the water, her green dress floating around like seaweed in the pool.

"What the *fuck*," shouted the woman in the pool, and she lunged up, grabbing the woman in the pink dress from her ankles and dragging her into the pool with her.

Subconsciously, Connor took a step back as she fell in. The woman's hot pink dress rippled in waves around her in the wind before she hit the water. It looked like hot pink smoke had exploded in the air before turning into liquid ink in the pool. It was mesmerizing, like a car crash you couldn't quite look away from.

An older woman rushed out onto the deck of the pool. "What is going on out here?"

"Stassi! Ava! What on earth are you doing?" the older woman continued.

"This psycho pushed me in!" said the woman in the green dress, climbing out of the pool water.

"Watch who you call a psycho, bitch," said the woman in the pink dress. She was still treading water in the pool, hot pink waves moving around her like the tentacles of an octopus.

"Stassi!" the older woman reprimanded. "You are disturbing the peace –"

The older woman looked up suddenly, seeing Connor. She looked horrified at having an audience.

The woman in the hot pink dress - Stassi - turned her head to look up at Connor. Their eyes met. Cerulean blue eyes met his, sharp and unapologetic.

Whoever this woman was, Connor didn't want to mess with her.

# CHAPTER ONE

## *Stassi*

### TAIPEI

The taxi stopped at the intersection. The cab driver, an older man who looked to be in his late sixties, glanced at the narrow streets and then back at me. In the rearview mirror, his brown mala beads swung against his reflection.

"Are you sure this is where you want to go?" he asked me skeptically, no doubt wondering what I was doing on a narrow little street at seven in the morning in Taipei.

"I'm sure," I said, glancing at the taximeter before taking out my purse.

I desperately needed coffee, and if memory served right, this was the best place to get it.

I paid the cab driver, thanked him, and got out of the cab. Dragging my suitcase behind me, I let the smell of humidity and concrete fill my nostrils. I stifled a yawn, stepping into the narrow street.

Concrete buildings surrounded me on either side. It was early enough in the morning that some of the small shopfronts were just rolling up their garage-style shutters. One street-side breakfast shop already had a line of customers. The griddles and steamers of the shop sat close to the open street, allowing the smell of fried eggs and scallion pancakes to waft deliciously down the street. I would have to go back later. But first, coffee.

Some locals lined up at the breakfast shops turned to look at me as I passed. I liked to think they were looking at me because of my fabulous new Jimmy Choos, but it was probably the long, blonde hair that marked me as an outsider.

Finally, I found the black and white coffee shop sign I was looking for, tucked between a small hair salon and a breakfast shop that served sticky rice rolls with meat floss and pickled vegetables.

My stomach growled just as my eyes caught the sign on the door of the coffee shop - closed.

"No!" I cried, letting go of my suitcase.

Staring at the 'closed' sign, I bit my lip, trying to think. I hadn't thought of a backup plan. Should I just eat first? The taste of smooth, dark, nutty black coffee crossed my mind, pushing the need for food to the side.

No, I needed coffee.

I grabbed the handle of my suitcase, marching off to go to the adjacent street. It was Taipei. There was going to be a coffee shop open, even if they probably didn't have that same delicious hazelnut coffee with vanilla whipped cream that I'd been craving since -

My phone rang, and I pulled it out of my pocket to see Jenna's name calling me through our messaging app.

"Hey."

"Will you come to alpaca yoga with me?" asked Jenna by way of greeting.

"What is alpaca yoga?"

Stepping onto the adjacent street, I kept my eyes peeled for a coffee shop. This street differed from the first. The buildings were slightly taller, and the gates and metal doors at the first floor of the buildings marked it as a residential street.

There was an interesting mix of textures on this street. Though the buildings were old, featuring external air conditioning units and yellowing white tiles, someone had clearly added the gates on the first floor of some buildings later. Black metal formed the gates, and deep brown wood with decorative horizontal bars sat atop the metal frame, adding architectural charm to the street. Some residents had added little butterfly palms in concrete pots next to their doors, and I couldn't help but think about how much it reminded me of the Japanese-style teahouse I'd once tried to design in college.

"It's like a regular yoga class, except you're surrounded by adorable alpacas!" Jenna's enthusiastic voice pulled me out of my thoughts about buildings.

Ignoring the ache in my chest whenever I thought about architecture, I tried to focus on my erratic friend instead.

Jenna was a weird workout fanatic. She's done everything from fiesta-themed white water rafting, trampoline tango, to something called porcupine pilates. No joke. She loved any activity that was even just a little unconventional.

"They have that in L.A.?" I tried to imagine alpacas in a Beverly Hills yoga studio.

"Yes! Well, I found a farm just outside of L.A. that hosts alpaca yoga sessions."

I wrinkled my nose at the thought of a farm. With farm animals. "No offence, but I am not a farm person."

"You loved the vineyard we went to in France!" said Jenna.

"That's because vineyards equal wine tours. I like wine. I don't like stinky animals," I said, stopping at the end of the street next to a row of parked mopeds so that I could focus on Jenna.

Still no coffee in sight.

Propping my suitcase up, I leaned against a light blue moped. Hmm. Pretty comfortable.

"Come on, Stassi, please? Just once! If you hate it, we don't have to go again."

What the hell. "Okay, fine. Just once."

"Yes! Okay, I'll book the tickets for us. Trust me, it'll be so much fun," she said, her voice brimming with excitement.

I smiled, sighing, but as I did so, I leaned too hard on the moped, and it fell over.

I yelped, jumping up to avoid falling. The moped fell onto the one next to it...which caused the next one to fall over, and then the next one. The mopeds were now all slanted awkwardly on the ground, resembling a messy pile of knocked-over dominos.

"What's going on?"

"Uh, I gotta go," I said quickly, my cheeks flushing, speed walking away from the scene of the crime. My suitcase clattered loudly against the asphalt of the street.

"Where are you?"

"In Taipei."

"As in, *Taiwan?*" said Jenna, surprised. "I thought you were back in L.A. Aren't we flying out together on Saturday?"

"Yes, we totally are. I'm just picking up my dress for the Pink Party."

"Ooh, can't wait to see it. Send pics."

The Pink Party was a party that Jenna's cousin, a jewelry heiress, hosted every year. Jenna's cousin hosted the party at a different location every year. Last year, it was in Santorini. The year before, it had been in Gallipoli. This year, Ibiza. I loved that it was always in Europe. There was just something different about drinking in Europe.

My dress this year was a gorgeous pink dress with three-dimensional flowers sewn all over it. The designer was an up-and-coming Taiwanese dress designer whose work I'd seen for the first time at a fashion show in Paris.

After hanging up the phone with Jenna, I finally reached one of the larger intersections. There was a small urban park with tall, thick trees shooting up from each corner, and straight ahead of me, across the concrete path of the park, I saw the lit-up logo of a familiar coffee chain, the promise of caffeine finally in sight. People in work suits exited the coffee shop in a hurry, carrying paper cups in one hand.

With a sigh of relief, I made my way towards the coffee shop.

# Chapter Two

## *Connor*

### Taipei

My eyes wandered back to the building again. Taipei 101 was the first building that had inspired my interest in architecture and engineering. Having spent most of my life in a snowy little town where the tallest building was three storeys tall, it always felt surreal to be in such close proximity. Each rhythmic facet of the building shimmered in the afternoon sun, looking more blue than green today.

"This is amazing," said Dustin, tears forming in his eyes from shoving food that was still too hot into his mouth. "What is this called again?"

He tapped the clay pot between us as he scooped more rice into his bowl with one hand. When he was done, he used one hand to wipe away the tears still running down his nose.

"*San Bei Ji,*" I said in Mandarin.

"Three Cup Chicken?" Dustin translated, and I nodded.

"So, are you still enjoying New York?" I reached for the stinky tofu with my chopsticks, dipping it into chili sauce. The best stinky tofu was always at the night markets, but this restaurant did it well, too.

Dustin shrugged. "I enjoy living in Brooklyn. Work can be a bit of a grind, though."

"I thought you really liked your firm," I said, surprised.

Dustin and I had met in Los Angeles when we were both fresh out of college and junior designers at the same architecture firm. He had specifically moved out to New York to work at the boutique firm he was now at designing luxury homes.

Dustin brushed his slightly too-long hair out of his eyes. "Yeah, sure. When the projects are interesting. Lately, I've just been doing a bunch of kitchen re-tiles."

"Trade with me. Every project I've been on over the last six months has had building code issues. I've spent half of my time reading manuals." Saying this out loud made my stomach twist.

"This coming from *Singapore Today*'s Connor Fitzgerald?" Dustin's voice was teasing, almost mocking, and if it were anyone else, he'd have sounded like a dick, but I knew he meant well.

A year ago, I designed an urban city park in Singapore. The playground was designed to look like two dragons swimming in the ocean, and it had gotten enough attention that it had landed me a feature in *Singapore Today*. Now, I was worried I'd somehow peaked at twenty-eight.

"No, but seriously, I thought you were job hunting. Weren't you interviewing at the Salvati Group?" asked Dustin.

I put down my chopsticks. "Yeah, for almost a month now. Apparently, everyone who works there needs to interview with the whole fucking company."

I enjoyed being interviewed about as much as I enjoyed reading building code manuals. Actually, I preferred reading building code manuals. Having to talk to people and sell myself repeatedly was not something I enjoyed or was particularly good at.

Dustin winced. "Sorry, dude, I didn't mean to stress you out."

"No, it's all good. I actually have a final interview next week." I forced myself to loosen my posture, hating how much I cared about a fucking interview.

"No way. You got a final interview for the Head Architect position with the Salvati Group?" Dustin's eyes were wide.

I nodded, and my face twitched into a smile at the look on Dustin's face.

"Shit. That's fucking nuts."

"Well, I don't have the job yet," I said, not wanting to count my chickens before they hatched. Picking up my chopsticks, I stabbed the last piece of tofu, bringing it to my plate.

"Still. You're interviewing with the Salvati Group. Wait –are you meeting with freaking *Valerian Salvati?*"

"Yeah. I mean, at this point, he's probably the only person at that company I haven't met yet. Besides Anton Salvati," I added, correcting myself.

"Holy shit. Connor, what the fuck, man? You're meeting with Valerian Salvati? You should have led with that."

"It's not that big of a deal."

It *was* a pretty big deal, though, and I'd have been damn happy about it if I didn't feel like my entire career was riding on it.

Valerian Salvati was a real estate mogul and the CEO of the Salvati Group's North American division. He was extremely involved and hands-on with the Salvati Group's real estate and development projects. If Valerian Salvati was happy with your work, you were on the right track with your career. If he wasn't, you could potentially be blacklisted across the industry.

If I got the job as Head Architect, I would lead the project for the Salvati Group's latest luxury resort. Based on some articles I'd read online, the Salvati Group had recently invested in plots of land in Arizona, Colorado, and, in a surprising twist of fate, in my very own hometown in Fleurmont, Quebec.

When I first read the article, I thought it was a typo. Most people had never heard of Fleurmont. Fleurmont was three hours northeast of Montreal, with a population of just a little over 10,000 people. We were tiny, known to some Canadian tourists for our wildflower fields up in the mountains, but not to most.

As much as I loved Fleurmont, some irrational part of me was worried that being back in Fleurmont would feel like taking a step back instead of taking a step forward. It was a ridiculous thought. Even a junior architect position at the Salvati Group held prestige.

Despite a signed non-disclosure agreement and meeting with an entire team of architects, engineers, a marketing executive, and the CFO, it was still unclear which project I would be the head architect for. They asked if I was open to relocating anywhere else in North America, and I'd said yes. The only thing that was clear was that Valerian Salvati would be the one making the final decision, both on the location and on who'd be getting the job.

"Do you know if Harrison is still in the running?" asked Dustin, with one eyebrow raised.

I rolled my eyes, setting down my chopsticks for the second time. "I'm not sure, but I wouldn't be surprised if he got a final interview too."

William Harrison was the human equivalent of a compliance audit. He was annoying, a general waste of time, and appeared in my life roughly once a year. William was a senior designer at the first company I was at, and had openly mocked one of my earliest designs in front of my boss and ten other people. I was so surprised at how blunt and direct he was in his feedback to me in such a public setting that I knocked over my boss's coffee and caused her laptop to need repairs.

Despite being only a few years older than me, he liked to make passing remarks about how kids these days didn't know how to accept feedback in the workplace and needed to be spoon-fed criticism. Even after I left the firm, I continued to see him at conferences and events, and the animosity had only grown between us over time.

"Doesn't his grandfather go golfing with Anton Salvati or something like that?"

"Something like that."

On top of being a grade A asshole, William was also the grandson of a famous architect. In short, he was the definition of a rich, privileged douchebag.

"Don't even worry about it. You're a way better designer than Harrison. Trust." Dustin took a sip of his tea, leaning back thoughtfully in his chair. "Damn, so you could be, like, Head Architect at the Salvati Group in a few weeks. You think that means you could move back to Canada?"

"Maybe," I said, my voice still tight, conflicting, disjointed thoughts fighting for dominance.

"That would be sick. Where are you from again? Montreal?"

"No, but close. It's a small town called Fleurmont."

"Huh, is that in the mountains? I wonder if he wants you to build a luxury ski resort."

"That'd be cool, but there are a lot of ski towns in that area already."

Quebec had a ton of great ski towns –Mont-Tremblant, Mont-Sainte-Anne, Le Charlevoix...the list went on. Fleurmont felt different, though. With the massive lake on one side of the town, and the farms hugging against the mountains on the west side, it felt too serene to become a ski resort.

Dustin looked at his phone.

"Shit, I'm so sorry, I gotta go," said Dustin. "I have a train to catch in half an hour."

"No worries, it was good to catch up," I said.

Dustin signalled for the check.

"Kick Harrison's ass. Get that job, Fitzgerald." Dustin stood up. "I'll see you..."

He paused, tapping the table like he was thinking. "...at the Architect Gala! Yes, I'll see you at the Architect Gala in Los Angeles in August!"

"See you then, man. Have a safe flight back."

Dustin gave me one last wave and headed out.

I looked at the time on my phone.

Oh, shit.

I was about to be late too.

I was meeting my parents at their hotel before we headed out to the night markets. My parents were also in Taipei for the week. Dad –my stepdad, but my dad in the truest sense of the word– was a lawyer and had been talking about retiring for years now. He was slowly taking more time off and getting to the bucket list of places he wanted to visit. Coming back to Taipei with Mom had been high on the list.

After paying my bill, I got into the elevator, clicking on the button for the floor connecting me to the subway station.

The door was about to close when a young woman held up a bright yellow purse to the elevator doors, preventing them from shutting. The woman gave an annoyed huff before turning away from me and pressing the button to the first floor.

There was something about this woman that told me immediately she came from the same kind of wealth as William Harrison. It wasn't just the long, dark blonde hair that looked so perfectly coiffed it could have been a wig. She was also wearing an expensive-looking white patterned dress and sky-high heels that matched her yellow purse. The yellow was so bright it reminded me of the colour of a neon yellow highlighter.

The elevator went down.

Then, suddenly, it stopped, croaking out a sound as it did. The woman next to me shrieked, holding onto the sides of the elevator.

I looked at her again. She looked kind of familiar. Did I know her from somewhere?

We waited a couple of seconds, but the elevator didn't move. The woman leaned over to press the button again for the first floor, tapping at it impatiently.

"What the hell?" she said in English. Her long nails were hitting the button over and over again.

Tap, tap, tap.

Tap, tap, tap.

It was more than a little irritating.

"Are we just stuck here?" She asked loudly to no one in particular.

I was the only other person in the elevator, but I wasn't sure that she was actually talking to me because she wasn't looking at me. She was probably talking to herself.

Tap, tap, tap, tap.

Unable to stand it anymore, I leaned over and pressed the emergency button. She jumped back as if I were a piranha. I tried not to roll my eyes.

"Hello?" the voice on the other end asked in Mandarin.

"Hi, the elevator seems to be stuck," I said to the operator.

"Yes, I see that. Apologies for the inconvenience. We are sending someone to come get you," said the operator.

"Do you know how long it will be?" I asked.

"We're working as quickly as possible. Apologies, it could be another ten or fifteen minutes."

"Thank you."

The line on the other end disconnected, and I took a few steps back.

"They're sending someone to fix the problem," I said to the woman in English. "They said it would take ten or fifteen minutes."

Sharp blue eyes met mine.

I've definitely seen her before. But where?

"Fifteen minutes is way too long," she said, and she let out another huff, whipping out her cell phone from her tiny purse.

Was she Canadian? American? I tried to pinpoint the places I could have met her before.

"I'm stuck in a freaking elevator, and now I'm going to be late for my appointment," she said loudly to someone on her phone.

Yeah, okay, American.

"Can't you just drive the car in circles until I get out of here? I don't care if the traffic is bad," she said.

Jeez. She was worked up.

"Do you know how important a final fitting is? What if they got my measurements wrong? I don't want my boobs to suffocate. Do you know how annoying underboob sweat is?"

I tried hard not to look at her chest.

"No, it's for the Pink Party. Yes –no."

I remembered suddenly.

The pink dress. That's where I'd seen her before. She was the woman in the pink dress I saw at my parents' wedding anniversary party in Los Angeles six months ago, the one who pushed another woman into the pool.

"Do you have a problem?" she said suddenly, looking at me.

Shit. I hadn't realized I was staring at her.

"No," I said, turning away quickly.

American. She was definitely American.

Turning my attention to my phone instead, I dialled, amazed that we still had reception in an elevator. Shifting away from the incredibly loud, obnoxious woman next to me, I leaned against one side of the elevator.

Mom picked up on the second ring. "Connor, where are you? Dad and I are already in the lobby."

"Sorry, I'm going to be late. I'm stuck in an elevator with a loud American," I said to her in Mandarin.

"A loud American? Are you okay?"

"Yeah, I'm fine. Someone's coming to fix this, but I'll be at least half an hour late."

"That's okay. As long as you're okay."

"Can't wait to hear about the loud American," came Dad's voice cheerfully in the background.

Despite being French Canadian and born and raised in Fleurmont, Dad had learned Mandarin since he married Mom. He was surprisingly good at it now.

"Loud and rude," I muttered, still in Mandarin.

When I hung up the phone, I found the woman full-on glaring at me, a hand on her hip. When we made eye contact, she looked away in complete dismissal, letting out yet another huff of air.

I put my phone away, shaking my head.

We stood there in silence.

It was the definition of an uncomfortable silence. It was the kind of social interaction that I hadn't experienced in years. This was -

Suddenly, the elevator started to move again.

Slowly, the elevator moved and opened onto the first floor. Two technicians in uniform greeted us as we stepped out. The woman who was with me marched forward ahead of me, yellow stilettos clicking sharply on the marble floor.

"We are so sorry for the inconvenience –" one of the elevator technicians said in English.

"That's alright. Thank you for rescuing me from that unbearable situation," said the woman in perfect Mandarin.

She threw me a look of pure hatred.

Well, shit.

Didn't see that one coming.

Without another word, she marched towards the exit of the building.

"Is everything okay?" one of the elevator technicians asked me. "We're so sorry about that. That's never happened before."

"Fine." I cleared my throat, shaking away the awkwardness of what had just happened. "Sorry, which way do I go for the subway?"

"The closest entrance is just down those stairs," he said.

"Thank you," I said, and headed towards the stairs.

For the rest of that afternoon, I couldn't stop thinking about the rude American with cerulean blue eyes who spoke perfect Mandarin.

# Chapter Three

## Stassi

### Los Angeles

My new pink dress hung in my walk-in closet next to my pink dress from last year, and I admired the silhouette of the dress. Narrowing my eyes, I held up two pairs of shoes up against the fabric, careful to avoid touching the three-dimensional flowers. Gold was always a good option, and I was obsessed with the rhinestones at the ankles, but...maybe it was better to fully commit to the pink theme with the pink satin stilettos?

As I dragged my laptop closer to me to get the internet to decide for me, my laptop created a fuzzy line over the carpet. It was the kind of little thing that would have driven Nya crazy when we still lived together.

Nya was my roommate throughout college, and to say she was a bit of a neat freak was an understatement. She'd moved back to Kenya a few months after we graduated, and since then, I've hated coming back to the apartment.

A notification popped up on one of the tabs on my laptop, and I shifted the laptop onto my lap to look at it. As I suspected, my email inbox now showed a single unread email. It was the weekly email I received from my alma mater with the newsletter of new job listings.

I clicked into it.

**New!** Junior Architect (applications must include uploaded work samples)

**New!** Landscape Architect (on-site position, downtown L.A.)

**New!** Architect - Project Designer (travel up to 10% of the time)

Clicking into each of the listings like I did every week, my eyes scanned over the job descriptions, my stomach knotting and twisting. The 'apply' button stared back at me, a bright green rectangle that occupied a good chunk of the web page.

"You can click on a button," I said out loud.

*But what about what happens after?* A nasty little voice said in my head, and just like that, without fail, every negative, intrusive thought trailed through my mind.

I squeezed my eyes shut, clicking quickly out of my email before shutting off my laptop. Standing up, I grabbed both pairs of shoes and shoved them into my suitcase, which hadn't been stored away since I'd gotten back just a few hours ago.

I *hated* being in L.A.

L.A. was where I had to say goodbye to Nya. L.A. was where I had last seen my parents. It was where my parents had died in a freak car accident two years ago. Two whole years ago, and I was still not over it. Everyone else in my family had moved on.

"Fuck this," I muttered into the mocking silence of my apartment. I shoved my pink dress into its garment bag, zipped it up and folded it into my suitcase.

My phone rang twice before Jenna picked up.

"Hey, hey," she said cheerfully. "Are you back in L.A.?"

"Hey!" I said, my voice too bright. "Can I sleep over at your place this week until we leave for Ibiza?"

"Hell yeah. Get your ass over here -and bring olives. I'm kind of in the mood for martinis."

"Okay, see you in twenty!"

That's what I loved about Jenna. She never asked questions, unlike Nya, who would have tried to get me to talk about my feelings. Nya, who had stayed with me those first three months after my parents died, who had put her whole life and career on hold for me those months. Sweet, beautiful Nya...

I smoothed out the carpet in front of me, and dragged my suitcase back to the front of my apartment, wondering if my bed had started to collect dust yet.

# CHAPTER FOUR

## *Connor*

My interview with Valerian Salvati was held at the headquarters of the Salvati Group in downtown Los Angeles. The building was one of the tallest buildings in the metropolis, blue glass with a massive, three-dimensional green and white Salvati logo fixed to the top of the building's exterior. The building was the type of building that hired full-time security on the first floor, and you needed key card access just to get to the elevators.

The elevators were all done in a light gold colour, and there was a design to each of the elevator doors –transmission towers drawn in thin, elegant white lines. When the doors opened, it had the effect of displaying power lines stretching and connecting. It was a sick design.

Valerian Salvati's office was on the highest floor of the building. His private office was right on the corner of the forty-fifth floor, with his name at the front of the door in gold writing.

The elevator opened up onto his secretary's desk, and the metal plaque on her desk told me her name was Penny.

"Hi, I'm here to see Valerian Salvati."

"What's your name?" asked Penny, adjusting her monitor to face her more directly.

She was a middle-aged woman, and whether it was intentional, her pantsuit and blazer complemented the furnishing of the office space, creating a symbiosis that would make any interior designer happy.

"Connor Fitzgerald. I'm here for the interview."

Penny nodded and smiled at me kindly. "Yes, Mr. Salvati is expecting you. He's just wrapping up another interview. It shouldn't be too long now."

She gestured to the long couch at the wall opposite her desk. "Take a seat."

I had just sat down when the door to Valerian's office opened. The smell of an all too familiar cologne hit me, and it was enough for me to know who would be at the door before I even saw his face.

William Harrison strutted down the hall, Valerian's office door shutting behind him. His blond hair was slightly gelled back, emphasizing the razor-sharp lines of his jaw. Despite being a douchebag, he was objectively good-looking, and he was aware of it. I wondered if it was his family connections or his looks that gave him confidence and fed his ego.

He smirked when he saw me, his eyes darting quickly to Penny before looking back at me.

"Fitzy," he said, his voice low, his head dipping in a nod.

"William," I said, knowing I couldn't ignore him here, feeling my jaw tighten.

"Have a great rest of your day," he said more loudly to Penny.

"Good day!"

William pressed the button to the elevator, and he glanced back at me, a subtle shrug on his right shoulder, sucking in a breath through his teeth. "Better luck next time, kiddo."

My heart sank as his words registered and the elevator door opened. William stepped into the elevator, his face smoothing out to an almost blank expression as he looked away from me.

"Connor Fitzgerald?" called Penny, waving at me with one hand. "You can go right on in now."

"Thanks," I muttered, standing up, wondering if Valerian Salvati was about to reject me on the spot.

I opened the heavy wooden doors and found Valerian Salvati sitting at his massive desk. His office was exactly how I had pictured it: floor to ceiling windows, a massive oak desk, expensive carpeting, multiple seating areas.

"Fitzgerald, welcome," he said, and he gestured to a chair in front of him that probably cost more than all the furniture in my apartment.

"Thank you. It's a pleasure to meet you, Sir," I said, sitting down across from him.

Shit, was I supposed to call him that? Should it be Mr. Salvati? Should I just call him Valerian?

"Pleasure's all mine." Valerian looked at me with a slightly amused expression on his face.

At fifty, he looked young for his age, or at least was in good shape. His brown hair was greying just a little, and he had laugh lines around large brown eyes that suggested he might even be kind of easy-going in some contexts.

Valerian Salvati had worked at the Salvati Group his entire career and, despite his family ties that had gotten him in the door, he had helped increase the company's revenue in North

America tenfold in the last twenty years. He was the one who had helped the company reach a hundred billion dollar valuation just a few years ago.

He'd helped the Salvati Group reach this milestone at the age of forty-eight, and it was all over the news. On the same day the Salvati Group reached a hundred billion dollar valuation, his brother died in a car crash.

He observed me now with sharp brown eyes.

"So. You did a dual degree in civil engineering and architecture?" he asked, lifting a piece of paper that looked like a printout of my resume.

"I did."

He nodded, putting the piece of paper down. "And you spent two years designing rollercoasters for the Seattle Amusement Park?"

"I did," I confirmed again. Was I supposed to go into more detail? I must still have been jet lagged from the flight back from Taipei because it took me a second to remember the rehearsed monologues I usually gave about each of the projects I've designed and led. Before I could get into my first monologue though, Valerian was on to his next question.

"And you're from the town of Fleurmont, right?"

"I am," I said, surprised he knew that about me.

Salvati nodded. "I thought so," he said, and added by way of explanation, "I read the article about you in *Singapore Today*."

Valerian Salvati remembered the article I was in? I relaxed a little, surprised and flattered.

"I'll cut to it, then, Fitzgerald," said Valerian, and he took out a folder from his briefcase, putting it on the table in front of me, "because I know you've already gone through a shit ton of interviews, and frankly, I'm not really interested in asking you a bunch of interview questions."

My body tensed.

"I want you to be one of our Head Architects." Valerian smiled widely, pushing the mysterious black folder towards me.

Relief and excitement flooded into me, and I was about to thank him when I registered what he said.

"One of?" I repeated.

Valerian nodded. "That's right. That's what I want to discuss with you. As I'm sure you've discussed with the team, we recently invested in land in Quebec, Colorado, and Arizona. There's more, of course, across other countries. The Salvati Group has existed for over fifty years now, and we've operated in a very segmented way, usually by region."

I didn't get where he was going with this, but I nodded, and he continued.

"Well, we need to think through how we want to position ourselves as a brand in the next ten years. Should the resorts we have in North America really be separate from the residential buildings we're investing in Asia? Maybe. Maybe not. All to say that there's a need for a new role. We don't just need a Head Architect. We need a Creative Director who can spearhead all of our future development projects."

Holy shit.

Valerian smiled again at my expression. "The Creative Director will be responsible for leading all of our major development projects, and will work with our marketing team to help us come up with a vision for the brand as we evolve. I imagine this person would design some projects, delegate others, but they would be involved with all the major development projects to some extent. Is that a role that would be interesting to you?"

"Yes," I said immediately. "Absolutely."

Hell, yes. That would be the opportunity of a lifetime. Being Head Architect would have already been the opportunity of a lifetime. Being Creative Director of the Salvati Group? Insanity.

Valerian chuckled. "Good, good. So, let me backtrack. I'm not offering you the Creative Director position yet. I'm offering you the contract to be our Head Architect, specifically to design the resort up in Fleurmont. I've been following your career, Fitzgerald. The theme park in Seattle, the dragon playground in Singapore, the urban space in Montreal. You've got a real talent."

"I'm flattered," I said genuinely. "Thank you. I'm grateful for the opportunity."

"Considering your background and that you're from Fleurmont, I thought you would be the best person for the job."

Damn. Who knew growing up in Fleurmont would land me a job?

"Take a look at the documents," said Valerian. "When we bought the land over a year ago, I had a full site analysis done. The land is technically within the town lines of Fleurmont, but only legally. It's about a twenty-minute drive away from town, if I'm remembering correctly. It's close enough though, up in the mountains."

Fleurmont was in a valley surrounded by mountains on all sides.

I flipped through the photos in the folder. It looked vaguely familiar.

"Is this the abandoned mining town?" I asked.

There used to be an old mining town close to Mt. Aster, which was minuscule even compared to Fleurmont back when it still had inhabitants.

"Exactly," said Valerian. "This is where I want you to design the resort. I want you to lead it from start to finish. Concept, design, execution."

I opened the folder he had out on the table, but there were no mock-ups, no concept images, just photos of the old mining town and details about the geography.

"Do you envision this being a ski town?" I inquired.

Valerian shook his head. "Not necessarily. I want you to pitch me something great. I have a cabin up there. It used to be a miners' lodge, but I got the basics to work when I was up there last year. It's the only thing running up on Mt. Aster. I want you to go up there, really get a feel of the place. In a month, pitch me something great. Assuming you accept my offer, that is."

I nodded, trying to look thoughtful even though there was no way I wasn't accepting this job opportunity. "And you mentioned you have other Head Architects? Is there one for the project in Colorado and one for the one in Arizona?" William's reaction would make more sense if this were the case.

"Not exactly. I'm offering this contract to you and to one other architect. You might know him, actually. It looks like you were at the same company before."

I already knew what he was going to say before the words came out of his mouth.

"His name is William Harrison. Are you familiar with him?"

Viscerally.

"We've crossed paths," I said tightly.

"Good. He just finished designing a set of resorts in the Maldives. It was a pretty unique concept. You wouldn't expect something like that in the Maldives. Anyway, he's going to be the Head Architect for the resort in Arizona. Colorado is something I want the Creative Director to take on." Valerian scratched at his short, trimmed beard, still observing me. "I'd like to offer one of you the position within the next four months."

Fucking Harrison. I never seemed to be rid of that bastard.

"Sounds good," I said, trying to sound confident.

"Excellent. Here's your contract." He slid another stack of papers in front of me. "Take some time to read it over."

The salary was highlighted in yellow on the first page, and I tried to throttle back my physical reaction. When I glanced up at Valerian as I flipped to the next page, he looked amused again, no doubt having complete confidence in just how great his offer was.

"That's your base salary. The incentives are on page six."

I flipped through the contract in disbelief.

"I'll look it over," I said, unable to keep the smile from my face, "but I honestly can't think of a reason I would say no."

"Good," he chuckled. "I like you, Fitzgerald." He got up from the chair. "I want to move fast on this, so you have three days to think about it."

It was a dismissal.

I got up and thanked him. He waved me off, his phone already at his ear by the time I reached the door.

# CHAPTER FIVE

## *Stassi*

The alpaca spat in my face.

A spray of liquid hit the side of my head, and alpaca saliva dripped from the side of my forehead down the side of my face.

I was so disgusted and shocked that I couldn't muster a scream. I grabbed the towel next to me, wiping the spit off of my face.

Disgusting.

So. Freaking. Disgusting.

Jenna let out a giggle next to me, and I turned my attention to her. She was wearing blue leggings and a matching sports bra, her body still twisted in a position named after a bird –the pelican? The pigeon? Who knew?

Every fiber of my being was done with yoga.

"That was so gross, and I blame you entirely."

"Maybe it likes you," she whispered.

I glared back at the alpaca in question. It looked at me, and I swear its expression turned taunting, thick russet eyebrows raised at me in contempt. It knew what it had done, and it was antagonizing me.

"It did that on purpose!" I hissed at Jenna.

Jenna laughed, the charms on her bracelet tinkling together as her body shook.

"This is the last time I'm ever letting you take me to one of your cuckoo workout sessions."

"Fine, fine," she whispered back, unbothered. "I guess you'll be missing out on next week's goat yoga, too, then."

Missing goat yoga was completely fine with me.

Alpaca yoga was exactly what it sounded like. Jenna drove us to a farm an hour outside of L.A. We walked past the main barn house and past a gazebo to enter a large, grassy area for the yoga class. It was only partially fenced, with stacks of hay and decorative wooden fences surrounding the area. Ten alpacas of varying colours roamed around the area, stopping occasionally to sniff at the yogis. While people ooh'ed and aww'ed at the alpacas, I had placed my mat in the centre but towards the back, hoping to avoid interacting with these strange farm animals. Obviously, based on the state of my towel and the crusty feel on my face, I had failed in the worst way.

God, I couldn't wait to get back to my apartment and take a shower.

The yoga space was deliberately sectioned off from the rest of the farm, but it was impossible to miss the stench of the farm. The pungent smell of farm animals was unmistakable, and it was hard not to think about that throughout the class.

"...transition into your plank," the yoga instructor was saying, "and we're going to hold here for ten counts. Take a deep breath in. Eight...Seven..."

This was so painful.

Why weren't we done yet?

"Five..."

Four, three, two, one!

I collapsed onto my yoga mat, my arms feeling like jello.

"Four..."

It didn't help that I was hungover. Memories of tequila made me want to hurl right onto my pink yoga mat. I gripped onto the ridges of my yoga mat, trying to focus on the semi-squishy texture instead of my nausea.

Ibiza had been a full week of non-stop drinking, and Jenna and I had only flown back last night.

I pretended to hold a plank position on my elbows before I realized everyone was now in a downward dog position. Taking a deep breath, I walked my hands back to the front of my mat.

The tequila rose in my throat, and sweat dripped from my forehead. Immediately, I sat back down on my mat. Yep, no downward dog for me today.

Jenna continued metamorphosing into different animals next to me while I sipped on cold water. I sat cross-legged on my yoga mat, glaring at the alpaca who had spat on me earlier.

It stared at me head-on, its mouth chewing on a piece of hay like it was a piece of spearmint gum. I stuck my tongue out at it.

"Are you alright?" the yoga instructor whispered to me, and I jumped, not realizing she had somehow ended up right next to me.

"I'm fine," I said a little too loudly.

I smiled at her as a couple of people turned to look at us.

"Okay then," she said, giving me a small, awkward smile before walking away.

Jenna laughed, her brown ponytail shaking as her whole body shook with laughter.

"I hate you," I said to her.

My cell phone rang.

Shit.

The yoga instructor shot me a look of annoyance.

"Sorry!" I whispered, grabbing my phone and rushing away from the grassy field.

On my way out, I sidestepped an alpaca that was rolling around in the grass next to a couple. The couple was trying to hold some kind of flamingo pose while also trying to pet the rolling alpaca. Why do people think alpacas are cute? Alpacas are not cute.

I ran to the shaded gazebo, away from the alpacas and yoga mats. By the time I reached the first step of the wooden gazebo, I was panting and I wanted to vomit again.

My phone continued to ring, and I glanced at the screen to see who was calling.

Oh, crap.

I picked up the phone.

"Hello?" I said dryly. I did *not* need this today.

"Stassi," came my uncle's unimpressed voice.

Uncle Valerian was my dad's younger brother, and the CEO of the Salvati Group's North American division. My grandfather, Anton Salvati, was the CEO and chairman of the board. Together, they were the two highest ranking members of the Salvati Group, and also the two most annoying critics and gatekeepers of my life. At least they would be until my trust fund kicked in when I turned twenty-five.

"This is not a great time, Uncle Valerian," I said. "I'm in the middle of something."

"You're in the middle of something? You mean sinking a yacht in the Mediterranean Sea? Or do you mean getting arrested in Barcelona?" his voice was seething with anger. "Do you know how much you cost us over the last week?"

I sighed.

My head was pounding. It was like there were a thousand miniature alpacas hammering nails in my head. I *so* did not want to have this conversation right now.

Okay, yes, I sank a yacht. It wasn't my fault, though. It was a tiny, old boat with shitty maintenance, and who knew there was a section of the boat I wasn't supposed to jump on? I mean, sure, the guy mentioned it once. But why would you let a bunch of twenty-three-year-olds with a bottle of Licor 43 take your boat out to sea if it can't handle a couple of light steps? No single person on that boat weighed over a hundred and twenty pounds. Not sure that one was my fault.

The arrest was a little bit my fault. I was at a bar, and this crazy woman started yelling at my friend Quinn about sleeping with her boyfriend or something. It was ridiculous because I know Quinn, and Quinn would never sleep with someone who was in a relationship. So yes, I yelled at this crazy bitch that we've never seen before to back the hell off, and it got a little physical.

But again, it was cleared up super quickly, and I don't even think Uncle Valerian had anything to do with helping get it cleared up. He probably just heard about it from Jenna's cousin's friend's uncle. Everyone in our circle was way too well connected. It was annoying.

I didn't explain any of this to Uncle Valerian, though. He wouldn't understand.

"Uncle Valerian, can we please talk about this another time? I'm at a yoga class. An alpaca just spat on me. I'm really not in the mood –"

"You think this is some kind of joke, Stassi? This is serious. You've been completely out of control for much too long now."

"Uncle –"

"Stassi, stop it," my grandfather's commanding voice cut in from the background.

Great, Bad Cop was here.

"Grandpa, I'm sorry," I said.

I felt around for my water bottle, my mouth feeling dry. Shit. I left it with my yoga mat out on the field.

"You're coming to the penthouse this week," said Uncle Valerian. "Tomorrow. The driver will pick you up from your apartment at 2 p.m. This is non-negotiable."

"I can't. I have plans," I said.

This was technically true. Jenna and I talked about going back to the south of France.

"Did you miss the part where I said this was non-negotiable?" snapped Uncle Valerian.

"Uncle Valerian –"

"Stassi, I thought you were done with all of this recklessness. Was crashing your car in Vegas not enough of a wake-up call? Crashing it –"

"Dad," muttered Uncle Valerian.

My body went cold despite the heat of Southern California. I swallowed with some difficulty, my mouth feeling like sandpaper. Of all the stupid things I've done over the last few years, that was probably my one regret. Not because anyone got hurt –everyone was fine– but it hit too close to home.

My mind flashed with Mom and Dad's faces, and a wave of sadness hit me.

"I'll be there," I muttered finally.

"Good. Penny just texted you a confirmation," said Uncle Valerian.

Penny Winston was my uncle's secretary and has been for over fifteen years now. How that woman never got sick of Valerian Salvati was a mystery of the universe.

As I hung up the phone after the call with Uncle Valerian and my grandfather, I instantly received a text from Penny.

I sighed, feeling resigned.

Maybe it was the hangover talking, but it *was* a little exhausting running around all over the world. I hadn't meant for it to last as long as it did. When my parents first died, I allowed myself to do nothing besides cry and stay at my apartment in L.A. Nya being there with me made things better, but the three months went by much too quickly, and then she was gone, and I had that disastrous interview...

Then, Jenna asked me if I wanted to go to Italy with her, to get away and not think about any of it. I said yes, and I never looked back because every time I was in L.A. for longer than a week, I felt sad again, feeling restless and irritable.

But maybe this wasn't the worst thing. If I knew my uncle, and I think I did, he was probably going to make me work for the company. The Salvati Group was a global conglomerate that invested in everything from real estate to energy across four continents. Both my siblings worked for the Salvati Group's European division. Adrian was the Vice President of

Operations and lived in London, while Miranda was a Director of Finance and lived in Paris.

Maybe Uncle Valerian would set me up with an architect position in Paris, and I could reconnect with Miranda. We weren't close. None of us were.

Once upon a time, we might have been, but it was a long time ago, and we all knew why we weren't close now. With our parents gone, it felt even more pointless to try.

Hope and anxiety churned with the tequila in my body as I braced myself to face my family again.

# CHAPTER SIX

## Stassi

My family owned three residential properties in Los Angeles. My grandfather lived on an estate in Holmby Hills. The second property, just a few blocks away, had been my parents' before they passed. Now, Adrian, Miranda and I technically co-owned it, but none of us had wanted to do anything with it, let alone even go back. Selling it felt like an insult to their memory, but going back felt too painful, like it was taunting us with all that we could have been. It just sat there, collecting dust.

The third property was the Penthouse. It was where Uncle Valerian lived with his husband, Julian. Their apartment had private elevator access straight into their Spanish-style apartment.

"There she is!" Julian's warm voice greeted me when the elevator door opened.

Someone must have notified Julian of my arrival because he was standing in the foyer with a cup of espresso in one hand.

"Julian!" I cried, hugging him tightly.

"Welcome home, darling," he hugged me with his free arm.

Julian was probably the only highlight of being in L.A.

Julian was only a couple of years younger than Uncle Valerian, and the lines on his handsome face told the story of a man who loved to laugh and love. He had smile lines, and when he laughed, the lines around his eyes crinkled with joy. He was probably the only person in the world that Botox would do a real disservice to.

"How was your flight in?" he asked, pulling away to look at me, looking approvingly at my four-inch pink Manolos. If I were going to get scolded today, I might as well look amazing.

"Oh, fine, you know. As good as it can be when you're coerced into coming to Valerian and Anton Salvati's private tribunal. Or, you know, hell. Whatever is the appropriate term these days."

Julian laughed. "This is why you're my favourite."

We walked down the hall across Uncle Valerian's favourite hand-woven patterned rug. As much as I hated being here, the apartment was pretty incredible. The entire apartment had a rustic yet elegant appeal. The hallway was lined with oak console tables with geometric patterns and topped with muted gold sculptures by Isabella Alamilla, an up and coming Spanish designer.

A set of hand-carved walnut armchairs with a brass nailhead trim greeted us when we reached the primary living room. The burgundy velvet sofas perfectly paired with the armchairs, and the bougainvillea flowers subtly drew attention towards the exposed wood beams in the ceiling and subtly textured white walls.

"Do you want an espresso?" Julian asked.

Out of the corner of my eye, I saw one of Uncle Valerian and Julian's maids push a coffee cart behind us, also heading towards Uncle Valerian's office. I stopped to let her pass, and she glanced at me quickly before almost nervously looking away.

Yes, I suppose the prodigal niece has returned.

"I'm okay," I said. "So I guess I'm in some pretty deep shit, huh?"

"They're not the happiest with you right now," Julian agreed.

We paused now between the living room and Uncle Valerian's office.

"Is Grandpa here already?" I asked.

"He is," confirmed Julian, scratching at the stubble on face. He gave me a gentle smile, his brown eyes crinkling before he looked towards the office. A nudge towards the room of my demise.

I let out a laugh.

"Alright, let's get this over with," I said, and Julian and I continued to walk into the lion's den.

Uncle Valerian and Grandpa were sitting at Uncle Valerian's massive oak desk when we arrived. Sitting there, they looked shockingly alike —stony expressions, hard, unforgiving brown eyes, lips pressed tight into thin, disapproving lines.

They should do a photoshoot like this for the Salvati Group's hiring campaigns.

"You're late," said Uncle Valerian.

It was 2:02.

"The car came late," I lied, even though the whole thing was ridiculous. Who cares if I'm two minutes late? If you're within a five-minute arrival time, you're on time. Honestly, in most parts of the world, showing up at 2:02 was practically rudely early.

I sat down in the chair across from Uncle Valerian and Grandpa. Julian took a seat on the red loveseat by the window.

"Julian, you don't really need to be here," said Uncle Valerian, though his tone softened just a smidge.

Julian gave me a mischievous smile. "And miss this conversation? Not a chance." He crossed one leg over the other and took a sip of his espresso. "Don't mind me."

Julian grabbed a magazine from the coffee table in front of him, pretending to look interested in *Architectural Digest*, as if he hadn't already read it.

"Stassi," said Grandpa, his voice gruff, looking me straight in the eyes, "I'm going to give you one chance to explain to me what happened. One. And cut the bullshit."

His silver beard was trimmed short the way it had been my entire life, just barely longer than a stubble. He was wearing his glasses today, though the thin metal frame and lens did nothing to hide the continued hostility of his stare.

Grandpa was probably the intellectually sharpest, most lucid seventy-four-year-old you could meet. Nothing escaped him, and he was as sharp as he was when he took over the Salvati Group forty years ago.

"I'm sorry about what happened in Spain," I said.

Grandpa's eyes narrowed.

"Explain yourself."

"I was defending a friend," I said. "Some crazy person accused her of something she didn't do –"

"And this justifies your physically injuring a waitress? She needed two stitches."

Shit. I didn't know that. I didn't even know which waitress he was talking about.

"I'm sorry that happened. I didn't mean to hurt the waitress. She just got caught in the crossfire. I was trying to get that crazy woman in front of her, and that crazy woman just ducked out of the way –"

"Stassi, do you hear yourself?" Uncle Valerian interrupted. "You're not six years old pushing some girl into a sandbox. You're a grown ass-woman, and you assaulted a woman."

"Assault is a pretty strong word," I retorted. "It was an *accident –*"

"Yes, assault is a strong word. It's the word she used when she sued you," said Grandpa.

Well, no one told me *that*.

"Luckily, we were able to get her to drop the charges," said Uncle Valerian coolly.

In other words, he got someone to pay her off.

Okay, fine. That was not my proudest moment.

"I'm sorry! I'm sorry, okay? It was an accident. I seriously didn't mean to hurt her. I was trying to defend my friend. Did any of your reports talk about what that crazy bitch did to Quinn? Quinn had –"

"That's *enough*," said Uncle Valerian.

"Val, stop interrupting her. Let her talk," said Julian.

Uncle Valerian glared at Julian before turning back to me. "No. That's it. This conversation is over."

"Great," I said sarcastically, "because it was so long and comprehensive."

"You are completely out of control." Uncle Valerian ignored me, the vein in his forehead pulsing. "You want to spend tens of thousands of dollars over a weekend on clothes and God knows what else? Fine. You want to drink like a fish on your own time? Be my guest. But now you're damaging private and public property, getting physically violent with complete strangers, not to mention breaking into museums, and *don't* even get me started on the less than fucking appropriate clothes I had the displeasure of seeing from the Miami auction."

I forgot about the museum in Brazil and the Miami auction. Oops.

"I don't know how you don't seem to give a shit about your own reputation, but your childish antics are damaging the reputation of this company and this has to stop," said Uncle Valerian.

Grandpa gave a tight nod of agreement.

"So what? I'm on a time-out?"

"No, you don't get a time-out. You're going to work for the company. Effective immediately. You're going to Fleurmont for the next four months, and if you so much as put a toe out of line, we are cutting you off. For good."

"*Where?*" I squinted. Was that another name for one of the arrondissements in Paris? But the office was in the business district.

"Fleurmont. It's a town in eastern Canada."

I have never heard of Fleurmont in my life. And *Canada?* Who wants to go to Canada? Anger rippled through me at the false expectation I had somehow set for myself.

"So you're banishing me to the North Pole?" I said flatly.

Uncle Valerian blinked at me. He looked at Julian, and then he gestured to me, as if to say, see? See what I have to deal with?

Julian continued to sip his espresso.

"Here's the deal. You're going to Fleurmont. You're going to be an intern for my new development project in Canada."

"*Intern?* I think I'm past interning," I retorted hotly, humiliation and guilt fuelling my anger.

I had done four architecture internships throughout college.

"I don't give a shit. You're going to report to the head architect. You're going to put that degree of yours to use. If I hear a *peep* out of him that you are not cooperating or not working your damn hardest, I am cutting you off. Permanently. Then you'll really see what it's like to be banished."

My trust fund kicked in when I was twenty-five. That was fifteen months away, which was pretty much an eternity.

"Why are you sending me to *Canada?* Can't you send me to one of our offices in Europe, at least? Like in Paris where Miranda is?"

"No."

"And what exactly am I supposed to do up in freaking Canada as an intern?" I gaped at my uncle.

"You will do anything Connor Fitzgerald tells you to do. If he tells you to design a floor plan, you're going to design a floor plan. If he tells you to research a lamp, you're going to research the best goddamn lamp you can find in North America. If he tells you to make coffee, you're going to fucking make coffee."

"And when exactly am I supposed to do this?"

This can't be happening. I can't go to Canada. To Fleurmont. Wherever the hell that was. I don't want to be someone's freaking intern.

"Next week."

"*Next week?*"

"Yes, and before you argue, save your breath. This is non-negotiable. You're going."

I looked over at Julian.

"*Don't,*" snapped Uncle Valerian, and I don't know if he was talking to me or to Julian.

Grandpa sighed.

"Do not enable her, Julian," said Grandpa, crossing his arms over his chest.

"I am sitting over here drinking my coffee," said Julian calmly.

Uncle Valerian exhaled angrily, and then he looked at his watch. As if on cue, there was a knock on the door.

"Come in," said Uncle Valerian.

A maid opened the door. I turned to the door to look at her.

"Mr. Salvati, Connor Fitzgerald is here to see you," she said.

"Perfect, bring him in," said Uncle Valerian, and he exhaled a second time, though it seemed more out of relief. "You can meet your new boss."

Swell.

I glanced over at Grandpa. He held my gaze steadily.

"This is good for you, Stassi," he said, his voice calmer now. "You were at the top of your class throughout college. What happened?"

I said nothing.

I couldn't tell them I was still struggling with my parents' death. It had been two years, well past the time they would have given me a pass, and it seemed like the last thing on anyone's mind except for me. Besides, they wouldn't even believe me.

"Fitzgerald, good to see you again," said Uncle Valerian. "Come on in. Meet my niece, Stassi Salvati. She'll be your intern for the next four months."

"Intern?" A deep male voice entered the room, holding the unmistakable sound of surprise.

I turned back to the door to see who the voice belonged to.

"Stassi, this is Connor Fitzgerald. He's the head architect for the project in Fleurmont."

My eyes widened in disbelief.

*I knew him.*

Shock washed over me as I took in his features. Wearing a mid-priced cotton button-down shirt and black pants, he was at least six feet tall, with jet black hair and dark brown eyes. He was clean-shaven, with a straight nose and a small scar on the left side of his face. If I hadn't immediately recognized him, I might have thought he was kind of hot.

*But I knew him.*

He was the totally rude man I was stuck in the elevator with in Taipei!

Recognition flashed across his face as we made eye contact. He remembered me too. Just as quickly, his face turned neutral again. He held his hand out to me.

"It's nice to meet you," he said coolly.

"Right," I scoffed. I looked at his hand and looked away, not moving.

"*Stassi*," someone reprimanded, but I didn't hear who.

My new boss was the asshole from Taipei?! What were the fucking chances? This had to be the biggest cosmic joke on the planet. I had to go to *Canada* with this jerk?

"Fitzgerald, I apologize for my niece. She will not be like this when you two are in Fleurmont," said Uncle Valerian, giving me a hard look. "Fitzgerald, meet my father, Anton Salvati."

"It's great to meet you, sir. I'm grateful for the opportunity," said Connor Fitzgerald, reaching over to shake Grandpa's hand.

Pfff. An asshole and a suck-up.

"I've heard great things about your work," said Grandpa.

Julian let out a cough in the corner.

"And this is my husband, Julian Salvati," said Uncle Valerian wearily, gesturing to Julian, who was now smiling brightly at Connor Fitzgerald. "Julian, this is Connor Fitzgerald."

Julian stood up, and he and Connor shook hands.

"Nice to meet you."

"It's a pleasure."

I looked at him again. Connor Fitzgerald.

He glanced at me as Uncle Valerian explained something incredibly boring to him. His expression was completely unreadable. I caught just a flicker of something, but his expression remained completely serious, and he nodded at my uncle's words, like he was thinking deeply and all of his thoughts were a series of highly intelligent thoughts.

I looked right back at him, staring him down. There was no way I was going to be the one to look away first. He looked away first, breaking his neutral facial expression, looking almost embarrassed, and I almost smiled with satisfaction.

"Excuse me," I said suddenly, standing up. "I think I need to go pack."

No one stopped me, although I'm sure the vein in Uncle Valerian's forehead had developed into its own entity at this point. Unable to sit there any longer, I headed out of the room and down the hall towards the guest bedroom, still processing.

Nothing came to mind when I tried to picture Fleurmont. Fleurmont. I had to go to Fleurmont. For four whole months. I had to be an *intern*. And for a complete jerk.

"Stassi."

I turned around to see that Julian had followed me out of the office.

"Are you okay?" he asked, a solemn expression on his face.

"No, I'm getting shipped off," I said.

Julian sighed. "I love you, but you gotta admit, they might have a point. Maybe this will be good for you."

"You think I'm going to come back all sweet and polite because I'm forced to spend four months in Canada?"

"No, I think there's a lot going on in that head of yours. I think maybe this could be good for you, to give you some perspective."

"On what? Maple syrup?" Why was I being like this? Especially with Julian. My frustration only climbed further, and I squeezed my hands into fists at my sides, forcing myself to stop talking.

"Fleurmont is actually known for wildflower fields, not maple syrup."

Julian laughed at my expression.

"No, I mean with everything you've been doing," he said more gently. "That's not who you are. Not in here."

He put his hand to his heart. Julian gave me a small smile before heading back to his room.

Slowly, I closed the door to the guest bedroom and leaned against the door for a moment. It was almost three in the afternoon. One in the morning in Kenya.

Worth a shot.

I dialled my best friend's number.

"Stassi?" said Nya's voice as our call connected.

I knew she'd be up.

"The most tragic thing in the world has happened," I declared, plopping down onto the duvet covers of the guest bed. The duvet was a soft, creamy beige, and surprisingly comfortable.

"Tell me everything."

Unlike me, Nya had never gone off the rails. She was a fully functioning adult. In fact, she was so fully functioning that she had started her own startup in Nairobi to empower more women to work in the renewable energy space in Kenya.

Yeah. Nya was a badass.

Sometimes, I felt a little bit of shame thinking about that, thinking about the differences between us since we graduated. I couldn't seem to break out of my toxic cycle.

"So now you are banished to Canada?" Nya said as I finished explaining, but I could hear the little laugh in her voice.

"Yes," I said.

"Are their winters not ten months long?"

"Probably. Apparently Fleurmont is up in the mountains somewhere," I said. "And did I mention that the guy I'm working with is a complete jerk?"

"Twice now. Is he at least hot? You might as well have something nice to look at if you have to be there for so long."

"I don't know. Maybe a little, but I can't tell because he seems so boring. He's all serious and sucks up to Uncle Valerian and Grandpa."

"Wow. Stassi Salvati living in a small town, up in Canada. Who would have thought?"

"Come rescue me!"

"I wish I could, but I can't."

"But you're my best friend!"

"I am your best friend," said Nya. "You know what? I will pray for you."

"You're going to have to do a whole fucking lot of praying to get me out of this one."

Nya laughed. "It's only four months. This could be really perfect, actually."

"How? How is this perfect?" I said, baffled.

"It's perfect because I'm going to see you in August for the Architect Gala. You're going to spend four months up in eternal winter, and then you will have so many stories to share with me. Then we'll be back in L.A. together, and you can tell me all about it."

"If they even let me back," I retorted. "What if they don't even have cellphone reception up there? How am I supposed to text you every day? How am I supposed to call you if I'm actually dying of boredom and you have to send an emergency helicopter to fly me out of there?"

"First of all, it would be an emergency private jet, not a helicopter," said Nya, and then she gasped in delight. "You know what would be fantastic?"

"You flying to L.A. right now in a private jet to come rescue me?"

"We can write letters to each other!"

"Write letters?" I sat up in my bed.

After I had moved to L.A. from Nairobi in middle school, Nya and I wrote letters to each other for years before we were reunited in college.

"Yes, it will be just like old times. We will keep each other updated through letters. You can write to me about all the dramatic tales of your sentence in Fleurmont, and I will write to you about all the happenings of the world from Nairobi. Then, we shall reunite in Los Angeles and all will be well."

I sighed.

"Fine, I suppose that sounds just dramatic enough to be fabulous."

"Good," said Nya.

I heard voices from outside my bedroom. Grandpa was asking one of the maids to bring him a drink.

Crap. I guess that meant it was almost time for dinner.

"I think I need to go," I muttered.

"Is it family dinner time?"

"Yes, unfortunately, I believe it is."

"Good luck, my friend."

I hung up the phone, and let myself stare up at the ceiling for a few moments before dinner. I hadn't done design work in so long.

But maybe Julian was right. Maybe I had fucked up too hard this time. I did feel really bad about hurting that waitress. I hoped she was okay.

I exhaled, sliding reluctantly out of the bed to go to dinner.

# CHAPTER SEVEN

## Connor

"Mr. Salvati, Connor Fitzgerald is here to see you," said one of Valerian Salvati's maids.

Valerian said something I couldn't completely hear, and then the maid turned back to me with a polite smile, opening the door wider to let me in.

"Thanks." I stepped into Valerian's home office, and I slowed my steps when I realized it was more than just Valerian.

Unlike his office at work, his home office was warmer, with intricate wood coffers all over the ceiling. There wasn't time to look at it more carefully, though, especially as I immediately recognized Anton Salvati sitting next to him, a cold, humourless expression on his face.

"Fitzgerald, good to see you again," said Valerian. "Come on in. Meet my niece, Stassi Salvati. She'll be your intern for the next four months."

"Intern?" I asked, surprised, and my eyes shifted from Anton Salvati to the well-dressed man sitting next to the window before landing on the blonde head of the woman who was still turned away from me. Did I hear him right? Did he say niece?

Valerian continued. "Stassi, this is Connor Fitzgerald. He's the head architect for the project in Fleurmont."

The woman sitting across from Valerian turned, and the moment I saw those cerulean blue eyes, I knew it was her.

Fuck.

She looked exactly the same as she had in the elevator, only her dark blonde hair was straight now, and her shoes were pink instead of neon yellow.

She was Valerian Salvati's niece? What were the fucking chances? Why was she here? I didn't need an intern.

She glared at me, clearly recognizing me too.

Making a mental pivot, I put out a hand to shake hers. "It's nice to meet you."

"Right." Her eyes dropped to my hand before looking back up at me, the rest of her unmoving.

"*Stassi*," snapped Valerian. He turned to me, shaking his head. "Fitzgerald, I apologize for my niece. She will not be like this when you two are in Fleurmont."

I furrowed my brow to form the question I wanted to ask, but Valerian didn't stop, turning instead to Anton Salvati. "Fitzgerald, meet my father, Anton Salvati."

"It's great to meet you, sir. I'm grateful for the opportunity."
We shook hands.

"I've heard great things about your work," said Anton, though his tone was clipped and his eyes were still hard and calculating.

Something about the way he was looking at me made me feel like this was another interview, and one I wasn't doing particularly well at.

Valerian introduced me to his husband Julian next, but I barely registered our interaction. Stassi Salvati was still looking at me. Her face was mostly sharp angles –the arched brows, the defined cheekbones, the sharpness in her eyes.

Shifting away from her, I looked away. What were the odds of this? Why hadn't Valerian mentioned an intern before?

I'd already met with the marketing team and the cost estimator since signing the papers. No one had said anything about an intern.

"Did you get the itinerary Penny sent you about your trip out to Mt. Aster?"

"Yes, I just got the email," I said.

Stassi stood up abruptly. "Excuse me. I think I need to go pack," she said, and without waiting for anyone, she left the room.

Julian followed her, closing the door behind him.

Valerian sighed again, shaking his head, and I took the opportunity to jump in.

"To be honest, I don't need an intern at this stage of the project," I said. "The next few weeks are just going to be design work. If anything, I might need to consult with some experts for structural or environmental factors, but I don't need an intern."

"The intern is not negotiable, Fitzgerald," said Valerian firmly, "but don't worry, it'll be good. Think of it as having your personal assistant. Stassi is...well, she's something."

"Stassi was at the top of her class at UC Berkeley," Anton cut in sharply, looking unimpressed with me.

Valerian nodded. "Yes, she's a smart cookie, but she could really use some structure. She did her undergraduate degree in architecture, and she's licensed, so you can do with that however you see fit."

Nepotism. Great. She'd better not be the female version of William Harrison.

"I see." I tried to think of anything else I could say to dissuade him from this. It seemed unlikely, though. Based on Stassi's reaction, and the fact that she was from one of the wealthiest families in California and certainly did not need an internship, this was not exactly her idea, either.

Still. An intern could set me back weeks of work. What tasks was I supposed to give her?

"Anyway," continued Valerian, "I want to dive into part of the site analysis with you today."

I tried to focus on Valerian, but it was difficult. Having to come up with a pitch in a month was work enough, and no doubt, my first few days back in Fleurmont would mean spending time with my parents and the town.

My parents couldn't be more thrilled that my job was taking me back to Fleurmont. I thought about the rest of the town –Arielle's diner, Raphael's grocery store, Aunt Suyi's restaurant, the town square...

It had been eleven years since I had lived in Fleurmont. As much as I loved L.A. and travelling the world for work, it would be nice to be in Fleurmont again.

# CHAPTER EIGHT

## *Connor*

"Did you eat enough? Here, have more food," said Mom, shoving turnip cakes and shrimp dumplings onto my already very full plate.

"I know you have a lot of great dim sum options out in L.A., but you gotta admit that Suyi makes the best turnip cakes in the world," said Dad, dipping his turnip cake into chili sauce.

We were at Chez Suyi's, the only Asian restaurant in Fleurmont.

Chez Suyi's was owned and operated by one of my mom's closest friends, Aunt Suyi. She was the first Asian immigrant to Fleurmont, and had originally opened a small Asian-fusion poutine shop. Her family had owned a proper dim sum restaurant in Hong Kong, and she was determined to bring some of her culture into her cuisine. She made BBQ pork poutine, curry fish ball poutine, and even a seafood poutine.

It was Mom, actually, who had inspired Suyi to turn the place into a dim sum restaurant. During Mom's divorce from

Sebastien, Aunt Suyi had made Mom a bunch of traditional dim sum dishes. Mom had encouraged her to add it to the menu, and slowly but surely over the last twenty-five years, Chez Suyi's had evolved from an Asian-fusion poutine shop to a small but mighty dim sum restaurant.

Everything looked exactly the same as the last time I was here. The building was the same as most buildings in Fleurmont, charming and with the exterior painted in a bright colour, but the moment you stepped inside, it was full-on Chinese family restaurant charm and nostalgia. Paintings of lotus flowers hung on the walls all around the room, which was covered in thick curtains of gold and red. There were small round tables covered in white and gold patterned tablecloths, each with its corresponding rotating glass turntable. They were smaller than tables you'd find in a big city, but that added to the atmosphere. The seat cushions were the same as the ones I was familiar with growing up, cushioned and covered in the same pattern as the tablecloths.

My parents and I were now seated next to each other at one of these round tables. I took another bite of turnip cake. This had to be my fourth or fifth piece.

"This is pretty amazing," I nodded.

"Have more, then!"

"Mom, Mom, that's enough, thank you."

"I'm so happy you're back home." Mom patted my arm warmly.

Her gold bracelets jingled on her slender wrists, her engagement ring and wedding ring always glittering so brightly you would think they were trying to send out SOS signals.

"I'm really happy to be home too."

"I have an empty nest," said Mom dramatically. "It's been over ten years and I still can't get used to it. If only you and Michael were home more."

"I thought you were always busy with town events."

Mom was heavily involved in all town activities, including the upcoming Spring Festival, a festival our town hosted every year. Mom had always been determined to thrive in small-town Quebec, and throughout my entire childhood, she was on every parent committee and involved herself in as many town events as possible. Now, she was also a good friend of the town mayor.

"She has been busy. She's basically orchestrated the whole Spring Festival herself this year," said Dad.

"Oh, please." Mom waved her hands in dismissal, but I saw the small smile on her face.

In the last few years since I'd graduated, she had entrenched herself even more in town business.

"You know," said Mom after a while, "I know someone that you'll be working with soon who would be perfect for you."

"Cece," Dad chastised, like he already knew what my mom was scheming.

"You know someone I'm working with?" I asked, baffled.

There was no way Mom knew someone at the Salvati Group. My mind flashed to Stassi. Could they have met already somehow? I still couldn't believe that the woman I met in the elevator, in Taipei of all places, was the same woman I was being forced to work with. We'd barely exchanged five sentences between us, and already I knew we couldn't stand each other. She so clearly had no interest in this project, and the last thing I needed was a distraction that could derail my whole career. I bet Valerian hadn't saddled Harrison with an intern.

That, and Stassi Salvati seemed like a train wreck.

"Elodie Gendreau. She's an environmental consultant, and I believe she's the one your boss connected you with."

"How do you know *that*?"

"Your mother knows anything she wants to know about," said Dad.

"I have my ways," said Mom smugly.

"Elodie is on the Spring Festival committee with your mother," Dad whispered to me.

Oh, of course.

"You don't remember Elodie?" Mom asked me, frowning.

"No, Elodie Gendreau?" I repeated.

The name didn't even faintly ring a bell, at least not beyond the list of collaborators Valerian Salvati had sent me over email.

"Well, she grew up here, so you went to the same high school, but she's three years younger than you, so maybe that's why you don't remember her."

I shook my head no.

"Anyway, she's gorgeous now. I just saw her last week. She's really smart and really pretty, and who knows, maybe the two of you will hit it off," said Mom cheerfully.

"But you don't have to," added Dad. "You can also just keep things professional."

"*Owen,*" said Mom, annoyed.

"Cece, they're going to be working together. That might make it a bit awkward, don't you think?"

"Oh, please. Workplace romances are all the rage these days."

I decided I didn't want to know how she knew that, focusing instead on my shrimp dumpling.

Mom wasn't far off base exactly. I'd been single for longer than I cared to admit.

My last real relationship was in college. Work kept me so busy that dating was just...never on my mind. The few dates I had been on in the last five years were awkward and kind of uncomfortable. I never connected with anyone, and the conversations always felt like networking at a conference. Same small talk, same questions, same topics.

"Are you sure you don't want more turnip cake? I'm going to eat the last one." Dad had his chopsticks ready to snatch up the last turnip cake.

"Go ahead. I'm getting really full, I promise," I said.

"Full? Who's full?" came Aunt Suyi's voice from behind me.

I turned to see Aunt Suyi carrying two more bamboo steamers towards us.

Aunt Suyi wasn't really my aunt, at least not by blood, but that's what we called her growing up. She was a shorter, plumper woman with large eyes and a permanently kind expression. She had also successfully bullied all three of her children into continuing the family business, and I could see her youngest son, Alexi, pushing a dim sum cart to the other side of the restaurant. The dim sum carts were really only at the restaurant for fun. The restaurant was almost too small for dim sum carts, but Aunt Suyi had gotten them for us anyway. I still remembered playing in them when I was younger.

"When your mom told me you were coming back to Fleurmont, I just knew I had to make chicken feet today," said Aunt Suyi, setting down the bamboo steamers at our table.

Did those steamers get bigger somehow? My stomach was going to burst. *But* Aunt Suyi's chicken feet were pretty great.

"Thanks, Aunt Suyi. You're the best," I said, opening up the lid.

Steam rolled out, and the delicious scent of the dish somehow pushed open more room in my very full stomach.

"I only make it for you, Connor. No one else in this town likes chicken feet. Well, except your dad." Aunt Suyi gave Dad a smile.

Dad grinned, his blue eyes twinkling.

"Connor? Is that you?" said a voice, and I turned to see Abel Boivin coming in through the front door.

"Abel!" I said, surprised, swallowing my last bite so that I could stand up.

Abel Boivin was the town's Everything Guy. He was technically trained as a vet, but there wasn't enough business for him to be a full-time vet, so he also worked as the town handyman and substituted as a driver for all town things —snowplows, Zambonis, even school buses. He lived right above his small storefront, which had a massive hand-carved sign at the front that read "APPELLE ABEL —VÉTÉRINAIRE, BRICOLEUR, CHAUFFEUR, TOUT AUTRE" which translated to "Call Abel —veterinarian, handyman, driver, everything else."

We gave each other a half hug, clapping each other on the back.

"So good to see you," I said. "How have you been?"

Abel had to be past sixty now, but he looked the same, dressed in jeans and a flannel shirt. When I was in high school, I worked for him for a couple of seasons plowing snow.

"So good to see you back in town, *mon gars*," said Abel, eyeing the food on our table.

"Hopefully he's here to move back for good," said Mom, folding her hands together in front of her. She lifted an eyebrow at me and threw me a smile.

"We'll see," I laughed, "but I'm here for at least the next four months for work."

"Good, good. You should move back. Keep your parents company. Keep us company. We're all getting too old in this town."

"Do you want some?" Dad asked Abel, who was still eyeing the food at our table.

"What is it?" Abel asked, watching Dad suckle on the remains of some chicken feet.

"Chicken feet."

"Oh, er, no thanks."

"See?" said Aunt Suyi, jabbing a thumb at Abel. "No one else likes chicken feet except for you two."

"I like everything else," said Abel quickly.

"I know, I know. Grab a table. You want the usual?"

"Yes, but I'm actually waiting for –*ah, les voilà!*"

"Connor Fitzgerald? Is that you?"

We all turned to see a group of my former high school teachers at the door. Mr. Tremblay, Ms. Richard, and Ms. Simard waved at me and Abel.

It felt as if the whole town was here. Mom gave me another smile as we chitchatted and caught up.

I knew she wanted me to move back to Fleurmont. A small part of me wanted to too, but I still had too much to accomplish to make a move back here permanent, at least for now.

It was nice to be back in Fleurmont, though. I had only a few days before Stassi arrived to spend time with my family and get the cabin set up. It didn't feel like enough time, and suddenly, sitting there at Chez Suyi's, I realized just how much I missed this town and the people in it.

My friend Arden drove me up to the cabin on Mt. Aster the next day.

Arden Lee was an old family friend who had also grown up in Fleurmont. The Lees were the only East Asian family in Fleurmont besides ours and Aunt Suyi's. Arden and I were the same age and had grown up together.

Our families used to come together for all the major holidays. Holidays like Lunar New Year, Christmas, or any time traditionally spent with family were times our mothers thought would be spent best as a community. Arden and I were the youngest of our generation, and after we graduated high school, these holiday gatherings had become less and less frequent. Seeing Arden always made me a little nostalgic for those times.

Arden lived in Montreal now, but we were still close friends, so she made the three-hour drive to help me move over the weekend and visit her mom. Arden had a complicated relationship with her mom, so she usually kept her visits here short and infrequent.

I met Arden at her mom's house, and her mom surveyed us as we put my suitcases in the trunk. Aunt Janie was the same age as Mom, but the permanently serious expression on her face always made her look a little older.

"Hi, Connor."

"Hi, Aunt Janie," I said. "How are you?"

"Good. I hear you're moving back."

"He's only here for work for four months," said Arden.

"At least he's here for four months," said Aunt Janie. "I don't know what you're still doing in Montreal."

"Mom, I work there," said Arden, exasperated, and then turned to me. "Okay, let's go."

"Arden, let Connor drive," said Aunt Janie.

"Mom, I can drive," Arden said more sharply.

"Arden, he's a man. Let him drive."

Arden's right eye twitched.

"Arden's actually a much better driver than I am," I said in defence of my friend.

Arden looked at me gratefully.

"Fine, fine. But at least put your hair up, Arden. Your hair is a mess," said Aunt Janie.

"Okay, bye Mom, see you later," said Arden, plastering on a big smile.

"See you later," I said.

"Okay, okay, bye."

Arden ran to the car, and I got in the passenger seat. Arden turned out onto the road.

"God, I hate coming back here," shuddered Arden. "Did you hear? Apparently, my hair is a mess."

"Yeah, jeez, what's up with your hair, dude?"

Arden shoved me, and I laughed as we made our way up the mountain.

"Thanks for the sacrifice," I said to her. "It's good to see you."

She smiled. "Yeah, it's good to see you too. I wish you'd come visit me in Montreal instead of this, but hey, happy you're going to be the freaking Creative Director of the Salvati Group. You think they'll give you, like, a private plane to fly to all of your super important international business trips?"

I snorted a laugh. "I doubt it. And I don't have the Creative Director job yet."

"Oh, please. You're a badass designer. I've seen your designs."

"Thanks. I just wish I knew more about what he wanted. I mean, he says he's open to anything in the luxury resort space, but it's Valerian Salvati. He probably already has a very specific vision for this place, and he's just testing me."

"Do you have any ideas so far?"

"A few, nothing crazy. I definitely don't want to make it a ski town."

"Yeah, Fleurmont doesn't really feel like a ski town," Arden agreed.

"I think I'm more pissed off that I have to compete with William Harrison again."

"Screw William Harrison. You got this. Who wants to go to a stupid resort in Arizona, anyway?"

"I mean, Arizona has the Grand Canyon, but okay," I laughed. "Thanks for being supportive."

"Yeah, chin up, future Creative Director," grinned Arden. "And hey, looks like we're here."

I looked outside, and I let out a low whistle. We were at the old miners' town.

Arden parked the car at the front of the renovated Salvati cabin —the only structure in sight that wasn't actively falling apart— and the two of us took a breath in to admire the surrounding view.

The old miners' town was breathtaking. I couldn't believe I had never been here before. It was completely surrounded by the Aster mountains, the same way Fleurmont was encircled by mountains. Unlike Fleurmont though, the village grounds had no lake, just a small pond, and it was higher in the mountains than Fleurmont. The mountains were half green forest, half stunning rock formations of rich brown and blue hues.

Instantly, I could see it.

The resort.

We could have a set of luxury yurts with private fire pits. A lodge for stargazing on the west side. We could build it so that the first two floors could serve as a venue space.

We could have a wooden track ride around the east side of the mountain that would allow people to view the wildflower fields without stepping into the ecosystem. It could be a low-velocity ride, peak lateral g-force of 1.0g at most, but fast enough that it didn't feel like a gondola ride, maybe at a speed of around thirty kilometres per hour. That was fast enough to be almost exciting, but slow enough to enjoy the view. I'd have to sketch out a layout and run a simulation.

The sunrises and sunsets would be breathtaking.

The ideas flooded in, and I was so excited my hands almost shook with anticipation. I needed to write this down.

"I can see the wheels in your brain whirring," smiled Arden. "Do you need a notepad?"

"You know me too well," I grinned, and I fished my phone out of my pocket to take notes. "This place is fucking incredible."

"Yeah, it's gorgeous," said Arden with an exhale.

The resort could be a romantic destination. We could build out an observation deck where you could see out into the mountains. Maybe it could be made of glass so you could see the rock formation underneath. I would need to think about the insulation implications, though, for the hotter months and the cold winters.

My fingers shook with excitement as I typed.

# CHAPTER NINE

## *Stassi*

The driver, Davy, took me straight to Mt. Aster. We technically never passed by the mysterious little town of Fleurmont everyone kept talking about. Penny sent me their tourist flyers for their upcoming Spring Festival. The Fleurmont spring festival sounded like greasy fast food stalls and outdoor games that would take place on top of stacks of hay.

The drive from the closest airport to Mt. Aster was several hours long. The entire drive was just trees –a blur of endless trees. Everything was bright as the car made its way upwards on an incline up the mountain. It was the first week of May, and spring had apparently not quite sprung yet. The trees were almost bare, with dark branches stretched out and twisted in every direction towards the sky. Little neon buds pebbled at the tips of the branches, causing the blur of trees to take on a strikingly bright, almost neon hue. If I cared more, I might have had ideas about how to incorporate this kind of visual into a design.

But I didn't care.

I was being exiled and put on a time out.

Like a child.

Part of me was furious that Uncle Valerian had pegged me as an intern. Another part of me was reluctantly a little relieved. It meant I didn't need to be back in L.A. for a while. And another part of me was terrified. This internship meant I had to design again...What if I *couldn't* design anymore? What if I were just blocked for the rest of my life?

I stared out the window for the first forty minutes, just thinking. It was the first time in a long while I hadn't been surrounded by people. I'd spent months surrounded by groups of people, not thinking, just going with the flow.

Want to jet off to Paris? *Yes.*

Want to shop for a ten thousand dollar Japanese tansu chest that we'll never use? *Yes.*

Want to go to a party in Vegas? *Why the hell not?*

If it weren't for Uncle Valerian, I could have kept going. I felt like I was at a club at four in the morning. It was the feeling of pushing yourself past the point of being tired and feeling almost invincible, like you could keep on dancing forever, like you could keep moving to the beat of the music and let it carry you away forever.

The first time I went clubbing, I was eighteen, and Jenna had gotten all of us fake IDs. I felt like such a badass taking an Uber to a club with my friends. I wore a black one-shoulder dress and pink heels and drank enough tequila that my feet only killed me the next day. The four of us had matched our outfits –black dresses, pink heels. Nya had just moved to L.A. for college, and while I was happy to have my best friend in the city with me, our dynamic was still a little new for us after our seven-year separation. We were still slowly getting to know each other again, this new version of ourselves that was eighteen now and not eleven.

We arrived at the club, fake IDs either totally clearing with flying colours or the bouncers not actually giving a shit because we were a group of girls wearing skimpy short dresses –honestly, it was probably the latter.

We started dancing, and a song by The Veronicas came on. It was the same song Nya and I had been obsessed with before I had moved back to the U.S.

Nya and I looked at each other in surprise, and then we broke out into massive, identical smiles. It felt like fate connecting us again –and just like that, we were close again, and everything was going to be okay. We danced to The Veronicas, and when the song was over, we begged the DJ to play it for us again and again.

It was one of the best nights ever, and it made me a little sad to think that maybe that phase of our lives was over now, too.

The car jolted, pulling me out of memory lane. The road had changed. We were no longer on the paved road. Instead, the car was bumping along upwards on a dirt path.

I felt nauseous about thirty seconds later.

Clearly, no one had maintained this road for a very long time, and Davy navigated the car around fallen branches and massive rocks.

"You okay back there?" Davy asked.

"Yeah, I'm fine, thanks," I said, even though I was ready to hurl.

"We should be almost there," he said, looking at the GPS screen.

I nodded and tried to focus on looking outside.

The trees bumped unsteadily in my vision, and then, I saw it. A wooden house. We bumped our way across the dirt road, and more houses appeared.

Old, decrepit, disgusting houses that were as unkept as a campsite on the last day of a music festival.

This must be the old mining town.

The wooden houses were faded, with broken windows and sagging porches. They leaned against each other like a group of drunk friends at a pizza parlour at three in the morning after a night out. Green moss and rust spread out in equal measure across the loose surfaces. Even from inside the car, I felt like I could breathe in the scent of the rust.

This place was *disgusting*.

Uncle Valerian invested in this?! How was this place not a complete health hazard? Didn't he already have the site analysis done? Was air quality part of the site analysis? Maybe this whole place cost less than a pair of Jimmy Choos. How could anyone pay more for a –

Oh my God, *what the fuck was that slime* –

I looked away from the house at the edge of what I assumed was a swamp.

A swamp.

I was in a Shrek movie.

This could not be happening.

The car slowed as we reached the edge of what looked like the old town limit. A log cabin that was significantly less decrepit –but still gross-looking–stood at the edge of a hill. I was about to look beyond it when the car stopped.

"We're here," said Davy.

Oh my God.

Someone save me.

Davy got out of the car and took my suitcases out of the trunk. My beautiful, vulcanized fiberboard and leather cream and brown suitcases were sitting in the dusty, rusty, swampy dirt of Fleurmont.

Slowly, I got out of the car. Some kind of enormous bird screeched overhead as the door to the cabin opened.

Connor Fitzgerald stepped out of the cabin. He was wearing jeans and a red plaid button-down. Like a full-on Canadian lumberjack. Except it wasn't sexy, because he was frowning and looked at me like Silicosis Personified had just showed up at his front door.

His black hair was mussed like he had just run his hands through it, and his dark eyes glanced over at the mountain of suitcases that were piling up at the foot of the porch before roaming over me.

I shut the car door.

"You're here," he said coolly.

He sounded disappointed.

"Obviously," I retorted.

"Do you need the suitcases carried inside?" asked Davy.

"Yes, please." My voice was icier than I wanted it to sound, thanks to Connor.

Connor opened the door wider for him. "It's the bedroom on the right."

The bedroom on the right? Right of what? I watched in horror as Davy brought the suitcases into the cabin. It didn't seem to take him long to reach 'the bedroom on the right'. Was there only *one* floor in this cabin?

I was about to ask Connor about the cabin when I saw him looking at my shoes.

"You're wearing heels," he said flatly.

"Do you always just state the obvious? I thought you were supposed to be some fancy, creative architect."

His eyes narrowed in on me in what I could only assume was a glare.

"Wearing expensive shoes is not practical here, especially if we visit construction sites."

"First of all, it's Sunday, so I wasn't expecting to visit construction sites. And second of all, these are Club London heels; they're not Christian Louboutins."

Connor Fitzgerald blinked at me.

Davy came out of the cabin, heaving a sigh of relief.

"Alright, you're all set now," he said with a small exhale. "I'll be on my way now."

No. Take me back with you.

"Thank you," I said.

He tipped his hat to me in goodbye.

Before I could muster enough courage to beg him to take me back to the airport, Davy and the car were gone in a trail of mud.

"Well," said Connor, his arms still crossed in front of him, "this is it. There's a garage on this side, and then a shed out on that side towards the mountain. They're both a bit of a mess right now, but I'm going to clear them up for storage."

I stepped closer to the front door of the cabin. It was hideous. The exterior, while not falling apart like the rest of the mining town, was so old the wood looked almost grey. That Connor Fitzgerald was standing next to it only made it look that much more oppressive and atrocious.

"So, this is the...cabin," I said dryly.

"It's also our office," said Connor. He stepped into the cabin with me, and I was viscerally aware of his physical presence as I stepped into the cabin with him. He shut the door behind us.

"Well, this is the living room, or one of the workspaces, if you will. The Wi-Fi password is on the table. I just set it up. Internet speed is good. Then you have the kitchen, simple enough." Connor gestured to the kitchen, even though he didn't have to.

I could see it from where I was standing. It was tiny.

How was this even a kitchen? I've been in bathrooms larger than the living room and kitchen combined.

Connor pointed down the hall.

"There's a closet there, a bathroom, and then your bedroom is on the right. Mine is at the end of the hall."

"End of the hall?" I repeated in disbelief. "We're sleeping in the same house?"

"I'm sorry, did you think this was a multi-unit gated complex?"

"Is this place even a thousand square feet?" I snapped back.

I had to sleep...*twenty feet* away from my boss? How did HR approve this? Was this Uncle Valerian's shitty new Stassi prison? Rich people are such assholes.

"I'll have you know it's actually three thousand square feet," said Connor, "which you would know if you bothered to read the PDF I sent you last week."

He had sent me an email or three that I hadn't read.

Connor walked down the hall away from the prison cell bedrooms towards the kitchen. I followed him reluctantly.

He walked to the back of the cabin –should I be calling it a hut?– which was bright from the afternoon sunlight. There was a massive wooden table in the middle of the room. Drafting paper and pencils were arranged in a neat pile to one side, and there were two desks set up in parallel next to it, monitors and keyboards set up. There was a coffee mug and a laptop on one desk, and the monitor was open to the image of a detailed site plan.

I looked out onto what I assumed was a sad excuse for a backyard. A deck was out back, but fallen tree branches and leaves from the previous autumn covered the backyard. In one corner, there looked like there was a hint of snow stuck between the branches.

"Is that *snow?*"

"It can snow until mid-May here."

I looked at him, appalled.

Connor offered nothing else, and I looked around the space again.

"Food's stocked up. There's stew for dinner if you want it. I already ate."

It was five o'clock. Who eats dinner before five o'clock?

Another horrible thought entered my mind.

"So I'm just stuck here with you in this tiny cabin for four months?" I blurted.

Connor looked at me coldly, the hate and irritation clear in his eyes. "Look, princess, I'm not happy about this either. Babysitting isn't exactly in my job description. You're not stuck here, though. No one is keeping you hostage. You are welcome to leave at any time."

The invitation was clear in his tone.

"I don't exactly have a car."

"You can rent one in Fleurmont. It's only a three-hour walk from here. Easy hike."

I couldn't tell if he was joking.

"Two hours if you wear proper shoes."

Dick.

"Work starts tomorrow morning at nine o'clock," continued Connor. "There will be other people here, eventually. We'll be working with an environmental consultant, and in about a month, there will be demolition technicians and engineers working on site to start clearing out the old mining houses."

"Great," I said sarcastically.

"I'm going to work," said Connor, and he walked to his desk, not sparing me another glance.

It was *Sunday*. It was five o'clock on a Sunday.

Connor plugged in his earphones, opening up a new tab on the monitor.

Freaking workaholic.

I walked away and went to my bedroom.

The room was simple. A queen bed with white bedding. A desk and chair by the window. Log cabin walls all around. The bedroom had the smallest closet I've ever seen in my life. This closet was clearly designed by a straight man. Or by a person who was designing for a toddler.

I saw the bathroom connected to my bedroom. At least there was that. If I had to share a bathroom with that man, I would die.

I unpacked what I could. My belongings from one suitcase barely fit into the closet. Connor was unsympathetic to my dilemma.

"Are there storage compartments I can put under the bed?"

"No."

"Can I use the storage rooms in the hallway?"

"Yes." A not so subtle silent 'duh' was implied.

"I was asking to be polite."

"Didn't know you were capable."

"More capable than you."

"You're interrupting my work."

I shoved the rest of my belongings across the storage space in the hallway. The hallway extended all the way to Connor's room. The door was closed, and I was half tempted to look inside to see if he had a bigger closet than I did. If he did, he probably had it stuffed with work. Or love letters to Uncle Valerian. I should tell Julian he had competition.

After I unpacked everything that I could, I changed into my pajamas and climbed into bed with a sigh. I guess it wasn't the most uncomfortable thing in the world. With my non-stop travelling, I hadn't stayed anywhere long enough in the last year for me to be too particular about the type of bed I had, anyway.

I pulled out my phone and checked my social media apps. Quinn had posted a photo of her and Jenna and a few of our other friends at Dry 66, the new club that had opened up downtown. There were about a dozen messages from my friends asking me where I was.

I didn't reply to any of them. I fell asleep uneasily in my new bed, falling asleep earlier than I had in over a decade.

When I woke up the next day, Connor was already working at his desk, with a pitcher of fresh coffee next to him.

*Did he even sleep?*

"Good morning," he said, glancing in my direction. His eyes lingered on the shorts and tank top I was wearing.

I felt myself shiver involuntarily at his gaze. Connor looked away.

"There's coffee if you want." He pushed the pitcher of coffee half an inch towards me.

He was wearing a simple button-down shirt today and dark pants. He was surprisingly fit for a workaholic, and I wondered if he worked out.

"Sure," I said. "Thanks."

There was an awkwardness in the air between us as I silently grabbed a clean mug and poured myself coffee next to his desk. Connor clicked around on his computer, but I got the sense that he was laser-focused on me. I tried not to look at him.

I failed a second later and looked at him.

He looked at me, and we both looked away quickly.

Why was this so weird?!

Maybe we were being too polite with each other, and that was wrong. My heart beat a little faster as I went to sit down at the large worktable in the middle of the room. There was a plate of croissants and fresh fruit in the middle of the table. I took a croissant and sipped my coffee.

"So, what do you want me to do today, Boss?" I asked wryly.

"Please don't call me that," said Connor, frowning, "and it's not nine yet. You can take your time to eat."

"I'm ready to work," I said, biting off a piece of croissant.

Damn, that was good.

Connor looked at me again, and he looked almost embarrassed when he said, "You can take your time to get dressed or whatever. There's no rush."

I glared at him.

"What do you mean, get dressed?" my irritation returned, saving us from the weirdness between us. "I *am* dressed. I'm not naked."

"I never said you were naked," Connor flushed, his face turning pink, "but this is a workplace –"

"This is a random cabin in the woods," I snapped. "And I don't recall seeing a dress code in your *seventeen* page long PDF."

"Fine, wear whatever you want," snapped Connor.

"I don't see what the big deal is," I said.

That was a bit of a lie. I was wearing a tiny cherry print V-neck camisole that hugged my tits together and exposed most of my stomach. My shorts were made of the same soft cotton material and rode up against my ass. Still, it's not my fault men are intimidated by women's bodies.

"I was just trying to create the *semblance* of a work environment here."

"It's not like I'm flashing you my nipples."

I was wearing a bra. A very cute one, in fact. With polka dots.

"Please do not talk about your nipples when we're working. Or ever," Connor said, biting out each word, his voice carefully controlled. He looked straight into my eyes. I wondered if he was afraid of being caught looking at my tits.

"Fine." I held his gaze, trying not to raise my eyebrows in a challenging way.

"We need fucking HR here," muttered Connor under his breath.

I took another bite of my croissant. "Okay, so what do you want me to do?"

*You will do anything Connor Fitzgerald tells you to do. If he tells you to design a floor plan, you're going to design a floor plan. If he tells you to research a lamp, you're going to research the best goddamn lamp you can find in North America.*

Something about Uncle Valerian's words suddenly felt a lot dirtier now. Maybe it was because I was just talking about my nipples.

"You can do research today," he said. "Research the topography and the natural elements in the area."

"Isn't that just in the site analysis?"

"Yes, I need you to study the site analysis so that you understand how we'll be orienting different buildings and creating access paths."

"O-kay," I said, "and what will you be doing?"

"Designing."

So descriptive.

He turned away from me and went back to his work.

*May 2*

*Dear Nyambura,*

*I am trapped in a small village in eastern Canada called Fleurmont, and I request that you come and save me immediately.*

*I'm not even really in Fleurmont. Apparently, it's a twenty-minute drive from Fleurmont, so I haven't actually been to this town everyone keeps talking about. Instead, I am stuck in a wood cabin with the most serious, insufferable workaholic I've ever met in my life. It's only been two days, and already I'm going crazy. All I do the entire day is a bunch of dumb, boring research tasks. I even tried looking for some tequila or wine so that my meaningless tasks could be more amusing, but alas, my warden's drinking habits are as dull as he is.*

*Connor Fitzgerald speaks in one-word sentences half the time, and all he does is drink coffee and work. The only time he isn't drinking coffee and working is early in the morning when he goes to work out in the backyard, which, by the way, is not even a backyard. It's a pit of dirt with gross leaves and snow. There's snow here. In May!*

*I am miles away from civilization, and I don't even know if I'll be able to send you this letter because did I mention I'm in a mining ghost town with ONE OTHER HUMAN BEING? I have no idea where the post office is, and I may die before you ever see this. If I am dead when you read this, bury me by the jacaranda trees.*

*Love,*
*Stassi*

# CHAPTER TEN

## *Connor*

**Dustin:** Yo! How is being back in Canada?

**Me:** Not bad actually, except that I got stuck with an intern.

**Dustin:** Isn't that a good thing? I heard Harrison is all by himself in Arizona.

**Me:** Lucky bastard.

**Dustin:** That bad, huh?

**Me:** It's fine. At least it's a cool landscape.

**Me:** What about you? What have you been working on?

**Dustin:** I've moved on from kitchen re-tiling to elevators for some rich person's expensive, douchey cars.

**Me:** Rough.

**Dustin:** Seriously.

The hot water felt good against my skin. I had sat in my chair working for probably two hours longer than I should have, and the combination of sitting in one place for too long and then trying to go on a run after had not been a good idea. My muscles were cramping.

I let the hot water run down my back. The water pressure in the shower was surprisingly good in this cabin.

As it had been for the last four days, the day had been frustrating.

Stassi was by far the messiest and most frustrating person I have ever met in my life. She was messier than my college roommate, Tom, who played rugby and came home trailing in mud. All she was doing was research on a computer, and yet she was the messiest person in the world.

Socks trailed over the cabin. Breadcrumbs from croissants and cherry stems littered every table in the cabin. Somehow, within the first twenty-four hours of her arrival, she had occupied every single surface of the storage area available in the cabin. Sequins, cashmere, feathers, suede, and more shoes than most shoe stores carry lined every drawer and every shelf.

Stassi sang to herself while she worked –or rather, pretended to work. Mostly, she flipped through different music playlists on her phone. But every couple of minutes, she seemed to be unable to stand the silence, and started to talk, usually by asserting herself into my work. And usually, in incredibly inappropriate ways.

"What are you working on?"

"Is that structure to scale with the welcome sign?"

"Why is the welcome sign so big? Do you have a complex? Are you overcompensating?"

"You're keeping the disgusting swamp in your proposal?"

I wanted to lock her in her bedroom and throw away the key.

I groaned, not wanting to be thinking about Stassi Salvati in the shower. It didn't help that she was always wearing those tiny tank tops.

Despite how frustrating it was to have her here in the cabin, it was impossible to deny how painfully attractive she was. It wasn't even just those magnetic blue eyes, or her full, voluptuous breasts. It was every inch of her. Her legs were long and golden. Her hair was somewhere between brown and blonde and looked softer than silk. She had her hair up in a neat bun in the mornings, but in the afternoons, she took out the massive hair clip that held her hair together, and her hair would spin out onto her shoulders like a spiral staircase of gold.

My dick hardened.

Yep. It had been too long since I'd had sex. Maybe I should think about dating again. Not that there was anyone to date in Fleurmont. Maybe in the next town over.

No, that was a ridiculous thought. I needed to stay focused. I was so close to finishing the draft of the main lodge. I went down a rabbit hole yesterday looking up different materials for the exterior façade. Despite how daunting a blank canvas could be, it was also the best kind of project, especially with a budget like the one the Salvati Group had. It was easy to get lost in a single building, a single design. Every building of this resort was an opportunity to innovate, to pitch something out of the ordinary, and with only a month to draft a pitch, I had probably wasted a little too much time yesterday in my research.

I looked down. My cock was still hard. I pumped liquid soap into my hand, and put my hand over my cock. Just as I was about to relieve myself as quickly as I could, there was a knock on the bathroom door. I jumped.

"Connor?" came Stassi's voice.

Jesus fucking Christ.

"What?" I shouted irritably, forcing my hand away from my cock.

"Is there a blowjob here?"

She did not just say that.

"What?"

"Blow dryer! Like, to dry hair?" she said impatiently.

Oh. Blow dryer. Blow dryer. Right.

"Can this wait? I'm kind of in the middle of something -I'm -I'm showering," I added unnecessarily in case she could somehow tell through the door that I was a pervert. I rubbed the soap off my hands as quickly as I could.

"But my hair is wet," she said, and I could practically see her rolling her eyes and crossing her arms over her chest, pushing her tits up...

"Going to bed with wet hair can cause hair breakage and scalp issues –" she rambled on while I stepped out of the shower, still sporting a partial as I quickly wiped the water off my skin with a towel.

I dried myself just enough to pull on my T-shirt and sweatpants. Getting dressed as quickly as I could, I adjusted my hard-on before grabbing the blow dryer under the bathroom sink.

Regret at trying to be a gentleman and letting Stassi take the bedroom with a private bathroom washed over me. If only Valerian had had the time to really renovate this place and have this bathroom connected to the bedroom instead of being out in the shared hallway, exposed to all the elements and Stassi's every question.

"–which is why if you want your hair to be healthy, you should really do that every time you wash it," Stassi continued.

I opened the bathroom door a little aggressively.

Stassi stood there, arms crossed exactly as I pictured, her wet hair dripping down her tanned arms and chest. She was wearing what looked like silk shorts.

I should try to turn down the thermostat to see if that would force her to wear more layers. Should have thought of that earlier.

Stassi looked up at me, glancing first at the steam rolling out of the bathroom before her gaze drifted back to me. Her irritated, bored expression turned into something different when she looked at me –an expression I couldn't quite pinpoint. She looked at me almost slowly, from my face all the way down to the sweatpants I was wearing.

"Here." I shoved the hair dryer into her hands.

"Did you get fully dressed just to hand me a blow dryer?" she smirked suddenly.

"You know, 'thank you' and 'I'm sorry for interrupting' are still perfectly acceptable phrases," I bit out.

"Fine. *Thank you*." She turned around, silk shorts dancing around the curves of her ass.

I was about to close the door when she spun around again.

"Oh, wait, wait," she said, speed-walking back.

"Jesus Christ, what the hell is it now?"

"Do you have floss?" asked Stassi, bouncing back up to me, her blue eyes all warm and sparkly.

"Floss? Are you kidding me right now? You've been here for four days. Why are you asking me about floss right now?"

"I ran out."

"Who runs out of floss?"

"Umm, people who actually care about hygiene and flossing every day?"

"Says the person who took four days to take a shower and finally ask for a blow dryer."

"Are you accusing me of being dirty?" Stassi put a hand on her hip, her weight shifting to her left leg as she popped her hip.

Fuck, she was driving me insane.

"If I give you floss, will you finally go away?" Without waiting for a response, I went back to the bathroom to look for floss. I opened the mirrored door of the cabinet in the bathroom, searching for an extra box of floss. I quickly found the box of floss and then opened the bottom drawer of the bathroom to find the other thing I was looking for.

"Besides, I *do* shower every day, not that it's any of your business. I just don't wash my hair every day, okay? I don't know why you're judging me for running out of floss when –"

"Alright, Stassi, here." I shoved the floss and the bottle into her hand. "Here. Now you have everything that you need. Please go away."

"Jeez, you don't need to be so fucking grumpy –what is this?" Stassi inspected the bottle as I started closing the bathroom door again. "Extra strength melatonin?! You gave me fucking sleeping pills?"

"Well, an actual sedative would work better for you, but this is the best I've got. You're welcome." I shut the door behind me, locking the door this time.

"You are so fucking rude!" shouted Stassi from the other side of the door.

"Goodnight!" I called back.

"So fucking rude. And here I thought Canadians were supposed to be nice," I heard her continue to grumble as she headed back down the hallway. I waited until I heard her bedroom door close again before I let out a sigh of relief.

And despite my annoyance at her, it didn't stop me from needing to fuck my own hand a minute later when I could finally finish showering.

"I'll see you later tonight," I said to Stassi on Friday morning, putting on my shoes.

I fought a smile as I watched Stassi from the corner of my eye. Dressed in long black leggings and a cream sweater, she was wearing significantly more clothes than usual. Spring was slow to arrive in Fleurmont, and the weather was still cool and crisp for most of the day. I should have turned down the heating in the cabin earlier.

"Where are you going?" she asked, sipping coffee.

"I'm meeting Elodie, the environmental consultant, in town," I explained.

"Alright," she murmured, her expression unreadable.

I headed out and made the drive back into town, shaking off the weird feeling I had of wanting to know what she'd been thinking.

Stassi was technically my intern. Technically was the operative word here. Over the last week, it was clear that I was the maker of coffee and procurer of shitty meals.

I shook my head again, not wanting to think about her any longer than I had to. Getting distracted by her was exactly what my career didn't need. There were three more weeks before my meeting with Valerian, which meant I had three weeks to come up with an amazing pitch.

Inspiration, at least, was not a problem. The mountains and the entire landscape were breathtaking, and it wasn't hard to come up with new ideas. I wanted it to be unique, but still bring out some of the more traditional elements of a Quebec resort.

Valerian had sent me a draft of the job description for the Creative Director position a few days ago, and it had only gotten me more excited and determined.

I met Elodie Gendreau at Le Robinet, the most popular local bar in Fleurmont. The owner of the bar was Florian Desrosiers, my former, now retired, high school art teacher, who, incidentally, had been good friends with Sebastien.

My father didn't have many friends. He'd been a workaholic until his dying day. Work always came first for him. It came before me and my brother, and I guess it came before Mom, too. Sebastien travelled for work my whole life, but he practically lived in different countries after he and Mom got divorced. He used to always say that we would have more time together when he retired. Of course, by the time I was in high school, we barely spoke, and when he died when I was eighteen, it had been almost two years since I'd seen him. I would probably spend more time at his friend's bar than I would with him in my lifetime.

Le Robinet looked and functioned more like a quirky cafe than a bar during the day.

The theme, as the name of the bar suggested, was faucets. There were little sculptures of faucets on the walls, flowers growing around the metal pieces, and every drawing and painting in the bar was of a different faucet. The bar had opened just a few years ago after Florian finally pursued his dreams of owning a bar. He had painted and created every art piece at Le Robinet.

Elodie waved at me from a booth, and she got up to greet me.

She dressed pretty formally for someone meeting at a small-town bar. She wore a navy blue dress that looked like it had a built-in blazer, and the colour reminded me of a particularly sheer and pornographic navy blue shirt Stassi had worn yesterday.

"Connor?" said Elodie. "It's nice to meet you."

"Hey, nice to meet you."

We shook hands.

"I hope this doesn't sound weird, but your mom told me a lot about you," said Elodie as we sat down together.

"In Fleurmont, not at all," I said wryly. "Actually, my mom told me we went to high school together?"

"Yeah, I remember you," said Elodie, and her cheeks turned a little pink.

"And you're back in town now? From where?" I asked, trying to smile politely as the server came.

We ordered two cappuccinos.

"I just moved back home, but I was living out in Vancouver for school, and then I stayed for work."

"Oh, nice. How was that? I lived in L. A., but I never had the chance to go up to Vancouver."

"Oh my gosh, we were so close then," said Elodie, "or, you know, on the same coast. I loved living in Vancouver."

Elodie continued telling me about life in Vancouver, and while it sounded nice, the conversation felt oddly stilted. Being with Stassi over the last week had already completely desensitized me from what a normal conversation should look like. It felt weird not to have an irrationally sassy woman talking to me.

"So, I've read through all the files you sent," said Elodie after an awkward pause once we'd exhausted small talk around our living experiences in Vancouver and L. A., "and I think it's brilliant. Your designs are so good."

"Oh, thanks," I said awkwardly.

Elodie smiled at me, looking genuinely excited.

"I hope you don't mind, but I've organized how I think we can work together over the next few months." She tucked her brown hair neatly behind her ears as she took out her laptop. "Do you mind if I show you?"

"Not at all, please."

Elodie opened her laptop, showing me a colour-coded set of folders on her screen.

"First, there's all the regulatory stuff we have to go through. The resort is going to be built close to protected land, so we'll need an environmental impact sign-off from the government. Next, I thought we could go through some of your sustainability goals. This can be everything from carbon emission tracking to sustainable materials used for construction, but anything really."

"You are very organized."

"I try." Elodie flushed at the compliment. "I also already put together an environmental impact assessment and a list of recommendations for sustainability goals based on some of your initial design concepts."

Damn, Valerian Salvati knew how to pick out an environmental consultant.

"That's incredible. I'm really grateful to have you here," I said, feeling relieved at having someone so competent to be a sounding board. "Can I run some initial ideas by you?"

I had been pretty in my own head over the last week, and getting feedback from someone else might actually be nice.

"Yes, of course!" she beamed at me.

We spent the next two hours going over some initial design ideas I had and how that worked with her environmental impact assessment, which covered everything from minimizing ecological impact during and after construction, as well as all the regulatory things I wasn't familiar with.

Elodie's passion for the environment and the ecosystem was palpable, and our meeting was the most productive I'd felt all week. We each had two coffees before we left Le Robinet with plans to meet up again soon.

I felt more focused after my meeting with Elodie, and talking to Elodie gave me the additional confidence to pitch my initial concept ideas to Valerian's marketing team and cost estimator team that same afternoon.

Three weeks.

I had three more weeks to refine this idea and make it an idea that Valerian Salvati would go nuts for.

# Chapter Eleven

## Stassi

"We're out of coffee," grumbled Connor.

"No coffee this morning?" I gasped, walking into the work space. I inspected the room, even though it's not like coffee was magically going to appear in one of the crevices.

"Yep, looks like we're officially out." Connor took a swig of water from his water bottle and set it down on the table, looking disappointed by the taste.

He walked back towards the kitchen. I followed him.

"What? How can we be out of coffee? It's been six days."

Connor shrugged. "I was here a week before you. It's fine. I'll go into town and buy some more."

"Do you even function without coffee?" I asked him suspiciously.

"Of course I function without coffee," he snapped back irritably.

I laughed despite myself.

Connor bit back a smile at the irony. He shook his head and went to the front door. He put on his shoes, and I noticed that his hair was still wet from his morning shower.

Connor was like a machine. Wake up at six. Go to the bathroom. Work out. Shower. Coffee. Work. More coffee. I had his entire schedule down pat. If I were a corporate spy or an assassin, he'd be fucked.

He put on a fleece jacket, and as he did, his shirt lifted slightly, showing just a quick flash of abs and a hint of a V-shape. Interesting.

"You're going into town right now?"

"Yep," he said, checking his pocket for his car keys.

"Okay!" Turning, I grabbed my shoes.

"You don't need to come," he said in a clipped tone.

"I'm coming with you," I said, and then I ran into my room to grab the letter that I'd written for Nya.

"You have work. I told you, you need to –"

"Do research, yes," I said, resisting the urge to roll my eyes. "I promise you the research will be done."

"Well, I –"

"I'm coming with you. If I stay here, I'm going to get cabin fever, and then I'm going to go crazy and kill you or something."

Connor blinked. "Did you just threaten to murder me?"

"No, I very kindly warned you so that you may live." I gave Connor my sweetest smile.

"How generous of you."

"Yes, exactly. So are we going, or what?"

My bag was ready. My shoes were on.

"Fine," said Connor reluctantly.

I got into the passenger seat of the car. Yes. Finally, I could get out of this freaking cabin.

The cabin wasn't actually all bad.

I discovered I had a stunning view of the mountains from my bedroom. It was the same view that you could see from the porch. The mountains were kind of beautiful. There were peaks and valleys of bright green, and the mountains never seemed to end. The mountains further away just looked dark blue instead of green. The whole thing was very picturesque.

And for the first time in a long time, I felt just a little calmer.

My parents' death felt further away. My sister's death felt further away. Everything felt a little less overwhelming from a little wooden cabin in a remote town no one I'd known in my life had ever heard of. I felt far away from that. And even though I was mostly alone, it was freezing in May, and the food here mostly sucked thanks to Connor's subpar cooking skills, I felt far away from the intense loneliness I had been feeling for so long.

The drive across the mountain was less bumpy than I remembered it being on the way in. Connor drove the way he did everything else in life –carefully and seriously. His hands were literally on the steering wheel in the nine and three o'clock positions.

I wondered if he'd ever had sex.

If he hadn't, it would seriously explain a lot.

And if he had, then he was clearly due for some more. Maybe that would finally help him loosen up and chill out.

"Why are you staring at me?" asked Connor. He glanced at me quickly, dark eyes meeting mine before turning back to the road ahead.

"Just wondering if you're this uptight because you haven't had sex in too long."

The car swerved slightly, and Connor swore.

"Jesus, Stassi," he snapped. "I know this is your first job –I *assume* this is your first job– but piece of advice? Don't talk about sex with people you're working with."

"You asked me. I was just trying to be honest. And it's not my first job."

"Fucking hell," muttered Connor, shaking his head.

"Besides, this is hardly a job. My uncle forced you to put up with me for four months because he didn't want to deal with me himself."

"And why doesn't he want to deal with you himself?"

"Because he thinks I'm a loose cannon." Might as well continue to be honest.

"Are you?"

"Only to myself most of the time."

Connor glanced over at me again.

Shit. Maybe that was a little too honest, even for me. Connor actually talking to me and asking me questions was throwing me off.

"What did you do?"

I sighed, looking out the window at the trees. The leaves were growing; they looked less neon green than they did a few days ago.

"The usual privileged, rich girl crap. Drank too much, partied too much, sank a boat, broke into a museum. The usual."

I was surprised Uncle Valerian hadn't led with that in the "Supervise Stassi" clause of his employment contract. She sank a boat! She's going to sink the whole company! Make her do useless research tasks so that she's so bored out of her mind that she can't do anything crazy!

"Why did you do it?"

My parents and Sylvia flashed in my mind.

"Boredom," I lied. I shifted uncomfortably in my seat, trying to focus on something outside.

"Hmm."

I don't know if he could tell the lie for what it was, but Connor switched the topic.

"I never thought I would be back here," he mused, and I saw the ghost of a smile on his face. "Back in Fleurmont, that is."

I looked over at him curiously. "Why's that?"

Connor shrugged, letting out a long exhale. "Fleurmont is a small town. My family was one of three Asian families living here, and most people are nice, but it could still feel kind of alienating at times, especially being half Asian. Kids can be assholes, so I was excited to get out and actually live in cities with more diversity, more culture."

I was surprised at his surprisingly vulnerable admission. "Are you half Taiwanese?"

"Yeah," he smiled, "through my mom. She moved here after she met my dad."

"And your dad is from here?"

"Yeah, both my dads are from here, actually. My biological father, Sebastien, was born in Fleurmont, and he was an investment banker. My stepdad, Owen, is also from Fleurmont. I think they actually used to be friends for a bit."

Connor's expression had softened.

"That sounds like an interesting love triangle story," I mused. I loved hearing about other people's love stories.

"Yeah, I'd rather not think about that," he said with a tight smile.

"Fair," I smiled. "Is your biological dad still here?"

"No, he died when I was eighteen." His voice was harder now, tighter than before.

"I'm sorry," I said softly. So Connor had lost a parent, too. I wonder if he and his dad had been close before he died.

"All good, it was a long time ago now." He looked over at me and flashed me a genuine smile.

Something fluttered in my chest.

"What are your parents like?" he asked me.

My smile faded.

"Worm food," I said, and I instantly regretted my words. I cleared my throat. "My parents died in a car crash two years ago."

"Shit. I'm sorry. I think I knew that, and I forgot."

*You don't have anything to apologize for. I'm the one always saying stupid things.*

"No, it's fine," I said instead. "My older sister Sylvia died in that car crash with them too."

"I'm sorry to hear that. Were you close?"

"No, not at all. My sister actually had a lot of health issues growing up. My parents were always taking care of her, and we didn't really interact that much...in the end," I finished lamely.

I felt a lump in my throat at the thought of my parents, my emotions a jumbled mess in my head. I didn't want to think about it anymore.

"Do you have siblings?" I asked Connor, forcing my voice to sound brighter.

"I have an older brother, Michael. He lives in Toronto now."

"What's he like?"

"He's a bit of a slut."

"What?" I laughed, not expecting that response.

Connor laughed, too.

I bit back a smile. He was cute when he laughed.

"Nah, I'm joking. Well, I'm not joking. He does have a very active dating life, but he's a good guy. He works in business, and he's super outgoing, good with people."

I smiled, trying to picture Connor with his brother. I wondered if Connor ever had 'a very active dating life'. It didn't seem like it, but maybe it was just because we were up in a remote cabin.

The car turned the corner, and that's when I saw the real Fleurmont for the first time.

The first thing I saw was the lake. A massive lake glittered in the distance. It was beautiful, with little islands scattered across, the biggest one in the middle covered in trees that formed almost a crown-shape.

"There's a lake in your town?"

"Yeah, that's Lac Fleurmont. It's really nice, especially in the summer, but I think even now, there'll be people out in their boats."

The lake was huge. The blue of the lake glittering under the morning sun was so pretty that it took me a while to notice the rest of the town. As we made another turn down the mountain, I finally started to see the buildings in the town.

It was surprisingly...cute.

I had expected dingy and rundown, the way the old miner's town was, but seeing the town from where we still were on the mountain, it actually looked kind of charming. The buildings were mostly small and rustic, nothing standing out in particular besides the white church building, but the buildings were all painted in vibrant colours –bright white, blue, red, green. There were rows of houses that were a more traditional brown and grey, but they had a similar architectural design that made them look cohesive.

"*This* is Fleurmont?" I said in disbelief.

"This is Fleurmont," nodded Connor.

We pulled into the town, and Connor drove us to what looked like the town square. The town square was a neat square that was a clean park with a white gazebo smack in the middle. The streets on every side of the square were cute little stores, and there was a massive clock tower in the church on the north side of the square.

Connor parked on the street. We unbuckled and stepped out of the car, and I followed Connor a little absentmindedly as I took in the surroundings. The air felt different in Fleurmont. Up on Mt. Aster, it was all forest smells. Here, I could smell the stone pavement, petrichor from last night's rain, maybe. I smelled flowers and something sugary and –

"Coffee!" I cried as Connor and I reached a small, green diner. The outside was painted a deep forest green, and through the floor to ceiling windows, I could see sets of warm orange booths lined up inside. There were people sipping coffee inside, mostly groups of older people, and they looked out at us curiously as we made our way to the door. The sign on the front told me the diner was called Le Petit Toast.

"Exactly," laughed Connor.

We walked into the diner, and Connor headed straight for the counter.

"Connor!" A plump, middle-aged woman with red hair greeted him at the counter, her eyes flitting over to me with interest.

Connor switched to French. "Good morning, Arielle. Can we get two coffees to go, please? And two bags of medium roast?"

Fuck, that was hot. Why did he sound so hot when he spoke in French?

"Absolutely. Who's your friend?" Arielle winked, not being subtle at all.

"She works with me," said Connor quickly, still in French. "She's from the U.S."

I wanted to roll my eyes. He didn't have to say it like *that*.

"Oh, you are American?" Arielle called to me cheerfully in English, her accent thick and pleasant.

They probably thought I was a dumb American who couldn't speak French.

"I am. It's nice to meet you. I'm Stassi."

"Welcome to Fleurmont, Stassi. I'm Arielle Audet. You're in good hands with Connor here," she added, handing us our coffees, offering Connor another wink.

"Jeez," muttered Connor, handing Arielle a handful of colourful bills before swiftly trying to make his way out.

"See you soon!" sang Arielle.

"Bye, Arielle."

"See you soon!" I chimed.

Connor and I stepped outside of the diner, stopping at the same time to take matching sips of coffee. The coffee was hot and smooth, with an almost nutty taste.

"Oh, fuck that's good," I muttered, exhaling, taking another sip and trying not to burn my tongue.

"Best coffee in town," nodded Connor. He blinked as he sipped his coffee, the steam getting in his eyes.

We stood there for a few moments drinking coffee, ignoring the table of old people who were still looking at us from inside the diner. One older man in a sweater vest grinned at us, waving at Connor and then pointing to me with a suggestive smile.

Connor groaned, giving him a half-hearted wave back before moving us further down the street, out of their field of vision.

"Fucking busybodies." Connor rolled his eyes.

I held back a smile. I was still only halfway done with my coffee when Connor seemed to have finished his.

"Alright. The post office is right over there," said Connor, pointing to a pale blue store at one corner of the town square.

"I'm meeting Elodie Gendreau in town to go over the materials I've listed out in my initial proposal for the resort."

"List of materials?" I asked curiously.

"We're trying to be sustainable in the construction process, so Elodie is helping make recommendations on lower impact, sustainable materials. There's also a lot of work that needs to be done talking through our energy efficiency goals, and the water management plan, so I'm not sure how long we'll be today, but you can have the car and drive back up when you're done. I'll borrow someone's car and grab some groceries on the way back."

He handed me the car keys.

I was surprised and thrown off at once. I was surprised at how weirdly, inexplicably irritated I was that I was not a part of the 'we' Connor was referring to, and also completely thrown off by being given a set of car keys.

"I - I can't drive," I said.

"You don't know how to drive?" Connor frowned at me.

"Of course I know how to drive," I snapped.

"You *just* said –" Connor looked at me irritably again.

"I know how to drive. I just can't," I clarified. "I don't have a license anymore."

"What happened to your license?"

"It was indefinitely revoked when I crashed into a tree in Vegas."

I was sharing way too much with him today. It felt strangely unnerving.

"You crashed a car into a tree?"

"It was an accident."

"Were you okay?" His tone was a little softer.

"No one got hurt," I said.

Connor nodded. He was being too nice. It was freaking me out.

"There's a map of the town in the middle of the square," said Connor, pointing. "If you're okay with hanging around by yourself, I can meet you later in the afternoon and we'll head back together. I'll text you when I'm done."

Something fluttered again inside of me when he said 'together'. A few minutes in a car with Connor Fitzgerald having a normal conversation and I was feeling all weird and static-y. Must be the effect of being stuck with someone for a whole week.

"Okay, bye," I said quickly.

I headed to the post office, running away before my heart could beat any faster.

I reluctantly admitted to myself that Fleurmont was cute. It was clean and neat, with little gardens at every other intersection. After going to the post office, I walked all the way down to the lake. Sailboats and kayaks were dotted across the lake, and people were running and laughing.

We had beaches and waterfront in L.A., but something about this lake felt drastically different. Maybe it was all the little pastel storefronts with pretty, artisanal crafts. Maybe it was the mountains that hugged the lake and the town in a protective little bubble. Or maybe it was the people.

People looked more relaxed here. There weren't dozens of people showing off their latest investments in plastic surgery, or flaunting fifteen-dollar superfood smoothies while eating a bag of kale chips and calling it lunch and dinner. The people I saw were also a little older here, and it was kind of...comforting, seeing older couples out walking, or what looked like a small group of old friends out on a sailboat on a lake.

I hoped that Nya and I would be like that when we were old, out drinking wine on a sailboat on the lake, surrounded by beautiful mountains. That would be nice.

I sat on one of the public lounge chairs close to the lake and stared out at the water. I felt strangely relaxed. In fact, I felt so relaxed that I apparently fell asleep, because the next time I was conscious, someone was calling my name.

"Stassi. Stassi!"

I opened my eyes to find Connor looking at me.

The sun was directly in his face, and he looked concerned. It was warmer today than it had been the first few days in Fleurmont. Connor had taken off his jacket and was wearing a classic white T-shirt. His arms looked kinda good. Muscular and a little veiny.

"Are you okay?" he asked as I sat up straighter.

"I fell asleep," I said, still looking at him.

I looked back at his face, at the defined cupid's bow of his lips. His eyes weren't brown, I realized.

"What's wrong?" he asked me, because I was full-on staring at him now.

"Your eyes aren't brown," I said almost accusingly, standing up to look closer at him. "Are your eyes green?"

I inspected him closer, but he backed away from me, holding out a hand to prevent me from getting too close.

"I don't look at my eyes," he said self-consciously. "What's wrong with you? Why are you being weird? And why are you sleeping out here?"

"I was done with my walk," I said, still looking suspiciously into his irises.

His eyes were not the dark brown I originally thought they were. Instead, they were dark hazel, the outer part of his irises a beautiful blend of forest and apple green that fizzled in a radial pattern into the brown and black centre of his eyes.

"Okay, well, are you hungry?" asked Connor. He looked embarrassed at my staring at him.

My stomach growled in response.

"I'm starving," I said, the mention of food distracting me from the strange colour of his irises.

"Great, let's go to Le Petit Toast."

"Ooh, is that the diner we went to this morning for coffee?" I asked eagerly.

I would kill for a cheeseburger. Or curly fries.

"Exactly. They have the best milkshakes in town."

We walked together on the street to the diner, and a few people waved at Connor on the way. It felt like every other person in town knew him.

When we arrived at Le Petit Toast, Arielle was still there, and she seated us in a booth at the window, right next to an old jukebox.

"Two menus," said Arielle with a flourish.

"Thanks, Arielle."

"Can we get a plate of curly fries to start?" I blurted. I was starving.

"You got it," said Arielle with a big smile.

"Good call," said Connor as Arielle walked away.

"I'm *starving*," I said to Connor.

"I can tell," said Connor, looking amused.

"I'm going to die of starvation," I continued as I looked at the menu. "Ooh, what's a triple-decker burger?"

"You don't want that," said Connor, glancing up from his own menu.

"And how would you know what I want?" I huffed at him.

"Because I've seen you eat over the last week, and there's no way you can finish all of that. It's like, the thing that football players eat after a workout."

"Are you being sexist? You don't think a woman can finish a triple-decker burger?"

"No! I never said the football players had to be men. I just said that *you* –you know what, fine, order the damn burger. Just don't be mad when I get to say I told you so."

"I'm *starving*. I'm going to finish the whole thing. Don't be mad when *I* get to say I told you so."

Arielle came back with a tray, setting down two cups of water and a plate of curly fries. My mouth watered at the smell.

"There you go. What else can I get you two?" asked Arielle, and she gave Connor a suggestive look, glancing over at me quickly in a very unsubtle way.

"A meatloaf and a chocolate milkshake, please," said Connor.

He was so polite. It was kind of cute. I wondered if it was because he was Canadian.

"And for you?" Arielle asked.

"I'll have the triple-decker burger and a vanilla milkshake," I said happily, handing Arielle the menu.

Arielle's eyes widened at me in surprise. "Are you sure? It's uh...quite large."

"I'm sure," I said confidently.

"Do you want it with a side of soup or salad?"

"Salad, please."

Connor looked at me with dark, amused hazel eyes, shaking his head ever so slightly.

"Coming right up," said Arielle.

"Thanks, Arielle," said Connor.

Arielle walked away just as an older man walked into the diner, immediately spotting Connor.

"Connor," the man said, walking over to us.

He had grey hair and blue eyes and was wearing a sweater vest with a chequered shirt.

"Dad," said Connor, looking surprised.

"Hey, I don't mean to interrupt anything. Raphael said he saw you coming in, and I just wanted to say hi."

This was Connor's dad? I looked at him with interest, and he smiled at me.

"You must be Stassi," he said. "I'm Owen, Connor's dad."

"Nice to meet you," I said as Arielle brought out two milkshakes, setting them in front of us.

"Owen, I didn't know you were coming too. You want a milkshake?"

"No, no, just saying hi to my son."

"Alright," said Arielle with an easy smile.

"Do you want a sip at least?" said Connor, pushing his chocolate milkshake towards his dad. Connor smiled at his dad, another surprisingly cute smile.

"Oh, alright, maybe just a sip then," smiled Owen, and I got the sense that he and Connor were really close.

"Any excuse for a father to see his son before I take off," said Owen.

"Where are you going?" I asked.

"London. My brother lives there now, and it's been years since I've seen him. This year, I'm finally doing all the travel I've been waiting to do, so I'm hoping to spend a good two months travelling with him all over Europe."

"That sounds like a lot of fun," I said.

I wondered if Adrian and Miranda and I would ever want to travel together in Europe when we were older. Probably not.

"When are you leaving again?" asked Connor.

"Not until mid-June, I think, but we're still trying to figure out the right dates. I have to stay for the Spring Festival, that's for sure," grinned Owen.

"Well, we have to make the most of it while we're both in town then," said Connor.

"We will. I'll text you and we can set up a time to do a barbecue with your mom," said Owen, and he took one last sip of Connor's milkshake. "Alright, alright. I'll go now, just wanted to say hi. Really good to meet you, Stassi. I hope you enjoy your time here."

"Thanks," I said.

Owen left, leaving me and Connor with our curly fries and milkshakes.

I took a sip of my vanilla milkshake.

"Oh, God," I moaned. "This milkshake is insane."

Connor nodded in agreement, taking a sip of his milkshake.

A few moments later, Arielle appeared again, this time carrying two massive plates. I balked as she set the largest burger I had ever seen in my existence in front of me.

"One meatloaf, and one triple-decker burger," said Arielle brightly. "Enjoy your meal!"

Fuck.

Okay, maybe this was too big of a burger. The burger had three layers of everything: three burger patties, three slices of bread, three layers of cheese, three layers of tomato, three layers of onions...

"Now you won't starve," said Connor with a wicked glint of amusement in his eyes, "but hey, if you're still hungry after this, order whatever you want. We're way under budget as far as food expenses."

"Do you...do you think this burger ate another triple-decker burger before arriving?" I stammered, still looking at the freaking Thanksgiving turkey they were trying to pass off as a burger.

"I haven't asked it yet," said Connor calmly, pushing my plate a little closer to me, "Mmm, and don't forget about your salad."

Thirty minutes later, I reluctantly conceded to the monstrosity of a burger. There was more than half of it left. Slightly ashamed, I slurped up the rest of my milkshake.

Arielle looked over at us, glancing at my plate, which was still basically completely full. I could see the judgement forming on her face. I slid my burger over to Connor.

"Will you eat the rest for me?" I said quickly.

"You want me to eat the rest of your half-eaten burger?" said Connor, looking unimpressed.

"Why did I ask?"

Arielle looked over at us again, and I could see her wondering if she should come over.

I pushed the plate closer to Connor.

"Yes, yes, eat it, please. I don't want her to judge me."

"I think she finished judging you when you ordered this thing. No one orders this burger. I think someone I knew in high school ordered it once on a dare."

"You could have said *that* instead of making it seem like only big, strong footballers can eat this. Plus, I didn't know the curly fries would be so good."

"Just get a takeout box," said Connor unsympathetically.

"No, the bread is going to get soggy. I hate soggy bread. Come on, Connor, please? Just eat it for me," I whined, pushing the plate towards him.

"Fine, fine, stop pushing," he said, taking the plate from me.

I watched in complete fascination as Connor ate the rest of the burger. He chewed slowly, his cheeks heating as I continued to stare at him.

"Stop staring at me," he said as he chewed, covering his mouth with a hand.

"I can't help it," I said, putting my cheeks on my hands as I leaned closer to him. "This is so fascinating. I've never seen anyone eat, like, a whole chicken by themselves."

"I'm doing you a favour," he said, gulping down water between bites, "but if I pass out from eating this and you have to sleep on the road, don't complain about it."

"You would never let that happen to your innocent intern, would you?" I bat my eyelashes at him.

"There's absolutely nothing innocent about you," said Connor, taking a final bite of the burger before putting down one last bite. "You're a menace."

"You're not going to finish that last bite?" I asked, disappointed.

"I can't," Connor shook his head, slicing his hand through the air in an 'I'm out' gesture. "I'm going to explode."

"But, food waste."

"*You* finish it then."

"No, you said you were going to help me!"

Arielle came over to our table to clear the plates.

"My goodness, you put in some work here! I'm impressed."

I beamed at her, feeling kind of pleased with myself.

"Check, please," said Connor weakly, squinting with discomfort.

# CHAPTER TWELVE

## Connor

**Arden:** Hey, Town Stud. Just so you know, Arielle is already planning your wedding to Stassi.

**Connor:** How the hell do you know that from Montreal?

**Arden:** Arielle texted her daughter, who texted my sister, who texted me.

**Connor:** Fucking hell

**Arden:** I'm surprised your mom isn't all over you on this one.

**Connor:** Don't worry, I'm sure she will be.

**Arden:** Spicy, spicy. Keep me posted. I like to hear it directly from the source.

Walking to the grocery store was necessary after our meal at Le Petit Toast. My stomach still felt like it was going to explode from Stassi's burger as we made our way to Marché Fortin.

Stassi flounced around next to me, grinning wickedly from ear to ear, clearly enjoying my discomfort. I shook my head at her, but I couldn't help but smile back at her. She looked happier today than she had over the past week.

Marché Fortin was the only grocery store in town. It was two blocks away from the town square, and was owned by Raphael Fortin. The grocery store had been in the Fortin family for generations now, and Raphael, like my mother, was also someone who loved to be involved in town business.

Stassi and I got a grocery cart, and before Stassi could finish putting a box of strawberries into our shopping cart, Raphael had appeared out of thin air.

"Connor! Good to see you. I *thought* I saw you heading into the diner earlier," he said, clapping my back warmly.

"Good to see you, too, Raph."

"Yes, yes, and who's this?" Raphael smiled at Stassi. He wiggled his eyebrows at me.

Stassi beamed back at him, all pretty blue eyes and a sunny smile. I'd be lying if I said I didn't like how often people assumed we were together.

Of course, I had no business wanting a girl like Stassi. It wasn't even just that she was my intern, if we could even pretend that's what she was. She was so drop-dead gorgeous it couldn't be clearer that she was out of my league. Besides, she was a Salvati. Her family probably expected her to marry a Scandinavian aristocrat or something.

"I'm Stassi." She extended a hand towards Raphael.

"We work together," I explained.

"Good to meet you, Stassi." Raphael shook her hand, his brown eyes still flitting back and forth between us. "Welcome to Fleurmont. It's so good to see young Connor here with a beautiful young lady for once."

*Esti de calice.*

"Thank you. Your town is so beautiful," said Stassi sweetly.

Sure, she was nice to Arielle and Raphael. If she minded that people kept trying to push us together, she didn't let it show.

"Oh, we try to maintain it as best as we can. Our town is always full of fun events, that's for sure. It's almost wildflower season. Did Connor tell you about that?"

"No," said Stassi, shaking her head. She was playing it up, sounding almost disappointed.

I resisted the urge to roll my eyes.

"Connor," chastised Raphael.

"I'm grocery shopping."

I decided to ignore them and started piling groceries into our cart, needing to get back to the cabin as soon as possible. I'd had enough of the town for one day.

"Well, Fleurmont isn't very well known, but we do have visitors from all over Quebec in late spring, and they come here to see our wildflower fields. There are multiple hiking trails, and what you get is the most incredible mountain views with the most beautiful flowers."

"That sounds beautiful."

"It really is," continued Raphael enthusiastically. "We also have a Spring Festival coming up at the end of May. It's a celebration of our wildflower season. Arielle tells me you're here for a full four months, so you should really come to town for that."

"Uh, yes, I am."

Our cart was sufficiently loaded with fruit and vegetables before I reached for more bags of ground coffee. It seemed safer to get more, just in case.

"Connor can take you, of course –my goodness, Connor, that's a lot of coffee," said Raphael.

"He can't function without coffee," said Stassi. "He needs it to avoid being a grouchy bear."

"Don't I know it. You know, when Connor was in high school, he once had six espresso shots in one night to finish an essay."

"Oh, jeez. How do you remember things like that?" I said.

"Because you came to my shop in the morning! I still remember. You were with your friend Arden before school, and the two of you were shaking like chihuahuas in a snowstorm." Raphael stretched out his arms wide, mimicking our shaking, his eyes wide as his whole body vibrated dramatically, right there in fucking aisle 2.

Stassi giggled.

"They came in to get snacks, I suppose, for their day, both of them holding onto these essays they wrote. Connor was shaking so badly he accidentally ripped his essay right in half.

"I can believe that," smiled Stassi.

"He was so out of it, and he was talking non-stop the whole time."

"Talked non-stop? I find *that* hard to believe," said Stassi.

Raphael chuckled.

"Okay, I think we should go now," I said, quickly shoving our cart towards the checkout counter.

"Embarrassed I'm talking too much about your childhood to your girlfriend?" smirked Raphael in French.

I replied to him in French. "For the last time, she's not my girlfriend. We work together."

"Alright, alright," Raph switched back to English, not sounding convinced.

I looked over at Stassi, grateful she couldn't understand French at least. Unfortunately, she was looking at me with those sharp blue eyes again, and I wondered if she'd understood what I said anyway.

When we checked out, she grabbed two of the grocery bags, leading the way back to the car.

She threw me a quick smile over her shoulder. "I like your town."

Despite myself, I felt the corners of my mouth tug into a smile.

# CHAPTER THIRTEEN

## Stassi

*May 12*

*Dearest Stassi,*

*I was so overjoyed to find your letter in the mail. I nearly spilled hot tea at my desk, I was so thrilled.*

*While it is most unfortunate that your warden does not stock liquor as he should, I must request that you provide a much more detailed account of his physique. You say he works out in the backyard. Does he do so with his shirt on or off? How is this man working out? And you must confirm the most important detail - is he hot?!*

*Details, Stassi!*

*Everything is fine on my end. As you know, the rainy season is upon us in Nairobi. There's been so much flooding that it's been difficult to get to the office some days. Our internet was not working for almost two whole days, so we are behind. But! I finally found someone to be my head of Research and*

*Development. Her name is Mary Sankale, and she has a really strong background in systems engineering on the solar side of things. You'll never believe it, but she's from the same village my mother was from. (And don't freak out and worry, you crazy jealous lady, you are still my number one girl. I'm just a nerd who is excited about work).*

*In other news, as I know you are not checking your socials, Quinn got a boob job. They. Are. Massive. You could bounce a dime off of those melons. I'm not sure I like them, though. They look a little too fake. Stiff as a face smack in the middle of winter.*

*Anyway, I hope you are well. Write to me soon!*

*All my love,*

*Nyambura*

*P.S. Didn't I tell you how fabulous this whole letter writing thing would be?*

I looked at the photo of Quinn in my social media app. From the background of the photo, I could tell she was back in Spain. She looked good, even if her boobs did look stiff. Good for her. Lying back down on my bed, I briefly wondered what I would look like with a boob job.

I let out a long sigh. My tits were not the problem. I actually quite liked my tits. It was everything going on in my head that was never quite right.

Turning over to the side, I checked the time on my phone. I should probably get dressed. Sifting through my clothes in the two suitcases that carried most of my warm clothes, I found my favourite mocha-coloured loungewear set.

What the hell was I going to do today?

Connor was in Fleurmont again, meeting Elodie. Why did he have to meet up with this Elodie so much, anyway? And why was this consultant too lazy to drive up here to the cabin? Connor was so adamant about the cabin being 'a great workspace'.

After getting dressed, I paced around the cabin a little aimlessly. Connor was still giving me useless research tasks, and without him in the cabin for me to antagonize, there wasn't much to do indoors. I wish I had insisted on going into town with him again. It had been kind of fun, being in Fleurmont with him.

I smiled at the memory of Arielle and Raphael winking and wiggling their eyebrows at the idea of me and Connor together. Not that I liked him that way, obviously. It was just fun to see him squirm.

I decided to walk outside.

The trees had transformed completely in the two weeks I'd been here. It had rained a lot over the last week. Now, the neon buds on the tree branches had transformed into thicker, lusher, darker green leaves, and everything felt a little fresher than it had a few weeks ago. The air smelled fresher too, not just with the smell of crisp, cool wood and pine, but also with something more layered, something earthy and leafy on top of the crisp mountain air. That, or I was so bored all of my senses were getting heightened.

I walked all the way to the swamp Connor was planning to turn into a scenic picnic area. I mean, Connor called it a pond, but I was pretty sure it was a swamp. Green algae that looked like green boogers floated at the surface, and little bubbles occasionally appeared.

Ugh.

I tried to picture what Connor had in mind –a winding wooden bridge across the pond, with art installations that didn't disturb the ecosystem. I had seen his mock-ups of some sculptures made with driftwood, and I had to admit they looked pretty good.

Connor was a great designer. While he was anally organized in every aspect of his work, he was also kind of brilliant. His building sketches were really creative, blending different architectural styles in unexpected ways. He drew concept sketches in bright neon colours, which felt so different from his serious personality. It seemed to help him iterate though, and I found myself leafing through his drawings when he was working out in the morning and thinking through his design choices.

One building that Connor was designing was a welcome lodge, and over the last week, I tried to challenge myself to come up with a unique design for it in my sketchbook. I opened the sketchbook, and...nothing. I felt blocked again. I was brought back again to the time right after my parents died.

Three months after my parents died, right before Nya was going to head back to Kenya, I had a job interview at a boutique architecture firm in L.A. Everything had gone well at first. They liked my portfolio. I had gotten through the first two interviews. But then during the final interview, they gave me a sketch test. It was a design prompt asking me to design a greenspace next to a highway. I had twenty minutes, and I just...blanked. I couldn't.

I kept thinking about my parents and how they'd died on a highway. My sister had died on a highway. I couldn't think. I just froze. Nineteen minutes passed, and my page was still completely blank.

I bolted. I just left. It was the cringiest moment of my life.

Now, it was more of the same. It was a lodge, nothing like before, but I felt myself freeze up again, the same way I froze up every time in the last two years I've tried to design something. I couldn't get anything onto the page. After some time, I gave up, frustrated, and plugged my earphones back in, letting myself drown in the music.

I was about to leave the swamp pond when I saw something in the bush. I blinked in surprise as a tiny kitten appeared from the bush. It let out the smallest little mewl I had ever heard.

I barely believed in love, having not had much of it in my life, but it was at that moment that I experienced love at first sight. The kitten was black and white with a little black nose and the cutest black freckle on the right side of his nose. The fur on his back was mostly black, but his paws were white. His ears and the top half of his face were black, and the rest of his face was an inverted white heart shape. He was *adorable*.

He mewed at me again, walking closer to me.

"Hi, buddy." I squatted down next to him. I reached out my hand to let him sniff it. He was so tiny. He must be a kitten.

"Where's your mama, buddy?" I asked him, petting him gently. His back arched as I petted him, and he mewled again.

My heart ached a little at the sight of his ribs. His head and ears looked too big for his tiny body. He looked at me with the saddest green-blue eyes I'd ever seen.

"Awww," I cried, and I picked him up. I rocked the little tuxedo kitten in my arms, and instantly, he started to purr.

"Stop it," I said to him, my cold icy heart melting faster than a glacier. "You're too cute."

I scratched the top of his little head. He continued to purr, rolling in my arms onto his back. I rubbed his belly, and the purr became louder, like a little warm engine.

"Maximus, you're so sweet. But where's your mama?"

I looked around, but there was no sign of any other cats. I walked around the swamp with Maximus still in my arms. He looked like a Maximus.

"Maximus Constantine Romeo Salvati." I touched his nose softly with my index finger. "That's what I would call you if you were mine. You're such a handsome boy."

He looked like a boy, even though I didn't know how to tell with cats.

Maximus licked the tip of my finger, and he swatted at my finger with excitement.

"Ow, Maxi, your claws are so sharp." I pulled my hand away, setting him gently back down on the grass. I sighed. It was probably for the best. I shouldn't take him with me. What if he had a whole cat family somewhere?

Maximus ran over to me, climbing onto my shoe. He mewed at me again, round eyes staring straight through my soul. Long white eyebrow whiskers and nose whiskers tickled my leg. My entire soul melted.

"Screw it," I said, scooping him up.

He was so thin. There were no other cats around. What if I left him here, and he starved to death?

Maximus Constantine Romeo Salvati started to purr again, and he didn't protest the entire time I carried him home.

"What the fuck?" I heard Connor's voice.

I jumped, startling awake. Maximus jumped too, startled. He'd been asleep on my chest. We had both fallen asleep in my room after the afternoon that we'd had.

Shit.

I looked at my phone to check the time.

Double shit.

Maximus jumped off the bed as I made my way to the living room, where Connor was now staring at the cabin. Or what was left of it.

Turns out kittens really like to climb on things, and for someone as small as Maxi, he sure had some sharp, enthusiastic claws.

He had ripped into every surface of the couch, and half the curtains in the living room were now on the floor, hanging in disarray from when I had unsuccessfully tried to peel Maxi off of the fabric, causing half the curtains to come crashing down.

"What the hell happened here?" demanded Connor. He kicked off his shoes and marched into the kitchen, almost tripping over the plate I had left on the ground.

"Careful! That's his food!"

Connor swore again, jumping back.

"*His* food? Whose food?" Connor rounded on me, baffled. He picked up the plate from the floor, putting it into the extremely full kitchen sink.

The kitchen was a mess. Pots and pans were on each of the burners of the stove, half-cooked pieces of chicken scattered across the surface. Dirty dishes stacked in the sink, and I had spilt water all over the floor and only half attempted to clean it with a spare towel. Broken, raw eggs also littered the floor, and I had used spare pots to cover them up so that Maximus couldn't get to them.

"Don't be mad, I know it's a bit of a mess," I breathed, "but I didn't know what to feed him, and he looked so sad and hungry."

Damn, I couldn't believe I had slept for so long. I had fully intended to clean up before Connor got home.

"*Who –*"

Maximus appeared in the hallway right on cue. He let out a little cat cry before yawning, displaying a cute set of sharp little teeth.

"What the hell is that cat doing in here?" demanded Connor, looking between me and Maximus. "You let a cat in here?!"

"He's a kitten. And yes, I found him by the swamp -I mean, the pond, and he looked so sad and he was all by himself, and look how skinny he is! He was clearly starving."

"You let in a cat you found at the swamp?"

Sure, now it's a swamp to him.

"He's a baby," I protested, and watched as Maximus hopped onto the couch.

A little unhelpfully, Maximus chose that moment to scratch at the fabric of the couch.

"Anyway," I continued quickly, hoping Connor wouldn't fixate on that, "I'm sorry the place is a bit of a mess. It's just that first, I tried to give him tuna, because you know how in cartoons, cats are always eating fish? Well, it turns out that's a total lie and they can get mercury poisoning or something, so then I tried to make him chicken, only halfway through, I realized I had to *boil* the chicken, not pan fry it. So I boiled the chicken, only he was running around and he started climbing all over the place, and I knew you'd be mad because you're so uptight about everything –"

Connor let out an irritated exhale. He folded his arms across his chest, looking angrier than I'd ever seen him.

He looked weirdly hot when he was mad.

"Stassi," Connor warned, his voice low and angry.

Fuck, why was this turning me on?

I needed therapy. And not that 'go for a walk, it's good for you' crap. I mean, she hadn't been wrong. But still.

"Wait! I'm almost done, I promise. Anyway, I was trying to rescue Maximus –"

"*Maximus?*"

"Yes, his full name is Maximus Constantine Romeo Salvati," I said proudly. "Isn't he the cutest? He just looks like he could have been a little Roman emperor. You know, if Roman emperors wore tuxedos." I let out an involuntary giggle as Maximus trotted over to me excitedly. I picked him up and cradled him against my chest.

"Jesus fucking Christ." Connor ran both his hands through his hair.

Really, really hot.

"Anyway," I continued, "the water was boiling, and it kind of spilled everywhere, but don't worry, I put a towel on it, so there won't be any water damage. Ooh, but he *did* pee in the potted plant by your desk –"

"Stassi!" snapped Connor.

"Yes?"

"You cannot have a wild animal in here. That thing could have rabies. It could have fleas! And you let it shit and piss all over the cabin?"

"He's a baby," I protested, "and he was all alone. I couldn't just let him die out there. Look how skinny he is. And he doesn't have fleas. Look, his fur is so soft and so perfect."

"I don't give a shit," said Connor. "I don't give a shit. We can't have a cat in here. This is where we work. This is where –"

Connor seemed to have a sudden realization. He marched over to the workspace at the back of the cabin. I set Maximus down on the couch before following Connor into the workspace.

Drafting paper and pencils were scattered all over the floor. Maximus had also left a trail of mud over part of the work table.

"*Stassi!*"

I winced.

"Stassi, what the hell? I'm gone for what –*three* hours– and this place is a total mess. It looks like a fucking tornado passed through this place," growled Connor, picking up the pieces of paper and pencils from the floor.

"You were gone for *five* hours," I corrected. "Besides, what am I supposed to do for the next three and a half months? All you do is give me stupid, useless research tasks because you don't want me to get in the way. I'm bored out of my mind while you're off listing off how many sustainable toilet paper rolls you want or something."

"So that's what you do? You act out because you're pissed?"

"No! I wasn't acting out. I was just on a walk and I found him all alone."

"He has to go. We can't have a cat in here. Get him out of the house right now."

"No!"

"Stassi, this is insane. Get him out of the house right now."

"No! He could die if he's outside all by himself!"

"I don't give a shit if he dies. He goes, right now." Connor marched back into the living room.

"No!" I cried, running after him, feeling a sudden surge of emotion. I loved Maxi so much already. I grabbed onto Connor's arm before he could get to Maxi, pulling him back.

"Connor, *please*," I said, trying to grab his other arm.

"Stassi –" Connor turned to face me suddenly, without warning, and I was so surprised at his sudden movement towards me I took a step back, bumping into the wall behind me.

I looked up at him, startled by how close we suddenly were.

Connor looked at me. His eyes searched mine, anger and some other wild emotion swimming around in his eyes. "Stassi, he has to go. Right now."

"Please don't make me give him up," I whispered. I was still holding on to both of his wrists, but with my back pressed up against the wall, I felt like the one being held down.

"Stassi, it's just a cat," said Connor, more softly now.

His skin was hot against mine, and I could feel perspiration start to form all over my body. Tension and adrenaline and heat shot to my core.

"Not to me," I said hotly.

Connor's hazel green eyes drilled into mine. He was so close to me. He had never been so close to me before. I suddenly felt really overwhelmed.

Connor seemed to realize how close we were too. His eyes skimmed over my neck, then dropped to a tiny spot near my chest where Maxi had scratched me. His eyes moved to my hands, still around his wrists, back to my neck, and then to my lips before he looked me in the eye again. I tried not to shiver.

It had been all of five seconds, but something about the way he looked at me made me feel like I was being stripped naked. Heat pooled lower in my stomach.

Connor shook his head, pulling away from me.

I gripped his arms tighter, pulling him closer to me. His eyes widened, stumbling, not expecting me to yank him closer, and he broke free of me but caught himself on the wall. His hands fell onto the wall on either side of me, caging me in.

"*Please*, Connor," I said again, my voice softer this time.

Something heavy hung in the air between us.

Breathing became harder.

Neither of us dared to move an inch.

I could see him struggling to breathe too. His eyes searched mine.

Another moment of heavy silence between us.

"Fine," said Connor finally. "He can stay."

"Thank you," I whispered, still trying to breathe evenly.

"But you have to tell me these things. Text me, call me. We have to communicate. I can't come home to find random animals in the house again. Promise me that."

"Then you have to promise me something too," I breathed.

Connor let out an incredulous laugh.

"What?" His eyes were soft and heated at the same time.

Part of me wanted to say something else. Something dirty. Something I now couldn't unthink with him so close to me. The part of me that wanted to grab the front of his shirt and pull him even closer. My stupid brain won out on this one.

"I want you to give me a design project. A real one. I want you to stop giving me stupid research tasks," I said, not breaking his gaze, even as I felt myself getting soaked through.

Connor chuckled darkly.

"Okay, Stassi," he murmured. "Okay, fine. I will give you a design task. Are you sure you're actually going to work on it?"

"Yes," I said confidently.

His eyes dropped to my lips again for a second.

"It's going to be a lot harder than the research tasks."

"I like it when things are hard," I said.

"Good. Then I'll give you the hardest thing I've got."

I let out a breathless laugh. Was he...making a joke? Were we joking together? Was he...?

A loud meow came from near our feet, and we looked down to see Maxi looking up at us in protest. His black tail flicked behind him.

Connor took a step back, his arms dropping to his sides, the heat of his body finally no longer licking at my self-control.

"Hi, Maxi," I said softly, picking him up and cradling him in my arms.

Maxi purred again.

"We should get him proper cat things if he's going to stay here," said Connor.

I looked up at him in surprise as Connor moved back to the front door. He put on his shoes and offered me a gentle smile.

"Come on, there's a pet store in town. We should get him a litter box. And probably some scratch pads."

My heart caught in my throat. I found it hard to swallow. I stared at Connor Fitzgerald.

"I think the store closes at six, so we should get going," said Connor, checking the time on his phone. "Maybe the vet will still be in so he can get checked out."

"Okay," I smiled.

I put on my shoes and followed Connor out the door.

# Chapter Fourteen

## Stassi

"Congratulations! It's a boy!" said Abel Boivin enthusiastically.

We were standing in Abel's store. Maximus was walking around the wooden 'vet's observation table', sniffing his new surroundings curiously. He fidgeted when Abel inspected him, squirming to get away. It had taken five different treats to keep him occupied. His little tail swished back and forth as he ate, and Abel tried inspecting him for fleas before vaccinating him.

Abel Boivin was sixty, with a thick head of grey and brown hair. He had a kind face with a big nose, and when we came in, he enthusiastically ran to the back of the store to put on his white vet coat over his flannel shirt and jeans.

The town's 'pet store' was the vet's mishmash of a storefront. There was a wall of pet supplies, but the rest of the store was a strange combination of different things. One wall featured all of Abel's photos and credentials. He had his vet certification framed at the center, along with photos of himself next to a group of dogs, an unimpressed-looking horse on a farm, and a very chubby orange cat. Then, he had other photos and certifications and local news articles. Apparently, this man was not only a vet, a pet store owner but also a Zamboni driver and the local school bus mechanic. On the wall above his vet certificate, he had the same sign he had at his storefront, cheerfully reminding us to call him: "Appelle Abel!"

"Well, he's probably around six weeks old," said Abel. "He seems mostly healthy. No fleas or anything like that, but he is a little dehydrated and very underweight."

"How much should we feed him?" I took a cat toy shaped like a fish, waving it close to Maximus. His eyes went black and round, and he rolled over on his stomach, swatting at it enthusiastically. I dropped the fish toy as his little claws sunk into the fabric, and Maximus bit into the fish, looking like a little vampire with his front teeth exposed as he bunny kicked the fish toy that was almost bigger than him.

Abel chuckled. "He's a cute one, that's for sure. *P'tit minou.*"

I looked over at Connor, who was standing across the table from me, his arms crossed. He was looking at me, and I don't know if I was imagining it, but he had an almost smoldering look in his eyes.

Heat coursed through me, remembering our tense moment in the cabin.

Connor's arms tensed and tightened, and I tried not to stare at the veins in his forearms. He looked so good in that shirt.

I looked away first this time, forcing my attention back to Abel, who was now playing with Maximus with a feather wand toy. Abel continued to chuckle.

"So, for cat food?" Connor prompted him.

His voice was almost gruff, causing me to shiver again. Maybe I shouldn't have asked for a design task. Maybe I should have asked for something else.

"Oh, right, right. Sorry, he is just so cute." Abel's eyes crinkled.

I beamed at him, unable to agree more.

Abel walked over to his wall of pet supplies, scanning the wall. Not finding what he was looking for, he walked to the back of the store and pulled out a box.

"There it is. I knew I had this." He walked back and put the box on the table.

Maximus dropped his fish toy, standing up to sniff at this new box.

"It's canned kitten food. He should really eat food for kittens until he's a year old," said Abel, and took out a notepad shaped like a snowplow truck. He scribbled some notes. "Here is how much he should eat in a day. You can also supplement it with some dry food."

"Thanks." I glanced back at Connor.

He was still looking at me with those dark eyes.

"What about supplies? We have the litter box and the water fountain," I said, glancing over at the pile of things we had already picked out. I had also taken every cat toy available at Abel's store.

"Yes, well, I'm going to place an order for more food and litter for you, and you can come pick it up in the next week. You're going to need more than just this box. And if you want, you can place an order for a cat tree, too. Cats like to climb, you know. They like to be in high places."

Maximus let out a loud meow.

"Aww, okay, buddy, we'll get you a cat tree," I murmured, picking him up and giving him a kiss. He purred again as I cradled him in my arms.

I thought my heart was going to burst with how much I loved him.

"Thanks, Abel," said Connor as we finally finished up at the store. He carried all our things as I held onto Maxi and his cat toys.

"Thank you!" I called to him.

Abel smiled and waved at us, and then at Maxi.

"See you soon! *Au revoir, Minou Maxi!*"

*May 19*

*Dear Nyambura,*

*I hope the flooding has stopped in Nairobi. I'm really glad you found a new head of Research and Development! I know you've been trying to fill that role for so long. How is she doing? (And also, thanks for telling me I'm still your number one girl. I high-key needed that.)*

*To answer your question, yes, Connor is hot. He's got a dark energy to him and this crazy intensity when he works that is fucking sexy. He has gorgeous eyes that he won't let me stare at. He wears jeans most days, but I can tell he has a nice ass. Sadly, he works out dressed from head to toe, and he's uptight and a stickler for boundaries.*

*Work is still boring, but Connor promised me he would give me an actual design task instead of those stupid research tasks he keeps giving me. I'm happy about it, I think. I want to do design work. I really miss it. Remember when I was designing that tequila bar shaped like a pair of boots? How I spent like three days straight just designing? I miss being immersed in my work like that. But I'm also kind of nervous about it. What if I just can't design anymore and I have no more creative juices left in my body?*

*In other news, I have a new kitten! His name is Maximus Constantine Romeo Salvati, and he's the love of my life. He's my one furry little silver lining.*

*I miss you. August can't come soon enough.*

*Love,*

*Stassi*

# CHAPTER FIFTEEN

## *Connor*

**Arden:** You got a cat?! He's so cute!

**Me:** I did not get a cat. A cat was forced upon me. Stassi found him by a pond.

**Arden:** So when's the wedding?

**Me:** Please don't. Not you too.

**Arden:** Hey, if the shoe fits. Or if the collar fits? If it fits, it sits?

**Arden:** Whatever, I'll think of a better way to say it.

**Me:** Ignoring you now.

I stepped out into the living room after my morning shower. It had been another shower of unsuccessfully trying not to think about Stassi.

That night she had found Maxi, I had been shaking with how much I wanted her. I kept thinking about the way her face looked, so fucking determined and yet almost nervous, her lips trembling. And then she had grabbed my arms when she had pulled me towards her in that moment of frustration…All I'd wanted to do was bend her over the couch and fuck her. I wanted to bend her over and punish her for her insolence, for constantly talking back. I wanted to grab all that silky hair and yank on it.

I shook the thoughts away, walking into the workspace, but Stassi wasn't in her usual spot at the worktable. Frowning, I was about to call out to her when I saw her golden brown hair in the sunlight in the backyard. We were nearing the end of May, and the weather was warmer, some days almost hot. I stepped out into the backyard and almost had a fucking heart attack.

Because Stassi Salvati was lying naked on a lounge chair.

No, sorry, technically, she was not naked. She was wearing white bikini bottoms, lying on her stomach and reading a stack of papers. But she was topless, with no bikini top in sight. Just a plump, round ass squeezed into tiny bikini bottoms and an expanse of smooth, golden skin.

"What the hell are you doing?" I grit out.

Stassi turned her head towards me.

"We're sunbathing," she said, and that's when I noticed the cat lounging on the chair next to Stassi, both paws outstretched in the sun like Superman.

Stassi sat up slowly, carefully covering her nipples with both of her hands.

"Can you explain to me why you're doing this topless in the middle of a work day?" I asked, trying really hard to keep my eyes trained on hers and not on the rest of her body.

"Well, I don't want any tan lines, and you haven't given me a design task yet," said Stassi almost matter-of-factly.

She looked over her shoulder as if she were checking for tan lines, and that's when my willpower died.

I looked. I looked at the way her hands could barely contain her full, perky tits. I looked at the lines of her body, from her smooth, flat stomach all the way down to her legs. She was a complete knockout, so fucking beautiful it almost hurt my eyes. I was full-on leering.

"Can you pass me my shirt?" she asked, and then turned to look at Maximus, who yawned and turned his body into a little shrimp-like shape. "Aww, isn't Maxi so cute?"

I grabbed her shirt from the table and threw it at her, too afraid to get closer.

"Gee, thanks," said Stassi, and I turned my entire body away as she bent over to pick up her shirt.

About a hundred lewd, filthy thoughts passed through my head.

"I have a design task for you," I said, fighting to keep my voice controlled and not sound like I was about to come in my pants from just the sight of her.

"What is it?" she asked, and she walked past me to pick up her shorts.

"The accommodations," I said, turning to stare at the wall.

"Accommodations?"

"Yes, part of the concept for the resort is unique accommodations. Instead of regular hotel rooms, we'll have treehouses and yurts at the center of the resort space. It'll be luxury treehouses and yurts, though, so everything will have full plumbing. The plan is to plant native trees around the treehouses to really immerse people in nature. Maybe even have a few that have a wooden walking bridge between treehouses so people who are coming with friends or larger families can walk across the bridges to get to the other treehouse. The yurts would be in a different section, more in an open space, and each yurt would have its own private campfire."

I was rambling, but the words came spilling out. Anything to distract me from her body.

"That actually sounds really nice." Stassi walked in front of me suddenly, waving her arms in front of me. "Why are you turned towards the wall?"

"I was trying to give you privacy."

The pervert in me was disappointed that her bra was somehow back on, along with her T-shirt and shorts. Ocean blue eyes met mine as she smirked at me, a knowing look in her eyes.

Her confidence and defiance were sexy as hell, and it didn't help the hardness in my pants that was trying to pitch a tent down there.

"So you want me to design the treehouses and the yurts?" She touched the front of my shirt, removing a strand of long golden hair from my shirt. Her nails scraped against me.

My dick twitched. Was she doing this on purpose? She must know exactly what kind of effect she had on me. This wasn't even a fair fight.

"Yes," I coughed, tearing my eyes away from her, marching back to our work station. "I can show you the concept sketches."

I sat down at my desk, and she followed me, stopping close enough to me that her arm touched mine. I was so hard at this point that it was almost painful. I struggled to click through to the concept sketch page. The concept sketch showed what the treehouses and yurts would roughly look like, and where they would sit within the site of the resort.

"Here," I rasped, and I took a sip of water, begging my dick to calm down. "These are the concept sketches for the exterior, but feel free to change it up. You can do anything you want."

"Anything?" Stassi raised an eyebrow.

That shouldn't sound sexual. It wasn't sexual.

I nodded with difficulty. "Yes, just keep the square footage the same according to the estimates in the concept sketches. We need details for the interior and exterior, floor plans, all the materials you want to use, plans for insulation and ventilation, all of that."

"Do you want 3D modeling and massing?"

"Yes, but don't worry about any 2D site layouts with super precise layouts. We can worry about that once we agree on the high-level design concepts."

"Okay." Stassi nodded, a determined look in her eyes.

Something warmed in my chest at that look.

I sat back down at my desk. I was working on my pitch deck to Valerian and the stargazing lodge. The lodge would sit between the yurts Stassi was designing and the pond —or swamp, as she liked to call it. The stargazing lodge was going to be the main building for large events, like weddings or retirement parties. There would be two floors. The first floor would be the venue space, with high wood beam ceilings. The second floor would be split into two spaces for stargazing, one outdoors on the roof, and the other indoors so that they could still host events there in rain or snow.

I loved the summer months up in the mountains here, but there was something really special about the winters here. I glanced over at Stassi, wondering if she would ever get to see this place in winter, when thick layers of snow covered every surface and the sunlight bouncing off the white surfaces made everything so bright you had to squint.

Stassi was frowning. She was sitting at the table, Maxi now lounging on a cat pillow next to her, cleaning his paws. Stassi's sketchbook was open in front of her, and she was holding a graphite pencil in one hand, almost glaring at the blank page in front of her. She put down her pencil in frustration.

"What's wrong?"

"Nothing," she snapped back, avoiding my gaze.

I would have felt irritated at the harshness of her tone, but her expression was one I recognized.

"Do you feel blocked?" I was careful not to sound judgemental.

"No! I can do it. I've done plenty of design work before," she said quickly, flushing.

She picked up her sketchbook, holding it up to hide behind it, but I caught the pained look on her face. Something in me softened. I stood up from my desk and walked over to her.

"There's nothing to be ashamed of," I said, taking her sketchbook from her. I closed the sketchbook, tucking it under my arm. "Creative work isn't a linear path. You don't have to force yourself to come up with something amazing within the hour. People get creative blocks all the time."

"It's not...that exactly," muttered Stassi, looking down at her knees. She leaned forward at the table, sighing as she placed her elbows on the table, holding her face between her hands for a moment before looking back up at me.

"What is it then?"

Another pained look flashed across her face. It was the same look she had in the car when I asked about her parents. When she told me about her sister, who had died.

She was still grieving them, I realized.

"It's...nothing. It's stupid. Maybe I'll just take a break," she said. She gave me a forced smile, shook her head, and stood up.

"Stassi."

She stopped, turning around. "I'm fine, Connor. I'll just go walk around."

Hearing her say my name out loud was enough to make it impossible for me to let it go.

"Please talk to me."

She blinked at me, and she took in a shallow breath. She let it out again slowly, turning to face me again.

"I...I haven't been able to design since my parents died," she finally admitted. "I just...freeze up, and I can't think, and then I'm thinking about the fact that I can't think. I get frustrated, and then I just get even more frustrated...It's so stupid."

"Stassi, that's not stupid at all. Doing anything creative is tied to your emotions and how you're feeling. If you're still grieving, it makes sense that you can feel blocked."

"But it's been two years!" she cried, frustrated. "They've been gone for two years, and everyone's over it except for me. Adrian and Miranda both function and do their jobs. Uncle Valerian hasn't even talked about my dad in months, and that was his brother. It just feels like everyone's moved on, and I'm just this big fuck-up."

Tears formed in her eyes. She blinked them away angrily, like she was refusing to cry.

"Stassi, Stassi, hey." I moved closer to her, hating how upset she was. I was about to put my arms around her when I stopped myself.

Stassi exhaled in frustration, and I half-wondered if it was because I *hadn't* put my arms around her. I sighed, knowing I was probably screwing this up.

Then, an idea came to me.

"Alright, we're going outside."

"What?" she balked.

I took her sketchbook and grabbed my box of markers from the desk. I ushered her towards the front door.

"We're going outside. Come on, let's go."

"What? What are you doing?" she said, but she let me move us towards the front door.

"We're going to do some fucking design work together. Let's go. Put on your shoes. Even the spiky ones if you want."

Stassi let out a reluctant laugh, rolling her eyes. "Fine."

We put on our shoes and headed outside. I led her to the southernmost edge of the valley. At the edge of the valley, where there was a view of the mountain pass, there was a small stream. It was small, tucked between sloping tall grass and rocks, but it was a stream. I found a dry patch of grass for us to sit on. I sat down, and Stassi sat in front of me, crossing her legs and looking at me intently.

"Can't you feel the ideas flowing already?" I grinned at her.

"Ha-ha," she said dryly, but she cracked a smile.

My stomach tightened at the sight of her smiling.

"So what do we do now? Do you want me to visualize a treehouse here or something?" she asked skeptically.

"No..."

I looked around the stream until I found a large enough rock. I held it up to her.

"Here. I want you to draw this rock."

She took the rock from me, the tips of her fingers grazing mine.

"You want me to draw this rock?" she said in disbelief. She looked at me, a small smile forming on her lips as she fingered the rock in her hands, touching its smooth surface.

The wind bristled, making the dark blonde strands of hair flutter around her face. She was so fucking beautiful.

"Yes," I said. I opened my box of markers, taking out a bright, lavender-coloured marker. I handed it to her. "Draw this rock."

Her smile widened, and she rolled her eyes, but she took the marker from me.

"Yes, Mr. Fitzgerald," she said playfully, almost teasingly.

Stassi twisted off the cap of the marker and opened her sketchbook. She put the rock in front of me and eyed it again before she put the marker on the page. Slowly, she drew out the shape of the rock. She put the cap back on, holding up her sketchbook, and laughed.

"Oh my God, this is the worst drawing of a rock I've ever seen."

"Let me see," I said, taking the sketchbook from her.

It was a simple, slightly wobbly purple oval.

"What are you talking about? This is amazing. This is Louvre-worthy."

Stassi laughed, grabbing the sketchbook back from me. "You're so full of shit."

I grinned at her. "Okay, now write your name at the bottom."

Stassi giggled, but she didn't argue, and she wrote her name at the bottom of the page.

"There," she said, turning the sketchbook over so that I could see it. "Happy?"

"Yes," I said. "You just created something."

She sighed. "But it's not design work."

"No, but this is the first step. You just created something again. When was the last time you created something?"

She bit her lip, thinking, looking down at her drawing.

"I guess," she murmured.

"Alright, now flip the page." I handed her a leaf. "Now draw this leaf."

"Really?" she protested, but only slightly, taking the leaf from me.

Our fingers touched again.

"Really." I managed to keep my voice firm.

We spent the next thirty minutes drawing random things we found by the stream. Stassi pushed her sketchbook towards me and made me draw things too –a stick, blades of grass. We drew until we had used every marker in the box three or four times. Her sketchbook was full of colourful sketches now.

When we finally made it back to the cabin, she didn't exactly sit down and finish designing the treehouses and yurts on the spot, but she looked happier, lighter.

Seeing her happy made me smile, and I knew this couldn't be good. My attraction to Stassi was one thing. She was so beautiful anyone would have to be blind not to see it. She was funny and sassy, and anyone could see that too.

But caring about Stassi, caring what she thought, wanting her to be happy...those were feelings I couldn't let fester. She was my boss's niece. We worked together. She was a wealthy Salvati, and I was only starting to get close to where I needed to be in my career.

Stassi Salvati was off-limits, and I'd be a fool to give in to my feelings.

# Chapter Sixteen

## *Stassi*

Connor's exercise helped. I was sketching again. I almost couldn't believe it. When we got back to the cabin, I tried to sketch out a treehouse. At first, I froze up again. I didn't know where to start.

But then Maximus jumped back on the table next to me, and I sketched him out instead. I drew a little black and white tuxedo cat. Even in my drawing, he was cute.

And then I drew out my first treehouse sketch. It wasn't very good. I was almost copying exactly what Connor had already done in his concept sketch. But then I added a little detail to the exterior of the window. I imagined what the trees would look like surrounding the treehouse.

The next morning, when Connor was working out in the backyard, I went to sit outside and continued sketching. I stared at the texture of the tree trunks outside, imagining how I could bring that same texture to the outside of the treehouse. I looked at Connor's sketch again, and I imagined changing the curvature of the roof. What if I softened the edges a little? What if a treehouse had more than a single roof because there were two floors? What if the top floor was just a cozy little nook, following the A-frame of the roof? I drew it all out with the same purple marker I had used to draw out the rock. It felt like a lucky marker.

*I was designing again.* I was so excited and so relieved I wanted to cry.

The next week passed by quickly. Completely immersed in my work, I felt a determination I hadn't felt in years. My laptop was filled with different mood boards and brainstorms of names for each of my treehouses. These were going to be the best fucking treehouses in North America. No, they were going to be the best treehouses any resort had ever seen. It was going to make other treehouses sad that they even existed because these would be so fabulous. I was excited to work on the yurts next.

Finally, near the end of that week, I started turning my sketches into a digital model. I smiled at my laptop screen, taking a peek to where Connor was working at his desk with that serious, focused expression on his face.

I watched as Maximus jumped onto Connor's desk. Connor's face broke out into a small smile, and he petted him softly before reaching into his pocket, pulling out a cat treat.

My heart melted a little. I didn't know how to deal with Connor when he was being sweet.

It wasn't even just how sweet he was with Maxi. It was also in the subtle ways he was always taking care of me too. He brought me croissants or little fruit bowls in the afternoon while we worked. At night, when it got colder, he brought me blankets to keep me warm while I sat on the couch.

Our dynamic was changing, and I didn't know what to make of it, or what to make of him. All I knew was that it was getting harder and harder not to think about him.

I went to bed at night a little restless, thinking of Connor just down the hall and also eager to wake up the next morning to continue working. The only thing that helped me sleep was Maximus.

Maxi was the cutest cat in the world. No one could ever convince me otherwise. I was obsessed with him. Every night, he slept next to me on my pillow, snoring so softly it was just the softest little wheeze, like a tiny whistle.

When I crawled into my bed at night, not thinking about Connor and his smoldering eyes, I waited for Maxi to climb onto my pillow. He curled into a little ball, tucking his tail into his body before blinking slowly at me. Sometimes, he stretched out a paw, gently placing it on top of my head. He always fell asleep first, and I fell asleep to his soft little breaths against my face.

"I need to head into town today," said Connor on Saturday morning.

It was already the end of May. I couldn't believe I'd already spent a whole month up here.

"Are we out of coffee again?"

"No," smiled Connor, "but this weekend is the Spring Festival. My parents are both involved, so I need to make an appearance."

"Oh," I said, and I jumped up. "Can I come?"

"Sure," he said, his expression soft.

"There's going to be a lot of pastel," he warned. "People really like to go all out."

"Ooh, is it like a themed party?" I loved a good themed party.

"It's nothing fancy, but people do like to get dressed up in spring colours."

"So, like pastel blues, pinks, greens, and yellows?"

"Exactly."

I looked at Connor's dark jeans and black shirt. "Then why are you dressed like that?"

"It's really not a big deal." He moved to the front door to put his shoes on.

"No! Come on, we should dress up too! I don't want to insult the entire town of Fleurmont because we didn't take two seconds to change into a spring outfit!" I ran to the closet space to pick out my outfit, already knowing what to pick out.

See? This is why you always pack more than you think you need. You never know when you're going to be shipped off to a small town in Canada and get invited to a spring festival. You just never know.

I changed into a bright creamy yellow dress. It was vintage with a modest, square neckline, and it flared out in a satisfying way that made it look like the dress was twirling every time I moved. I opted for a pair of coral pink heels that I'd bought in Milan and had only worn once. Nya would be so proud to know I was getting some use out of them.

I bounced back to the front door, and I saw Connor's eyes drag over me. Something crackled in his eyes, and his Adam's apple bobbed once before he cleared his throat.

"Ready to go?"

"No, what about you? Come on, there must be something in your closet. Can I go look?"

"Fine," he acquiesced.

I went into his bedroom, still in my heels. Maxi ran after me, curious too.

It was my first time in Connor's room. The smell of him was almost overwhelming. He smelled like the forest, all pine and something warm and earthy. I felt heat pooling in my stomach when I saw his bed. There wasn't anything out of the ordinary in his bedroom. In fact, it was exactly as I'd pictured it. It was neat. His bed was made, and he didn't have any dirty clothes lying around. The only things on his desk were his sketchbook and a set of graphite pencils.

I forced myself to look away from the bed and looked through his closet instead. Hmm. No love letters to Uncle Valerian, after all. Well, at least my closet was technically still bigger.

"Are you almost done?" he asked, an amused expression on his face. He leaned against the door frame as he waited for me, looking like a snack.

"These things take time!" I huffed, but I felt my face redden, trying not to think about how his bed was right. There. Finally, I picked out a pair of light blue jeans and a light yellow T-shirt for him. It wasn't the best, but it was better than his current outfit.

"Here," I said, handing it to him.

Connor got changed, and we made the drive into Fleurmont. Connor had to park near a school and walk into the town square because the roads were all closed off to vehicles during the week of the Spring Festival.

The moment we stepped onto the closed streets, we were in a full-on celebration of spring. Music was playing throughout the streets, and most of the shops on the streets had their doors wide open.

We started walking down the street, and it was clear that changing had been the right choice. The townspeople of Fleurmont were committed to celebrating spring. Everyone was wearing pastel colours. I almost expected everyone to be carrying wicker baskets filled with flowers and bursting into song the way everyone was so perfectly coordinated. But I appreciated committing to a good theme, so it was fun to see everyone completely decked out in spring wear.

We made our way to the town square, where we saw Connor's dad at a large stand with a bunch of strawberry rhubarb pies. Arielle stood behind the stand wearing a pastel pink apron. Next to her, a middle-aged Asian woman was wearing a matching apron, and I thought it was Connor's mom before he greeted her.

"Hey, Aunt Suyi. Hi, Arielle," said Connor as he gave his dad a hug.

"Hi, son. Good to see you again, Stassi," said Owen warmly.

"Good to see you, too," I smiled, and was surprised when Owen leaned in to give me a hug.

I returned it, feeling myself warm. I couldn't help but compare him to Grandpa and Uncle Valerian, who were definitely not huggers.

"You remember Arielle. And this is Suyi. Suyi owns the dim sum restaurant just down the street," Connor introduced us.

"It's so nice to meet you, Stassi. I've heard so much about you," said Suyi warmly.

From the way she and Arielle exchanged looks, I could tell that they were close friends.

We all exchanged a round of hellos as Abel came running up to the pie stand.

"Here we go, here we go," he said, panting, his face red like he was out of breath. He placed a massive pie on the table.

It was a beautiful pie with intricate latticework on top, baked to perfection with a shiny, golden-brown crust.

"Relax, Abel, you still have time," said Suyi, checking the time on her phone. "The competition doesn't close for another twenty minutes."

"There's a competition?" I asked Connor, but it was his dad who replied.

"Yes, we have a pie competition every Spring Festival," said Owen excitedly, eyeing the pies with interest. "This year, it's strawberry rhubarb and, of course, Wild Pie."

"What's Wild Pie?" I asked.

"It's the category they came up with for whoever can come up with the most interesting flavour combination," said Connor.

"Yes," said Suyi, and pointed to Connor. "And thanks to this one's brother, we almost cancelled it altogether one year."

"What happened?"

Owen looked at Connor in confusion.

"The *durian*," Arielle puffed out.

"Ohh," Connor said, slapping his knee with a soft laugh as he remembered, and he looked at me with a smile. "That's right. In his senior year of high school, Michael and his friends made a durian and raisin flavoured pie for the competition."

"That sounds...disgusting?" I wrinkled my nose.

I had tried durian when I was in Thailand, and while I knew many people loved it, I just couldn't get behind the pungent flavour.

"It *was*," said Suyi sharply, glaring at Connor.

"That was Michael. That wasn't me," he reminded her.

"Oh, good God, I still remember that," said Abel. "I couldn't get the aftertaste out of my mouth for weeks."

"It couldn't have been that bad, could it?" said Owen. "I actually quite like durian."

"Trust me, it was," said Arielle.

Suyi nodded enthusiastically in support. She took a piece of paper and wrote a number, placing the tag in front of Abel's pie.

"This is your strawberry rhubarb pie?" Suyi confirmed.

"Yes, that's right," said Abel proudly.

"Good, good. Come back at one o'clock for the official judging," said Suyi, handing Abel back a number.

"Looks good, Abel. Can I try a bite?" asked Owen, pulling Abel's closer to him to take a whiff.

"Hey! No touching the pies until after official judging," said Arielle, whacking his hand away with a wooden ruler.

"I still don't understand why I can't be an official judge," grumbled Owen.

"You need to have official culinary expertise," said Suyi. "It's only fair."

"I'll make sure they save you a slice, my friend," said Abel.

Now I wanted some strawberry rhubarb pie.

"Hi! Would you like a flower crown?" a sweet voice said in French from behind us.

Connor and I turned to see a group of children holding baskets of flower crowns. They were all wearing pastel green outfits, and the sign on the baskets told us they were from the local elementary school.

Okay, was this super freaking cute or what?

"In English, please," Connor said to them.

In French, I responded, shaking my head. "It's okay, I speak French. And I would love a flower crown."

Arielle gasped out loud. "Connor! You didn't tell me she spoke French! Her French is perfect."

"You speak French?" Connor gaped at me, and I savoured the shocked look on his face. I smirked at him.

"What, like it's hard?" I said to him, doing my best Elle Woods impression.

Suyi and Abel cackled a laugh.

"You should marry her," Arielle whispered to Connor in French. Arielle threw me a wink.

Connor's face turned red, and I bit back a laugh. Suyi, Owen, and Abel burst out laughing.

"How much is a flower crown?" I asked one of the children, who were looking at each other, confused, probably wondering why it was a big deal that some woman spoke French when everyone else in town did too.

"One dollar, please!" said the little girl in the middle. She was wearing pigtails and had little green ribbons in her hair. She was freaking *adorable*.

Oh, wait, shit. I didn't have any cash.

"Do you take credit card?" I opened my purse.

The kids looked at each other again.

"Here, I got it," said Connor from behind me, and he handed the little girl two gold coins. "For two crowns."

Gold coins? Even their money was cute. Maybe being in Canada wasn't so bad after all.

"Thank you!" said the little girl, and her classmate picked out a flower crown from the basket.

He handed a crown to me and then another crown to Connor.

"Thank you."

"Happy Spring Festival!" they chorused, and then they moved over to Suyi and Arielle.

I put the crown of purple, yellow, and orange flowers on my head. It fit kind of perfectly. I glanced at Connor, who was looking at me with that smoldering expression again.

"Here," I said, taking his crown of flowers from him. I stepped closer to him, putting the flowers on his head. It was almost intoxicating being so close to him, and I took a step back nervously, aware we had an audience. Aware his dad was right there watching us. Seriously, what was wrong with me?

"Thanks," Connor said quietly, touching the flowers on his head.

"So, what are you kids up to? Are you hungry, or do you want to join me at the ring toss booth?" asked Owen jovially.

"I wanted to say hi to Mom, actually."

"Maybe go to the Honeycomb Stall. She was helping Ithier set up just a few minutes ago."

"Be sure to come back later for pie tasting," said Arielle.

"We will," said Connor.

We said our goodbyes and headed away from the town square.

# CHAPTER SEVENTEEN

## Stassi

"So what's the Honeycomb Stall?" I asked Connor as we made our way down the street.

"It's probably the most indulgent Spring Festival snack," said Connor with a grin. "It's really popular around here. Are you hungry?"

"I could snack."

We soon arrived at the Honeycomb Stall, which was a big, beautiful stall set up outdoors. It was set up like a rodeo-themed bar, and we took our seats at the outdoor bar counter, even though Connor's mother was nowhere in sight. I glanced at Connor, and he gave me a quick smile.

"Hey hey," said the bartender? Stall owner? The man who greeted us looked young, probably close to my age, and had a splatter of freckles on his handsome face.

"Hey, Ithier," said Connor. "I didn't realize you were doing this this year."

"Yep, officially roped into the family business," said Ithier, running a hand through his brown locks.

"Ithier's parents own a farm here in Fleurmont," explained Connor. "The Charbonneau Farm makes honey and maple syrup."

"Yep, local farm boy right here," Ithier smiled. He looked at me, a large grin on his face. "I don't recognize *you*. You must be from out of town."

"I am," I said, amused.

"Well, welcome to Fleurmont," Ithier flashed me a flirtatious grin.

"We were actually looking for my mom," said Connor coldly. "My dad said she was just here?"

"She was, but she left a few minutes ago," said Ithier, unbothered by Connor's tone. "So, you two want a board?"

"Sure," Connor conceded, though he continued to glare at Ithier as Ithier flashed me another flirtatious grin.

Ithier lifted a long tray from under the counter.

The tray had six different little pots, each containing what looked like different types of honey. Ithier took out another tray, this time looking like a small charcuterie board. It was topped with different cubes of cheeses and strawberries. He handed out little metal skewers to both of us.

"So basically, you take your skewers, you stab a cheese cube or a strawberry, and you try out different kinds of honey."

"So you just dip cheese and strawberries in honey?" I asked skeptically.

"Hey, don't knock it till you try it."

Ithier nodded. "There's a long story about each type of honey –you know, wildflower honey, orange blossom honey, and then a good story about the history of the farm, all of that good tourist spiel, but I know Connor's just in it for the eating."

I picked up my skewer and stabbed a piece of cheese. I dipped it into the pot of honey closest to me. The honey was a deep amber colour, and I twisted the cheese into it, scooping up a thick layer of honey. I put it into my mouth. Connor watched me as my eyes popped open.

The combination of flavours was insane.

"This is so fucking good," I exclaimed, still chewing. "What is this?"

"That's the eucalyptus honey," said Ithier, tapping the honey pot, "and the cheese is a special cheese we only make here in Fleurmont. You won't find cheese like this anywhere else."

It was a creamy and sharp cheese all at once, and that combined with the taste of the honey was just...insane.

"I think this is the best fucking cheese and honey I've ever had in my life."

"I'm glad you like it," Connor laughed quietly.

He turned towards me and reached for his skewer. Our knees bumped together under the table, and I was suddenly aware of how close we were again.

I stabbed another cheese with my skewer and leaned closer to Connor, our arms touching as I dipped the cheese into the wildflower honey. Connor's body was stiff and half-frozen next to mine.

"So you come here and eat honey and cheese every year?" I asked him.

"Almost every year," said Connor, "but I've missed more than a few spring festivals living out in L. A."

"We also sell full honeycombs," said Ithier. "Right, I should probably take those out."

Ithier bent down to take out a wooden crate and set out honeycombs on the counters along the stall. All the little boxes of honeycomb and jars of honey looked so pretty, and I wondered if I should buy any for Nya or Julian before I left Fleurmont.

Connor and I finished all the cheeses and strawberries within the next couple of minutes, and proceeded to twirl honey onto our skewers to get the remaining bits of thick liquid. I watched Connor dip his skewer into the eucalyptus honey and bring it to his lips. He missed by just a bit, and honey dripped onto the side of his lower lip.

I had a sudden urge to lick it off of him. I flushed.

"What's up?" asked Connor, those hazel green eyes back on mine. His tongue darted out to lick the honey off of his lip.

"Nothing."

"Stassi Salvati with nothing to say? That's a first."

"Just enjoying the honey." I took my skewer, dipping it in honey before holding it upside down. I licked the honey from the bottom of the metal skewer to the tip, keeping my eyes on Connor.

Heat flared in his eyes, and his whole body stiffened again as he watched me, his eyes on my tongue and then on my lips.

"I *love* honey," I said to him sweetly.

When we were done with the Honeycomb Stall, Connor and I left and made our way to more food stalls.

We people watched a little as we made our way down the streets. Life seemed so much easier in Fleurmont. People really seemed to take their time. No one was in a rush. I saw couples walking together down the street in matching outfits and matching flower crowns.

One young couple was dancing to the music in the streets. The sun was on them, drawing attention to the flash of gold on their hands –they were wearing wedding rings. They couldn't have been any older than me.

How did people just figure it out like that? How did people fall in love so easily?

I had never had a relationship last longer than...well, I had never really been in a relationship. Just a bunch of meaningless flings. I had never loved anyone easily, and no one had ever loved me easily either.

My parents had gotten married young. They must have been around the age of this Fleurmont couple when they met. They had met, connected, fallen in love, and gotten married, just like that. Why did it feel like they had loved each other more than they could ever love me?

Their love always felt just out of reach—close enough to touch, but never wholly mine. Something I was almost worthy of, but not quite.

I knew my parents loved me. I remembered all the times my mom would hold me in her arms when I was little. She used to sing to me, and we used to go on walks in the park on summer mornings, just the two of us. My dad used to make me waffle cakes for my birthday, and when he would tell me bedtime stories, he would show me pictures from all the amazing places he's travelled to. But those memories felt like another lifetime. Eventually everything became about Sylvia, and I was left in the background, half-forgotten.

Maybe I was the problem. Maybe I hadn't let them know how much I needed to feel loved. I was always joking and deflecting, and I never let people get too close.

That's what I'd always been like, and I was especially like that with my romantic relationships. It's never been a problem before. I'd never really connected with anyone. I'd never felt a crazy pull towards someone...until now.

It was a terrifying thought.

I didn't want to want Connor Fitzgerald. I could not want Connor and be nothing more than an inconvenience to him. That would kill me.

What if the connection I felt between us meant nothing to him? I mean, of course it meant nothing. I mean, how could this spark between us –if you could even call it that, if it wasn't just completely in my head– possibly mean anything more than just physical attraction? Right?

I was still overthinking all of my feelings when two women approached us suddenly.

"Connor," said the older woman.

The older woman was an elegantly dressed, middle-aged Asian woman. She wore a pale green pantsuit with a flower brooch on her right side, and delicate gold earrings. She was slender, and I immediately could see that she and Connor were related.

"Mom." Connor looked surprised, and then he looked at the young woman next to her. "Elodie."

Elodie? *This* was the environmental consultant Connor kept meeting up with? I looked at the woman standing next to Connor's mom. Everything about her was pretty and clean. She had straight, shiny brown hair. Her makeup was light and neat. Her dress was a light peachy pink, and she was wearing studded gold earrings and a matching necklace. She looked prim and proper. She looked organized and neat and like she would always be serious about her work. She was probably exactly Connor's type.

"I was wondering where you were. Who's this?" Connor's mom looked at me with some interest.

"Mom, this is Stassi. She's working with me on the *Fleurs de L'Étang* project," said Connor quickly. "Stassi, this is my mom, Cecelia Lin."

"It's nice to meet you," I said, feeling nervous for no reason.

Cecelia shook my hand, her eyes assessing me. She looked so much like Connor. Or rather, Connor looked so much like her.

"It's nice to meet you too. You must be Valerian Salvati's niece then."

"Yes," I said, and that's when I noticed Cecelia's shoes –she was wearing off-white Vivier pumps with a pastel green detail.

"I love your Viviers."

"Why, thank you." Cecelia looked pleased, and she looked at my shoes too.

I saw her subtle smile of approval, and my insides warmed.

Our bonding moment ended too soon.

"Have you met Elodie yet?" asked Cecelia.

Elodie smiled, and I didn't miss the way her gaze lingered appreciatively on Connor.

"They haven't had the chance to yet."

"Hi, Connor." Elodie smiled shyly at him, her cheeks turning just the slightest shade of peachy pink.

Who blushes and automatically matches their outfit? She must be a witch.

"Hey," smiled Connor.

Jealousy and irritation replaced my self-consciousness from a few moments ago.

"It's nice to meet you," I cut in a little icily, sticking out my hand. "I'm Stassi."

"Hi, I'm Elodie."

Her hand was weak and limp in mine, and I shook it a little more vigorously than necessary.

"Well, I'm so happy I ran into you both and got a chance to say hi. I was actually just going to go find Elodie's mom to catch up. Planning for this Spring Festival has been non-stop. But maybe you can all hang out while I go look for her," smiled Cecelia, giving Elodie's shoulder a gentle squeeze.

"I can text my mom for you," said Elodie eagerly.

"That would be great, actually." Cecelia clapped her hands together. "I don't know why I didn't think of that earlier. Must be all this running around."

"This is honestly the best Spring Festival yet," said Elodie. "You've really outdone yourself, Mrs. Lin."

Jeez, what a fucking suck-up.

"Oh, you're too sweet. Connor, isn't she sweet?" said Cecelia, patting Elodie's arm.

"Uh," said Connor awkwardly.

"Oh, *there* she is!" said Cecelia, spotting someone in the crowd. "Alright, I'll see you kids later."

"Bye!"

"See you later."

The three of us were left standing together awkwardly on the cobblestone street.

"I like your shirt," Elodie said to Connor. "It's perfect for the Spring Festival."

I hated this woman. I officially hated this woman.

"Thanks," said Connor, "I like your outfit too."

I huffed out an irritated exhale.

Elodie blinked, as if remembering I was still here, and turned her attention to me. She tucked her hair behind her ear and smiled at me, looking at my dress. "Cute dress."

*Cute?*

I gave her a tight smile.

When I didn't say anything else, she continued. "So, Connor tells me you're designing the treehouses for *Fleurs de L'Étang*?"

"Yep," I said shortly.

"How cute!"

That fucking word again. Did she think I was a child? I hated how condescending she sounded. Cute was how you described a stuffed animal.

"It must be so cool for you to get to actually design something as an intern," Elodie continued.

I almost sputtered.

"I've designed a lot of things," I cut in sharply, tossing my hair back. "This isn't my first design work. I am a *fully* licensed architect, which you would know if –"

"Okay!" Connor cut in. "Er, Elodie, it was nice to see you, but Stassi and I should really head back."

"Yeah, I should get going too," said Elodie, looking embarrassed.

"Bye," I said pointedly.

She looked at me, taken aback.

"See you next week," said Connor.

"Yeah, see you next week, Connor," Elodie smiled at him.

Elodie walked away from us, and Connor looked at me.

"What?" I said irritably.

Connor shook his head, and we made our way back to the car.

We didn't talk as Connor drove back up to the cabin. It was infuriating not to talk the whole car ride up. I don't think I've ever spent so long not talking.

Finally, when Connor parked the car, I rounded on him before he could get out of the car. "So, what, you're not going to talk to me anymore?"

"I never said I wasn't going to talk to you." Connor gave me an exasperated look.

"What's your problem?"

"*My* problem? Stassi, you were completely rude to Elodie. That was completely uncalled for."

"Oh, please. So I didn't give her a hug and a kiss goodbye," I said, rolling my eyes. "I think she'll live."

"That's not the point," said Connor. "You can't just talk to people like that."

"Like what?" I challenged.

"Like - like you look down on them because they're just small towners!"

"Look down on *her*? She was the one being totally condescending to me! She was the one acting like it's an honour and a privilege for me to even be contemplating design work."

"Stassi, she didn't mean it like that –"

"You're going to take *her* side on this? You know what, fuck this, I don't even know why I'm bothering to explain this to you," I fumed, and then I turned and got out of the car, slamming the car door behind me.

Connor followed me out of the car.

"Where the hell are you going? Is this how you resolve conflict? You can't just walk away –"

"Watch me!"

"Stassi!" Connor ran over to me, running up the porch steps.

I didn't let him continue, rounding back to face him before I could reach the door. "You have no idea how shitty it feels to always be underestimated, to have everyone around you think you're stupid just because you're young and you like tequila. Yeah, I'm only twenty-three and yeah, technically, I don't have a lot of work experience, but I know how to design a fucking treehouse. I don't need some prissy, condescending bitch who's not even an architect to tell me how lucky I am because I *get* to design something because I'm *just* an intern, okay? Do you know how demeaning that feels?"

I turned away from him to reach for the cabin door and wrench it open.

It was locked. Fuck.

I reached into my purse for the keys.

"*Stassi.*" Connor grabbed my elbow and turned me towards him.

"What?" I shouted. I was about to yell at him again, but his expression caught me off guard. He didn't look angry. Instead, he was looking at me with a different kind of intensity. It stopped me, catching me off guard.

"I *do* get it," he said.

"You don't –"

"I'm twenty-nine, and this isn't my first project. You think I spent the last seven years just constantly getting praised for doing a good job all the time? Do you know how many times I led projects and got dismissed as just being a dumb kid? Or how many times other people got credit for the work I did because I was younger and less experienced?"

I swallowed. I guess I hadn't really thought about it. Connor was such a brilliant designer that I couldn't imagine him ever feeling that way. When I'd looked him up online, all I saw was a mountain of praise.

But I saw how hard he worked every day. I knew he could get stressed out, too.

"I'm sorry." Connor exhaled, shaking his head.

"What?" I said, confused. "Why are you sorry?"

"Because I underestimated you when I first met you. I did the same thing that people used to do to me. I wrote you off as someone who had no interest in design and I gave you all those stupid research tasks instead of actually giving you a chance. I'm sorry about that. I've seen the work you started doing with the treehouses –they're better than anything I could have come up with. You're a hell of a designer."

The compliment was completely unexpected, and I felt tears prickling at my eyes. I blinked them away quickly, refusing to cry. I don't cry. Why was I being so emotional today?

"Well, I know I didn't exactly make it easy for you," I mumbled finally.

"It doesn't matter. It was my job to have an open mind, and I didn't. So I'm sorry about that. And I'm sorry that Elodie made you feel that way."

I exhaled, because I wasn't so sure that was really the whole reason I was so upset with Elodie. Or so upset in general. The thought of the young married couple dancing in the street came back to mind.

Connor's hand was still on my arm, and slowly, I reached to hold on to his arm as well. My fingers closed around his biceps. I saw Connor swallow, his breathing seeming to stop altogether.

"Is that the only reason you were upset? Was it just that comment she made, or was there more?" His voice was quieter now.

I looked up at him, and our eyes locked.

No, it was more. It was the way she was looking at you. It was the way she was smiling at you and you were smiling back at her. The way it looked so easy between the two of you.

Nothing was easy about me. I knew that. My family was a mess. I was a mess, and I couldn't even blame it all on them, even with Sylvia. I made things harder for people. I was always too much for people.

"It was just that," I said finally. I wanted to cry.

Connor's face softened a little.

"You're a great architect. Don't let me or anyone else make you feel otherwise."

I let out a heavy sigh. "You really think so?"

"I mean it. I know it's not done yet, but I saw one of your designs for the treehouse on the table before we left this morning. There was one with purple-tinted glass. I think you used it to create some kind of little reading nook? That looked pretty incredible."

"I wanted it to look like a jacaranda tree."

"Are those the trees that have purple flowers?"

"Yeah. There are a lot of jacaranda trees in South America and East Africa. When they flower and there's a whole row of them, they create this bright purple haze effect, and I wanted to recreate that in some small corner of the world."

"Sounds beautiful," said Connor.

"It is," I said.

We were still holding onto each other's arms. Our arms stayed frozen in place, as if we were both too afraid to move.

I took a step closer to him. Our lips were only inches away from each other.

Connor swallowed again, his eyes on my lips.

I took another small step closer, tentatively.

Connor took a step back away from me. He shook his head slowly.

"I -we should go inside," he said.

He disentangled himself from me, stepping aside, and I felt my heart sink. I felt the sharp sting of rejection.

The only thing that kept me from completely dying inside was Maximus greeting us loudly at the door. Maxi demanded for his can of wet food, and I beelined for the kitchen, grateful not to have to look Connor in the eye again after that moment.

# CHAPTER EIGHTEEN

## Connor

**Me:** How's the fancy car elevator designing going?

**Dustin:** LOL. Finally done with that shit now, thankfully. How'd the pitch go with Salvati?

**Me:** Haven't pitched him yet. About to have the meeting with him, though.

**Dustin:** Oh shit! Good luck, dude.

**Me:** Thanks, man.

**Dustin:** Let me know how it goes.

"How is it going with Stassi?" Valerian Salvati asked me when we connected over a video call.

It was the first thing he asked me, and it was a loaded question.

From a work perspective, Stassi was actually doing well. She was a talented architect, and over the last week, she had really gotten into it. Her designs of the treehouses were incredible. Stassi had incredible attention to detail, and her spatial thinking abilities were better than those of a lot of architects I'd met. For each treehouse design, she'd also created extensive mood boards for the interior design and had mock-ups of some of the furniture she envisioned.

On the other hand, things between us were…tense after the Spring Festival. We'd spent the last couple of days mostly working in silence, and when she spoke to me, it was about work or about Maxi.

I knew it was my fault. I knew I was the one pushing her away, but wasn't that what I was supposed to be doing? This was a four-month long arrangement. Internship. Whatever the hell we wanted to call it, and the next thing I knew, she'd be gone.

"It's fine," I managed to say to Valerian. My voice sounded tighter than I wanted it to.

Valerian looked unconvinced.

"Is she giving you trouble?" he asked suspiciously.

"No. I mean, she got a cat, but other than that, it's been fine," I said, feeling kind of bad for ratting out Maxi, who was, in retrospect, the least of the problems I had with Stassi.

Once we had gotten Maxi the things that he needed, he'd spent most of his time curled up next to Stassi or lounging about the cabin.

"She got a cat?" Valerian's eyes bugged out slightly before he regained composure.

"It's actually fine," I said quickly.

"Nothing's burning?"

"Nothing's burning."

Valerian nodded slowly, and then he seemed to refocus. "Alright. Give me your pitch."

I pitched my concept to him. The luxury resort would be called *Fleurs de L'Étang*. There was an experience pitch for every season, but the main difference would be between the warmer months and the colder winter months.

Guests would park right outside of the resort so that once you entered, you were completely immersed. There would be a free shuttle for guests to take them straight to Fleurmont. The first thing they would experience would be a welcome lodge to check-in.

There would be massive flower installations in front of the welcome lodge, an immersive piece of art that could also teach them about the wildflowers. Past the welcome lodge would be the entrance to the ride to view the wildflowers.

The entrance to the ride would also lead to the different hiking trails. In the winter, we would include snowshoeing and snowmobiling.

Then, there would be a set of treehouse cabins and the luxury yurts. We could plant more native trees around the treehouse cabins so that they could feel more secluded.

The pond across from the welcome lodge would be a picnic area, another immersive outdoor installation experience. In the winter, we could use it for skating. Next to it would be the stargazing lodge. In the back, we could create a fitness center where guests could do yoga or pilates with a view of the mountains. There would be a row of different restaurants for guests to choose from. We would shape the walking paths to look vaguely like a type of wildflower.

Valerian nodded thoughtfully as he listened to my pitch. He flipped through the initial schematic design pages, which had preliminary sketches I had done of each area of the resort and some of the buildings.

"The report from the marketing team is on page 20, and I have a separate spreadsheet with the breakdown of the cost estimates from your cost estimator," I continued.

"Hmm." I could see Valerian's cursor clicking through different tabs of the spreadsheet.

I held my breath.

"Well, Fitzgerald," said Valerian finally, "this is good work."

Relief flooded through me, and I fought to keep my face neutral.

"I like the ideas around the accommodations. That's exactly right for this kind of location. And the idea for the ride –spot on. I want to see the design more refined, but I love it."

I felt elated. My heart was pounding a million beats per second. Could this mean I was closer to becoming the Creative Director for the Salvati Group?

"My only issue is the plan for the back area," said Valerian, frowning at his screen.

"The fitness center and the row of restaurants?" My heart sank just as quickly as it had risen.

"Yeah," said Valerian, and I could see him tapping a pen against his nose. "Yoga and pilates...It's just so overdone, you know? And the restaurants in the back...Well, it's a little basic."

The veins in my body froze.

*Basic.*

It was the worst thing someone could say to a designer about their work. And this was coming from Valerian Salvati.

"I'll come up with something else," I said, my mouth feeling dry.

"Good. You know, you might want to reach out to William Harrison, see if a conversation can inspire anything."

Over my dead fucking body.

"I'll think about it."

"Alright, I've got to hop to my next call. Good work. I look forward to talking soon. I want to see what else you can come up with for that back area, but you can start refining the master plan for everything else."

I swallowed after Valerian Salvati hung up from our call.

*Well, it's a little basic.*

*You know, you might want to reach out to William Harrison, see if a conversation can inspire anything.*

Those words might haunt me for the rest of my career. Which may just be on its way to coming to its basic end. I could only hope that there was still time and that Valerian hadn't already offered the Creative Director position to Harrison.

I tried not to punch a wall on the way to the kitchen as I made myself a fresh batch of coffee. Fitness centres and restaurants. I should have known better.

I should head to the Chabonneaus' farm. Ithier had set up an outdoor axe-throwing range that was great for taking out anger.

I was about to have my first sip of coffee when Stassi appeared in the kitchen, her brown-gold hair in a messy, sexy bun on top of her head. She was wearing comfy-looking shorts and a loose pink sweater, and she marched in with purpose.

"Okay, I'm done with the first iteration of the yurts and treehouses. What's next?" she said, plopping down at the large table.

Maxi hopped onto the table next to her. He licked his paw, the residues of his breakfast still on his face. He lay down comfortably, spreading his body across the table, his white belly all round and fluffy. It was nice to see him gain weight over the last few weeks.

Stassi reached out a hand to pet him instinctively. A small smile formed on her lips as Maxi started to purr, and my chest tightened.

I had been so close to kissing those lips the other night. I must have the self-control of a Buddhist monk to have resisted that.

Even without her tiny shorts and tank tops, Stassi was breathtakingly beautiful. I had to be careful. If we ever crossed that line, there would be no coming back. At least for me. Because if I ever had Stassi Salvati, for even a second, I wasn't so sure I could ever let her go.

On the other hand, whatever pull she felt towards me was probably nothing more than a feverish cabin dream, the result of putting two hormonal twenty-somethings in a secluded cabin up in the mountains. Whatever tension we felt between us would no doubt disappear the second we stepped away from this strange, hazy bubble. I was doing both of us a favour by keeping my distance.

"We should do a final review of your designs together later this week," I said, and then I sighed reluctantly. "Sorry, I don't have anything else for you to work on yet."

"What about the welcome lodge?"

"That's done. I... have some work to do for the south side of the resort before I'll have more work for you," I admitted. "I just pitched the concept to Valerian, and he wants some changes."

"Maybe I can help," said Stassi.

"I'm open to any ideas you have."

"What are you stuck on?" Stassi poured herself a mug of coffee.

"Everything on the south side of the site."

"Show me," said Stassi, tapping the spot on the table next to her.

I obeyed. I took my laptop and sat next to her, careful to keep a healthy, professional couple of inches between us. I pushed my laptop towards her and showed her.

"There's this whole area on the south side that needs to be reworked. There's a lodge here that will be used as a venue space, with the top floors for stargazing, but there's a row of restaurants and a fitness area in the back that needs to be scrapped and replaced with something else."

Stassi observed the sitemap. After a couple of moments, she switched tabs to 3D massing models. She switched back and forth a few times, thinking. Her cerulean eyes were focused, and at some point, she cocked her head to the side.

"So how should the guests be feeling at the lodge?" she asked.

"Relaxed when they're stargazing, maybe a little in awe. Happy and excited when they're in the venue space." I opened up the mood board I had created for the space.

Stassi looked it over before she squinted again at the 3D models, clicking through each area of the resort.

"And the lodge, it's mostly made of wood?"

"Yeah, heavy timber structural frame, log siding for the exterior," I said, pointing to my screen with my index finger, gesturing lines in the building's orientation.

Stassi nodded, and then she looked at Maxi for a second, who had fallen asleep on the shirt Stassi had left scattered on the table.

Her eyes widened a little, and she cocked her head to the side.

"What if you had animals?" she suggested.

"What, like a petting zoo?"

"No, something more sophisticated than that. Like horses. Rich people love horses."

That was true.

"Horses," I repeated, thinking it through. "Like, horseback riding?"

"No. I mean, maybe, but I don't think you want this resort to be a heavy, intensive activity kind of place, and there isn't that much land. But this is just enough land to create a mini horse sanctuary. You know, like when racing horses retire? You could have a little old horse retirement home here and people could feed them apples and carrots."

"That's interesting," I said, trying to visualize it.

The land was perfectly flat on the west side of the mountains facing Fleurmont. There definitely was enough space for a large stable and grazing pasture.

"What about the back here?" I said, pointing to where the fitness centre would have been.

Stassi looked again, thinking.

"I'm not sure..." she said finally. "I'd have to think about it some more, but let me at least mock up the horse sanctuary so you can really see what I'm talking about. We can figure out the other section later."

She pulled open her laptop, and I pulled my laptop back to work next to her. We spent the next few hours in a complete state of flow. We researched different stable designs for the horses and brainstormed different fencing options to create a space continuum that could work for both the horses and the people.

A few hours in, I heated a casserole for us, and after a brief lunch break, we continued our design process.

I looked over Stassi's treehouse and yurt designs again to see if it would inspire anything to replace the fitness centre. I came back to her first design, the one with the purple-tinted glass in one of the reading nooks.

It was only when I glanced over at my phone and saw that it was five o'clock that I suddenly had an idea.

"Let's take a break," I said.

"Wait, but I'm almost done sketching out the feeding area!" she said.

"Just a little break," I said, standing up. "Come on, let's go. It'll be worth it, I promise."

"Where are we going?"

"It's a surprise."

"Ooh, we're leaving the cabin? Is this another sketching exercise?"

"Yes, and no," I said, and we walked to the door to put on our shoes.

Stassi put on her sneakers, and I took out the keys to the cabin.

"Wait, should I change?" asked Stassi.

"No, you're perfect."

It had slipped out before I could realize it. I saw her grinning at me out of the corner of my eye.

"Can Maxi come?" she asked.

"No."

"But where are we going?" asked Stassi, following me out the door.

I locked the door behind us, ignoring Maxi's whining. He would have to deal.

"Do you know what a *surprise* is, Stassi Salvati?"

"Is it a magical castle? Ooh, is it an existing horse sanctuary that only Fleurmont locals know about?"

"Just come with me," I smiled.

Stassi and I walked towards the northeast side of the old mining town. The demolition process had just started, and the charm of the old mining town was now juxtaposed with excavators and bulldozers.

We walked along the mountain, and I led her up the winding hiking path. Stassi talked non-stop as we made our way up.

"Are you taking me here to work out? If you wanted to work out, you could have just asked. I'm a great workout buddy."

"I'm sure you are."

"So are you finally going to be less secretive about your workouts?"

"I'm not secretive about my workouts."

She's been watching me work out?

"Then why are you always hiding out in the backyard?"

"I'm not hiding out. There's more room in the backyard. Are you spying on me?"

I gave her a look, and she shot me a look back, the corners of her lips twitching up into a smile.

"No, do you want me to spy on you? Also, are we almost there? And where are we going?"

"You know the expression, 'patience is a virtue'?"

"Have you heard the end of that expression? 'Patience is a virtue, but so is doing something about it.'?"

I laughed as we reached our destination.

"Okay, close your eyes," I said. "We're here."

Stassi, in typical Stassi fashion, opened her eyes wider, looking at the surrounding forest. "We're here?"

"We're *almost* here," I amended. "Close your eyes."

"Is this the part where you kill me in the woods?" she asked skeptically.

"I'm pretty sure that of the two of us, you would be the one to kill me first."

"Probably true," she agreed.

"Come on, a little trust?" I prompted.

Stassi smiled at me. It was an earth-shattering, breathtakingly beautiful smile. She closed her eyes, her smile still on her lips.

"Can I take your arm?" I asked her gently, unable to take my eyes off her lips now that her eyes were closed. I wanted to reach out and rub my thumb along her bottom lip to see if it was as soft as it looked.

"Yes," she breathed.

She held out her arm, and I took her elbow, guiding her into the clearing. She held onto my arm with her other hand, her fingers gripping my shirt sleeve.

I guided her upwards and then back down. We walked in a straight line as Stassi laughed, the grass tickling our ankles.

"Almost there," I promised, looking around to find the perfect spot.

Finally, I found it –a perfect flat rock in the perfect spot.

"One step up," I said, stepping up onto the rock.

She stepped up, and I helped steady her footing. She wobbled a bit, hands coming up to me to hold herself steady. Gently, I oriented her back towards the mountains.

"You can open your eyes now," I murmured.

# CHAPTER NINETEEN

## Stassi

I opened my eyes to the most stunning view I had ever seen in my life. Wildflowers covered every inch of land as far as the eye could see in yellow, orange, and purple. The colours were so vibrant it looked like someone had turned up the saturation in a photo editing software.

Thousands if not millions of wildflowers glowed and swayed in the afternoon sunlight. It looked like millions of fireflies were trying to recreate a sunset, and the effect could not have been more surreal or more mesmerizing. The sun hung low in the sky, and the backdrop was a gradient of stunning blue mountains.

The mountains closest to us had a purple hue to them, and they were so close I felt like I could reach out to touch their rough texture.

"This is amazing," I breathed finally.

I looked at Connor, and he was looking at me with a soft expression on his handsome face. He was standing close to me on the rock, and I could smell his soft, pine-like scent.

"Your design with the purple-tinted glass reminded me a little of the way the mountains look purple closer to sunset," he said, pointing at the purple-blue mountains.

"It's overwhelming how beautiful nature is sometimes," I said, feeling my eyes prickle with tears. I blinked them away, not sure why I was getting so emotional.

"Yeah," said Connor, and then added, "It gets even better at sunset."

"Can we stay here to watch?" I asked, still feeling breathless.

"Yeah," said Connor.

A gentle breeze brushed against us, and the fields of flowers bristled with quiet joy.

The whole scene was so beautiful I almost didn't know where to look.

"Purple jacaranda trees remind me of my parents," I blurted, feeling a lump in my throat. "They met in Kenya under a jacaranda tree, and my dad proposed to my mom under that same jacaranda tree."

I would never forget how much my parents loved telling the story of how they met.

"What were they doing in Kenya?" Connor asked.

My breath caught in my throat when I looked at him. The sun was in his face, and I could see the vibrant forest and apple greens in his eyes again. The small scar on his face shone brighter in the sun, and I wanted to reach out and touch it. I wanted to ask him how he'd gotten it.

"My dad was in Kenya for work. The Salvati Group has a division in Nairobi focused on sustainable energy production. My mom was in Kenya teaching English, and they met on a safari."

A pair of hawks soared across the sky overhead. It was a slow, graceful glide across the skyline, and I watched them fly in front of the sun.

"What were your parents like?"

I sat down on the rock we were standing on. Slowly, Connor followed my lead and sat down next to me. Our legs touched, but for once, Connor didn't move away.

"They were fun, and they loved adventure. They loved travelling, and they took us everywhere, or they tried to. I lived in Kenya for four years while I was growing up because they loved it there so much. Well, that was one reason."

"You lived in Nairobi?"

I nodded. "It's where I met my best friend, Nya. Her dad and my dad were best friends, and her dad also worked in the energy production sector. He and Nya both work in the energy production sector now, I guess."

"That's really cool. Is that a big industry in Kenya?"

"It is. Kenya is the biggest producer of geothermal energy in Africa. I think almost half of their energy production is from geothermal energy."

"Very cool."

"Yeah, it is really cool."

"Did you ever want to go into geothermal engineering? It sounds like you know a lot about the industry."

"No, that was always Nya's thing, not mine. It's just cool to learn about, and I was surrounded by that space when I was in Nairobi."

"What was it like to live in Nairobi?"

"It was fun, but it was because I lived in a bubble. I lived with my best friend in a very privileged community. Things got hard for my parents when I was six or seven. Their priorities changed, and I ended up not seeing them very much for those four years. I lived with Nya and her family instead."

"What happened?"

"My sister Sylvia was complicated. And not the way I'm complicated," I said with a self-deprecating laugh.

"Complicated how?" asked Connor.

He asked me cautiously, like he was trying to be sensitive, like he knew it wasn't the time to talk about all the ways I was complicated.

"She had a lot of health challenges growing up. Some were physical, and some were psychological. We didn't know what they were. She was misdiagnosed a lot when she was younger, and doctors sent her on all kinds of medication and therapy paths."

"Sylvia got worse as she got older. She threw tantrums, and sometimes, it would get physical. Our whole family walked on eggshells."

"That sounds really hard. On you, and on your whole family."

"It was, and it...kind of consumed my parents. Their whole lives centered around taking care of Sylvia, and finding out how to support and care for Sylvia. They tried their best, but the rest of us were kind of forgotten. Adrian and Miranda were older than me, so while I was with Nya's family in Kenya, they both went to boarding schools in Europe. That's why I'm not really close with either of them. We only ever saw each other in L.A. during the holidays."

"But then you moved back to the States?"

"Yeah, I went to a boarding school in California for high school."

I paused, letting my words sink in for both of us. It was the first time I had told anyone this. Nya knew, but it was because she had experienced it with me while it was happening, not because I was volunteering information to a stranger. Except Connor didn't feel like a stranger. Not to me, not for a long time now.

"It sounds like that was a really lonely way for you to grow up," said Connor.

I nodded. "It was. I think we all used to think —Miranda, Adrian, and I— that at some point, things would get better with Sylvia and then we'd be able to spend time with our parents and spend time with each other. My parents always made it sound so hopeful, like this new treatment plan Sylvia was on was really going to change things. And sometimes it did. But then, two years ago, my parents and Sylvia came to visit me in my senior year of college. We were going to spend time together before my graduation. They got into that car accident, and then it was all over. All those years of hanging on to the hope of one day spending time together were gone."

I let out a bitter laugh and shook my head. "I know it sounds so stupid and shallow. Rich people problems. I know my family was so lucky —*is* so lucky. So many people couldn't afford to go to boarding schools or afford to have their family go through so many surgeries and treatment plans."

My chest tightened, feeling regret course through me. Ibiza, Vegas, Miami... Did I really have to be so stupid and reckless? It seemed like such a shallow way to cope now, looking back.

Connor shook his head, his face in a thoughtful frown. "Wealth and privilege don't make your feelings or your experience less valid. You were a child growing up who needed to feel loved too."

"It gets worse though," I said.

The ugly thoughts I had gnawed at me, and something compelled me to tell him. I don't know why. Maybe I wanted to tell Connor so that it could be out there too, so that if he heard it and didn't leave, maybe this energy I felt between us could be more than just that. I felt a pull towards Connor that I could feel in my bones.

"Tell me," he said gently.

"The worst part is...I don't even think I was upset that Sylvia died," I admitted, my voice small. "When she died, I wasn't sad. I was angry with her. I - I feel like I'm still angry with her. I know it's not her fault. I know her life must have been so hard too, but I am so fucking angry at her because it felt like she had our parents her whole fucking life. It felt like I had waited my whole life to spend time with my parents, and Sylvia just got all of it. She had them all to herself, even their final moments. And I - I resent her so much for that."

I had never said those words out loud before. I had felt it in my core, in my soul, but I'd never dared say these words out loud, not even to Nya.

I turned away from Connor, bracing myself for him to hate me.

"I know," I mumbled, burying my face in my hands. "I'm a horrible human being."

Slowly, Connor peeled my hands away from my face, taking my hands in his. His hands were warm, a little rougher than I thought they'd be.

I looked up at him in surprise. He looked at me with a soft, almost tender expression. The shades of green in his eyes were bright in the softening sunlight.

"Stassi," he started gently.

I braced myself again, wrapping invisible shields around my heart.

Connor gave my hands a gentle squeeze. "That sounds incredibly difficult and painful. I'm really sorry you went through that, but you are not a horrible human being."

I shook my head, trying to blink my tears away.

"You are not a horrible human being," he repeated more firmly. "You're not a horrible human being for having feelings. It's completely normal and valid to feel angry and resentful in such a complicated situation."

I let out an exhale. It felt like a breath I'd been holding in for two years. Slowly, I let in another inhale, feeling Connor's hands still around mine. I felt relieved, like a weight had been lifted somehow, but I also felt a little anxious, a little jittery.

"Tell me something about you," I said, nudging his leg, feeling too naked, too vulnerable.

"Like what?" Connor slowly let go of my hands. He turned and faced the mountains again.

"Anything. Just...anything." My heart thudded unevenly in my chest, too aware of how vulnerable it had been.

Connor thought for a second, staring out at the wildflowers before finally speaking again.

"When I was eighteen, my dad passed away. He worked throughout my entire childhood, and we barely saw him. He was always on a business trip somewhere in the world. When he died, he left everything he ever owned to my mom. It was like Michael and I had never existed. But that wasn't the part that got to me."

Connor paused, a sad smile on his face. He looked out at the mountains.

"Right after his funeral, I found a letter he wrote to my mom when she was pregnant with me. They found out when my dad stayed stationed in Germany for business for a few months. In his letter, he begged my mom to get an abortion. He told her they already had Michael, and that whatever issues they had between them, they could work it out if she would just get rid of me. He said he couldn't deal with a second child, and he didn't want me. When I found that letter...I've never felt more devastated and unloved in my life."

My heart hurt, and instinctively, I reached for Connor, putting a hand on his. He didn't pull away.

"I'm so sorry," I said. "How did you find the letter?"

"It was at his house in Fleurmont, just sitting there in his desk. I don't know how it got there, but at the time, it felt like he wanted me to find it."

"That's terrible. I'm so sorry. Does your mom know you found the letter?"

"No. I was too afraid to tell her. My mom was very traditional growing up. She pushed us a lot, and I always felt like I was disappointing her compared to Michael."

"Why did you feel that way?" I murmured.

Connor sighed. "He was great in school and was good at sports. He was better with people and more confident. I didn't feel like I was enough for her growing up. I think in some twisted way, I was afraid that if I told her I found the letter, I would find out that she regretted keeping me. Paranoid, I know."

"Not paranoid, but not true, I bet. And your stepfather really seems to love you," I said, remembering the way Owen had interacted with Connor at the diner and at the Spring Festival.

"Yeah, and I'm lucky for that too," said Connor, looking back at me. "Owen is the best. I'm so lucky that I had him growing up. No matter how hard my mom was on us, I always had Owen in my corner."

I tried to picture a younger version of Connor, wondering if he was always quiet and serious. I hated that someone could ever have made him feel so unloved.

"Do you still think about the letter a lot?"

"No." Connor gave a small smile. "Not for a long time now."

I gave him a small smile back, and then I brought my feet up onto the rock.

"People are so complicated," I sighed, hugging my knees, staring out into the warm, multicoloured abyss of flowers.

A bee floated around a flower close to us, hovering for a while before disappearing into the petals.

"I think that's what makes places like this even better though," said Connor quietly, nodding out onto the flower fields. "People are so fucking messy and complicated, and despite all of that, places like this exist. There are just these insane, beautiful corners of the world."

I thought about the jacaranda trees in Nairobi, and how beautiful they looked in the fall months. It was pretty magical.

"That's pretty special," I agreed.

We sat there for a moment in silence, and then I nudged him again with my knee.

"Thanks for listening," I said to him.

Connor smiled at me, and my heart skipped a beat.

"Thanks for listening, too," he murmured.

I smiled back at him, and then we turned to look at the mountains again, waiting for sunset.

*June 10*

*Dearest Stassi,*

*Mary is doing a great job so far. I'm relieved because I'll be travelling for most of July to the villages where we want to expand our solar power reach. I need to meet with all the community leaders to convince them it's a good idea. Ahh! I am so stressed. Work has just been non-stop these past few months. I just want to soak in a hot bath and forget all my troubles. I want to put cucumbers on my face, drink a glass of wine, and just sit in a tub for three hours.*

*Separately, I completely believe in you. You are a great architect and a great designer! You can do it. Try not to overthink it. Unaweza!*

*Also, it sounds like you should be banging this Connor. Why have you not done it already? Go bang him and then tell me all about it. Don't leave anything out. Haha. You get it? Because you'd probably want it all inside? Haha. I am hilarious. Alright, hopefully that was some extra inspiration to help you design again.*

*All my love,*

*Nyambura*

*P.S.: I cannot believe you got a cat. Maximus Constantine Romeo Salvati is a great name —but why is he not named after his auntie Nya?! Also, please don't forget to feed him and take him to the vet.*

# Chapter Twenty

## Stassi

*June 12*

    *Dear Nyambura,*

    *Omg. I think I'm in love with Connor Fitzgerald. I'm not even kidding. We had this moment on the mountain together, and I just...I don't even know how to explain it. I think I love him. And not the way I loved Paul Walker when I watched Fast & Furious for the first time. Like, really love him. I think. I don't know. I've never been in love. I'm confused. But I definitely want to bang him now. Ahh, I wish you were here so we could talk about it in person. I need a proper debrief with you. What about you? Any hot men in Nairobi catching your eye?*

    *Also! NYA. I started designing again! I designed a bunch of treehouses and yurts. I love them so much I actually want to sleep in one. When this resort opens, you have to come for the opening weekend. We'll get a treehouse and drink wine together.*

*Ooh, and let me know if you ever want me to design your private office. I recently discovered a new fabric while I was doing research for the yurts I'm designing. It's waterproof, and one of the patterns I was looking at would really match that dress you wore at Auntie Ruth's wedding.*

*Okay, I have to go. Connor's just finished working out in the backyard, and I want to see if I can finally catch him with his shirt off.*

*Love,*

*Stassi*

*P.S.: Your work sounds so exciting. What villages will you be travelling to? And when are you leaving?*

I jolted awake in the middle of the night. The idea had come to me in a dream. Maxi jumped up, startled, bouncing off the bed.

I ran out of my room, running down the hall to Connor's room, the floorboards squeaking violently in protest.

"Connor! Connor! I have an idea!" I knocked excitedly on his door.

A groan came from the other side of the door, and then I heard slow footsteps. Connor opened the door. He had tousled hair, and he looked at me sleepily with half-open eyes. He looked so warm, his cheeks flushed warm from sleep, and he was wearing soft-looking sleep pants and a white T-shirt. Connor looked so warm I just wanted to melt into him.

"Stassi, do you have any idea what time it is?" he growled.

"I have an idea for the resort!" I said excitedly.

"Stassi. It's *five* o'clock in the morning."

"I know, I'm sorry, but it came to me in a dream, and I don't want to forget, and I actually think that it's perfect!" I cried.

Connor groaned. He leaned one muscular arm against the doorframe in exhaustion, closing his eyes. He looked hotter than any sleepy person had the right to look at five in the morning.

Maxi trotted over to us curiously, sniffing the doorway and peering around Connor's legs into the darkness of his bedroom. Stealthily, Maxi stepped into Connor's bedroom, disappearing into the darkness.

"Okay, okay, are you ready?" I said, jumping up and down in front of him, waving my arms around to hype him up.

"As ready as a 2% battery," grumbled Connor.

"Okay, so instead of having a fitness center on the south side of the resort, we should have a spa!"

The idea came to me from Nya's letter. She had talked about soaking in a hot bath with cucumbers and wine. I don't know why I hadn't thought about it when I first read it.

"A spa? Like a massage parlour?" Connor cracked one eye back open, standing upright.

"No, like a thermal spa, you know, with hot tubs and cold baths and resting areas? Have you never experienced hydrotherapy?"

I *love* thermal spas.

"No, what is that?"

"Hydrotherapy is when you alternate your body between heat exposures. It helps you relax."

"So, a thermodynamic non-equilibrium for your body?"

"Yes, nerd. It's the most relaxing and wonderful thing ever. I can't believe you don't already have a spa in Fleurmont."

"Wait…aren't those spas mostly a ski town thing?" Connor's other eye opened, and he yawned.

"I mean, yes, it's really popular around ski towns because it's like the ultimate après-ski activity, but this wouldn't be a *basic* spa."

Connor's eyes flickered with subtle interest. I wished I had my sketchbook there to sketch it out for him. But maybe a picture would do it more justice. He really needs to see the vibes. Spas are all about the vibes.

"Okay, hold on. Can I look something up real quick?"

Connor nodded, yawning again as he walked back into his bedroom to get his phone. I followed him excitedly and laughed when I saw Maxi sitting like a loaf of bread on Connor's pillow, clearly having found the most comfortable spot in the room.

"Aww, hi cutie," I said to Maxi, scratching the top of his head.

Maxi blinked up at me and purred. I couldn't believe I hadn't known I was a cat person this whole time. I sat down on Connor's bed next to Maxi. His bed was still warm, his brown blankets in disarray for once on the bed.

Connor handed me the phone, remaining standing. "Here."

"Thanks," I said, my heart skipping a beat when our hands touched.

I tried to focus on typing, but I could feel the electricity humming between us now. It was humming when we made our way back to the cabin after watching the sunset in the flower fields, and it was humming again now.

Connor shifted, and I could feel that his body was more alert, definitely no longer half-asleep. I felt his eyes on me in the semi-darkness. I was suddenly hyperaware that we were in his bedroom.

I continued my search on his phone until I found something close to what I was looking for.

"Okay, see how this sauna has a floor-to-ceiling window with a view? I think we can do something like this on the south side of the resort so that people can have a view of the mountain pass, and instead of a barrel, it should be an oblong, rectangular room. And wait, do you have photos from the –of course you do," I giggled, pulling up the images he'd saved to his phone on different areas of the resort, not missing the picture in his phone he'd saved of Maxi sleeping on his laptop.

I showed him one photo of the mountain on the south side of the resort. "Imagine if we had a lazy river here, but instead of a bright, synthetic lazy river you'd see at a water park, we built it against this side of the mountain. We can paint it to look like you're floating through a rocky tunnel of wildflowers –ooh, maybe we could even make it scented with wildflowers."

Connor stared at the photo on his phone, zooming in on a boulder. "And this would be hot water flowing in this lazy river?"

"Yes, hot water, and instead of floating around in hideous inflatable tubes or foam noodles, we could build a custom flotation device so that people can lie down on their backs."

He took his phone back from me, our hands touching in that electrifying way again, and he sat down next to me on his bed as he scrolled through different photo angles. I felt my body sinking slightly towards him on the mattress.

"This is a good idea," said Connor slowly, and I could see him really thinking it over, considering the idea. "I like the idea of taking advantage of the natural landscaping of the mountains."

"Yes, and the spa can be totally wildflower-themed, too," I said, moving closer to find pictures of spa hot tubs. "We could also have hot tubs shaped like different flowers. Or we could have a mud bath made from glacial marine clay from the St. Lawrence River."

Connor looked up at me in surprise.

"Well, when you told me to research the site analysis stuff, there was this one day I ended up doing a whole internet research on Quebec geography instead."

Connor smiled as we flipped through more pictures together.

"A spa...okay, this is a really good idea," he admitted.

"Of course it is!"

"I like it. Let's work on this later today. This really came to you in a dream?" Connor asked curiously.

"I had a dream that my friend Nya and I were in a hot tub drinking wine, and for some reason, I just knew that we were at *Fleurs de L'Étang*. Okay, I know that sounds super random, but Nya wrote me a letter, and I swear it makes sense if you read the letter."

I looked back up at Connor, expecting him to look at me like I was crazy...except he was looking at me with that intense expression in his eyes again. I caught the way he glanced down at the exposed skin from my sleep shirt before remembering I wasn't wearing anything underneath.

Oh, right.

"No, I believe you," he murmured. His eyes lingered back into mine, dipping to my lips for a fraction of a second.

I could feel my nipples harden as he looked at me. I wanted him to touch me so badly.

"Sorry for waking you so early," I said finally, feeling like I was going to explode with the tension between us.

"That's okay. You were right. This is a great idea."

"Really?"

"Yes," he smiled, and he looked at the time on his phone, letting out a breathy laugh. "Alright, I think I'm officially up. Do you want some coffee?"

I nodded. "Coffee sounds great."

# CHAPTER TWENTY-ONE

## *Stassi*

"I need to head out to take my dad to the airport."

I looked up from the table where I'd been working. Connor and I had spent the entire last week working on the spa design for the resort. Connor had the new pitch deck ready to go for his next conversation with Uncle Valerian, and I was having way too much fun designing the space.

I was obsessed with our spa, and I think it was already my favourite part of the resort. I wondered if that's what I should specialize in designing after this project was over.

But I didn't want to think about this project ending or not working with Connor anymore. As frustrating as it was that there was this heavy sexual tension between us that never seemed to let up, it was so *fun* working with Connor. Connor's background in engineering and his experience leading different development projects meant I was learning things beyond traditional architecture. We still had to consult with a mechanical engineer for the design of the spa's water systems, but Connor knew so much already, and he had a knack for helping me refine and revise my initial design ideas.

He was also surprisingly patient. He didn't hesitate to answer any and every question I had about the entire resort development process, even when we were in the middle of a very specific part of the design process. And unlike how I'd seen people like Grandpa talking to people who were less experienced or less knowledgeable, he never made me feel stupid when I asked questions.

"Airport?" I asked, confused.

"Yeah, my dad's going to London for a couple of months," he said, picking up his car keys from the table.

Oh, that's right. His dad was going to London to visit his brother.

"How long will you be out?"

"Probably close to three hours. I'm going to go into town to grab groceries on the way back. Do you want anything?"

"Yes, please. Strawberries. And bananas! And donuts from the Le Petit Toast. Ooh, and freeze-dried shrimp treats for Maxi. Oh, and –"

"Okay, maybe just text me a list," said Connor, but he was smiling.

He was wearing shorts today, and I could see the subtle thickness of his legs. Feverishly, I wondered what it would be like to kneel between them.

Connor caught me looking at him, and a dark, heated look flashed across his face. Heat pooled between my legs. He quickly adjusted his expression to a more neutral one, but I'd already seen the look in his eyes.

"I'll see you later, then," I said, my heart beating faster the way it always did now when there was lingering silence between us.

"Watch out for the rain this afternoon. We're supposed to get a big storm today," said Connor as he slid into his boots.

"Okay," I said, missing his presence before he could even shut the door behind him.

Connor was right about the storm. It started raining in the afternoon. I'd just finished feeding Maxi and making myself a second cup of coffee when the rain started tapping violently against the window.

Maximus ran up to the window in the living room. He pawed at the window as if he were trying to hunt the raindrops, his claws making clicking sounds against the glass of the window. I laughed, getting up from the couch to stand next to him.

"It's just the rain, buddy. I don't think you can hunt raindrops." I planted a kiss on his soft head. "But I still think you're a very scary apex predator."

Maxi continued to paw enthusiastically at the window, unbothered by the challenge.

I sat back down on the couch in the living room and sketched. With my coffee next to me, it was the perfect setup for sketching. The cabin was cozy and warm, and with the rain outside, I didn't even need music to focus.

Although Connor and a small team of other designers in L. A. had already decided on a concept for the stargazing lodge, I sketched out different ideas I had. I liked to reimagine what it could look like if it was in different parts of the world

–Bordeaux, Nairobi, Taipei... I sketched out design ideas for Nya's office and the chateau we were going to retire in.

My favourite professor in college used to end each class by saying, "And remember –sketch relentlessly!" It was a habit I had back in the day, and one of those lessons that actually stuck.

It was something I had abandoned when my parents and Sylvia died. It felt good to get back into it.

I felt more like myself than I had in years.

And I felt strangely at home.

If someone had told me even just three months ago that a small town in eastern Canada was going to feel like home to me, I would have laughed out loud. Now, it felt like the most natural place in the world.

Thunder boomed outside, and the windows shuddered as the wind howled against them.

Maxi jumped, and he dashed under the couch to hide.

"It's okay, buddy. It's just the wind," I said, trying to sound comforting. "Aren't you my scary little apex predator?"

Maxi poked his head out from under the couch, and we watched the rain together.

I wished Connor would come home soon.

Maybe I should text Connor to bring home a bottle of wine. It was Friday. Maybe if I could just get him to relax a little bit...

The rain outside seemed to stop. I frowned as I watched the clouds speed past us, and a few minutes later, the sun was back out and the skies were blue again.

Fifteen minutes later, it was suddenly hailing, and hailstones were hitting against the porch and the roof of the cabin.

"What the hell?"

I got up from the couch to look outside. The weather was too distracting for me to continue my work or scheme up ways to get Connor drunk enough to want to fuck me.

The weather was having a full-on temper tantrum.

After the hail stopped, the weather oscillated between unsettling, sunny blue skies and thunderous rain. The clouds outside were moving at what looked like an unnaturally fast pace.

A loud crack came from outside, and I jumped as something hit the side of the cabin.

I ran to the living room window, peering out to see where a tree had crashed down on one side of the cabin, hitting the shed. The door to the shed was now wide open.

"Shit," I muttered.

I ran to the front door, slipping on a pair of shoes and grabbing an umbrella before running out the door. I ran to the shed on the side of the cabin. The tree had smashed into the shed, but the shed had held its ground. It was just the door that had burst open.

The wind was so strong that it flipped my umbrella inside out. I let out a shriek as my umbrella flew away, hitting the side of the cabin before tumbling away.

I ran to the shed, shutting the door closed and ran back to the cabin as quickly as I could.

I had left the door wide open on my way out, and the wind was so strong that the rainwater drenched the front entrance.

"Shit!" Running inside, I shut the door behind me, shivering.

I ran to my room to change out of my wet clothes. When I came back out into the living room, something felt off.

I looked around the living room. My sketchbook and pencils were still on the couch, and so were Connor's oil pastels and markers. My coffee mug was still on the coffee table in front of the couch.

I surveyed the windows. They were still intact.

Something was missing.

I looked over at Maxi's cat scratcher. Maxi wasn't on the couch anymore.

"Maxi?" I called.

I looked under the couch, but he wasn't there. I turned around to see if maybe he had run back into my bedroom.

Nothing.

"Maxi?" I looked under the couch, and then walked to the back of the cabin where our workspace was.

Come on, he had to be here somewhere.

I went into the kitchen to grab his bag of cat treats.

"Maxi, snack time!" I shook the bag of treats, which normally had him sprinting to me.

Nothing.

Panic rose in my throat.

*The door.* I had left the fucking door open earlier!

In a panic, I ran back to the front door, flinging the door open. Rain splattered and sprayed into the cabin.

"Maxi!"

The wind howled back in response, but there was no cat waiting at the front door.

"No, no, no." Horror filled my veins.

Oh my God, what did I do?

"Maxi!" I screamed into the rain, running outside.

Connor's car came into sight on the road just as I stepped off the porch, windshield wipers moving furiously against the rain. Connor parked and ran out of the car.

"Stassi! What are you doing in the rain?" he asked, looking over at the door to the cabin.

"Maxi –I can't find Maxi," I choked out. "It was raining, and the tree fell on the shed, and I left the door open, and I think he went outside, and now I can't find him!"

"Okay, okay, calm down. Slow down," said Connor, holding onto my shoulders to steady me. "Are you sure he's not in the house?"

"Yes! I'm sure! I shook his treat bag, and he *always* comes running," I cried, feeling tears well in my eyes.

Rain was hitting me right in the eye, and I blinked the raindrops away furiously, trying to see around the porch.

"Oh my God, what did I do?" I sobbed. "He's probably so scared right now, and I shut him out of the house!"

"We'll find him." Connor's voice was muffled against the rain. He took my hand firmly in his, looking towards the shed. I squeezed his hand, needing to feel his steadiness.

"Connor –"

"We'll find him," Connor repeated firmly, and he marched us towards the shed.

"Maxi!" I screamed.

Connor opened the door to the shed, checking the inside. I ran along the perimeter of the cabin, checking against the crevices of the building, looking for places he might have gone to hide. I saw Connor peering into the clearing in the trees.

"Maxi!" called Connor.

"Maxi!"

He had to be okay. He had to be.

Please be okay. Please, please, please.

"Maximus!"

A small sound came from close by.

Connor and I looked at each other.

"Did you hear that?"

"Yes," I breathed.

We both froze, the wind and the rain too loud. We looked around.

Another small cry.

And it was coming from...above us.

Connor and I looked up at the same time into the trees.

"Maximus?" I cried out, but my voice cracked and the sound barely carried out.

"There!" shouted Connor suddenly, and he pointed to the tree next to the shed, next to the tree that had fallen.

Up in the tree, between two dark branches, was Maxi, his tiny black and white body stuck to the tree.

"Maxi!" I sprinted towards the tree.

"Hold on," said Connor, and he ran back to the shed.

Could I climb up the tree? How the hell did he get up there? I was about to climb on top of the fallen tree so that I could reach the one Maxi was on when I saw Connor running back with a ladder from the shed.

Connor set the ladder up against the tree, a splatter of rain that had accumulated from the tree hitting us in the face.

"I'll go," I said.

"Okay, be careful," said Connor, nodding, and he held the ladder steady for me.

I climbed up the ladder as quickly as I could. My feet slipped with the constant onslaught of rain, but I reached the top of the ladder.

Maxi let out a cry as I reached him. His pupils were dilated into two round black circles.

"Maxi," I cried, feeling tears well up in my eyes again.

He was completely drenched, his tiny body shivering as his claws dug into the bark of the tree.

"It's okay. You're okay now," I soothed.

I peeled Maxi off of the tree. It wasn't easy. He was so scared that he refused to move, his claws buried deep into the branches.

"I'm sorry, I'm so sorry. Come on, it'll be okay."

When I finally peeled his claws off of the tree, Maxi clung to my shoulder instead, his claws digging into my flesh through my shirt.

"I'm so sorry," I said again and again. I held him close to me, carefully making my way down the ladder. Maxi squirmed, claws digging in deeper.

Connor's steady hands reached me as I got to the bottom of the ladder.

"Is he okay?" asked Connor, concern in his eyes.

I nodded as Connor looked at Maxi, touching the top of his little head.

"You gave us a scare there, buddy," said Connor, and then to me, "Come on, let's head back in."

Connor stored the ladder back in the shed, and we went back into the cabin.

When we got back inside, we kicked off our shoes and set Maxi down on the couch. Connor grabbed a small towel as I inspected Maxi, checking for scratches or signs of injury on his tiny body.

Maxi let out a sad meow, and I burst into tears.

Hot tears dripped down my cold cheeks and stung my eyes as Connor sat down next to us on the couch.

"He's okay, Stassi," Connor said gently.

"It was all my fault," I cried. "I left the d-door open when I w-went outs-side."

"It's okay. He's okay. Look, he's fine. He just got a little wet," soothed Connor, rubbing Maxi's wet fur with the towel.

Maxi squirmed a little under the towel, and he started to purr.

"See, he's purring."

"Cats purr when they're self-soothing," I sniffed. "It doesn't mean that he's happy."

"The important thing is that he's okay." Connor set the towel aside.

Maxi's fur was in wet clumps, and he shook himself almost like a dog.

"I'm so sorry, Maxi." I reached for his cat brush to brush out his messy fur. Maxi continued to purr loudly as I brushed him as gently as I could.

Connor got up from the couch.

"Where are you going?" I asked, feeling panicked again.

"I'm just getting him some food. I'll be right back."

Connor stepped into the kitchen and grabbed a plate and a can of cat food. He sat down next to us on the couch, placing the plate on the couch.

"Normally, you're not supposed to eat on the couch, but you got your mom all worried, so today's a bit of an exception." Connor popped the can open, dumping the contents onto the plate.

Maxi jumped up instantly, his green eyes round with excitement, his tail instantly shooting up into the air.

Relief and warmth coursed through me, and I petted him gently as he slurped up his favourite canned food.

"Thank you," I said to Connor. I brushed a rogue tear off the side of my cheek.

Connor looked at me, his expression soft. "He's okay, Stassi. Look at him. Happy as ever."

"I feel so bad," I whispered.

"It's not your fault."

"I left the door open." I knew it was my fault. I could own up to that.

"He's a cat. You know, you kind of found him outside," Connor reminded me.

"I know, but still..."

Over the last few weeks, Maxi had completely acclimated to indoor living. He was a litter box-loving, canned food-eating cat who slept on silk pillows every night, for crying out loud.

"He's lucky to have you caring so much about him," said Connor, and he reached out a hand to pet Maxi.

I nodded, the guilt only slightly subsiding.

I watched Connor pet Maxi, that small smile on his face. My heart felt like a balloon filling with hot air. I felt like I was going to explode with emotion.

I had to remind myself to breathe.

I let the minutes pass, and while my breathing evened out, my guilt and anxiety were replaced with my fixation on Connor.

Watching him pet Maxi, I had never been so convinced that Connor Fitzgerald was the person for me.

I wanted to kiss Connor so badly. I wanted to hold him and never let go.

I took a deep breath, and let it out as steadily as I could.

Maxi finished his food. He licked his nose and then licked his paw.

He sniffed his plate again, as if to make sure he wasn't leaving anything behind, and then he hopped off of the couch. He stretched slowly in the living room, lowering his chest toward the ground and extending both of his front legs in front of him.

He yawned and then jumped into his little cat bed by the window. Maxi tucked his tail around him and blinked slowly at us.

I let out another sigh of relief.

I put Maxi's empty plate on the coffee table in front of the couch.

Connor and I looked at each other. Suddenly, the space between us on the couch felt like not very much space at all.

# CHAPTER TWENTY-TWO

## *Connor*

Stassi and I stared at each other on the couch.

Maxi was safe. He was fed and warm and happy.

Stassi and I were still sitting on the couch, facing each other in our wet clothes.

Suddenly, my heart was racing.

Stassi's hair was still wet, and dark blonde strands clung to her cheeks and neck. Her cheeks were pink, but her face was pale, and her eyes were wide with a whole concoction of emotions.

"Are you okay?"

Stassi swallowed and nodded quickly.

"Thank you," she said again, and she edged closer to me on the couch.

It was my turn to swallow next. I lost the ability to form words for a moment. Her white T-shirt was soaked through, and I could see her nipples through her shirt.

Stassi saw my eyes glance down, but unlike she normally would, she didn't tease me or openly taunt me. There was no more defiance, and no more open challenge in the way she was looking at me. Just a whole lot of raw, unfiltered, unprocessed energy between us.

She looked at me, her big blue eyes blinking at me in a way that almost reminded me of Maxi.

"How was the airport?" she breathed.

The airport. What was the airport? Oh. My dad. Right. I didn't want to think about my dad right now. Not with Stassi's full lips inches away from mine and her hard nipples pointed straight at me.

"It was fine. Smooth."

"That's good," said Stassi quietly.

"Yeah. Smooth is good."

Stassi nodded.

Maybe she was still in shock. I shouldn't be staring at her breasts while she was still in shock. Or at her lips. Or at her eyes. I felt like I might drown in them if I looked too long.

"Do you want a coffee or anything?" I asked, making a move to move off the couch.

"Connor," she said quickly, grabbing my hand with both of hers.

I sat my ass right back down on the couch.

"Yeah?" I was instantly hard from hearing my name on her lips. I liked the way she said my name a little too much.

"Will you stay with me for a bit?"

"Yeah, of course."

"Thanks," she murmured.

Her hands were still on mine. They were soft but firm. I wondered how they would feel around my cock.

"Are you sure you're okay?" I asked.

I had taken her hand and held it in mine when we were outside in the rain. I don't know why I did that. It was instinctive. It had felt right, even if it had lasted for less than a minute before we had separated for our search.

But now it felt different. Not wrong, but definitely different. It felt more intimate, more intentional.

"I'm okay," breathed Stassi, and some of her usual confidence and steadiness seemed to resurface a little.

"That's good...I looked at the materials you listed for the spa," I said, trying to change the topic.

"Oh. What do you think?" Her eyes trailed slowly over my lips and then back into my eyes.

"They look good. The lighting choices were interesting too," I said stupidly, not even completely sure what we were talking about anymore.

"Thanks," she murmured. She let go of my hand but adjusted herself on the couch. She was even closer to me now, and our legs touched.

I wanted to kiss her so badly.

It would be so easy, too. Just a quick lean into her already parted lips.

We looked at each other for a couple of breaths. She blinked at me again, and I don't think I've ever seen eyes so beautiful in my entire life.

And then the moment passed.

She blinked again as she pulled away, letting out an exhale. Her eyelashes fluttered more rapidly this time, blinking as if to clear her mind.

"I guess I should go take a shower." She sounded as disappointed as I felt.

"Have a good shower," I said lamely.

Stassi got up and went to her room, shutting the door behind her.

I heard the sound of the shower in her bathroom turn on. I sank back down onto the couch, exhaling. What the fuck was I doing? The lines between us were getting blurrier and blurrier each day.

It probably didn't help that every day, it was Stassi that I thought of as I got myself off in the shower. I hadn't needed to nut this much since I was eighteen.

"Fuck," I groaned, sexual frustration, logic, and unadulterated desire competing for dominance in my head.

I knew Stassi was attracted to me too. I could see it in her eyes. But a small part of me wondered if she was just attracted to me because I was the only person around and we were forced to spend so much time together in this cabin. And then there was the whole issue of us working together and her being my intern.

Maxi hopped onto the couch and positioned himself neatly next to me to clean his toes. I pet the top of his head, and he paused his toe grooming to lean into my touch. I scratched his chin, and he purred.

"What do you think I should do?"

Stassi burst out of her room just then, and I jumped. Maxi looked up at her in alarm for a moment before going back to grooming himself.

Stassi's hair was still wet, probably from her shower, but she had changed into clean, dry clothes. She was wearing those soft cotton shorts and lacy camisole again. She looked so fucking tempting.

She marched over to me with determination in her expression and sat down next to me on the couch. Maxi jumped down from the couch to move to the armchair across from us instead.

"What –"

"Are you ever going to kiss me?" Stassi blurted, popping the thick bubble of tension between us.

"I –"

"Is it just in my head? Am I actually secretly going nuts, and all of this mountain air is getting to me, or something? Am I the only one who feels something between us?" she demanded, her wet hair whipping around her shoulders and clinging to her skin.

"No," I said, shaking my head. "No, it's not just you."

"Then why –"

"Stassi, we shouldn't," I said thickly, mustering up any remains of self-control I possibly had left in my body. "There's...a power imbalance between us."

Stassi laughed out loud.

"Right," she said. "Yeah, I guess you're right. My uncle is your boss, so I *could* technically easily get you fired."

"You know what I meant. Be serious."

"I am serious!" she protested, her knees bumping into mine on the couch. "Do you really see me as your intern? Is that really how you see me at this point?"

"No, of course not," I said reactively before I could explain to her that even though it didn't feel like it, she technically was my intern. I don't think Stassi cared much about technicalities at this point. Not when we'd shared so much between us over the last six weeks.

Something glinted in her eyes.

"Then why?" she demanded. She stared at me, her blue eyes wide.

The extra dose of self-control I ordered can arrive any time now, thank you.

"I-I'm six years older than you." It was a terrible excuse, and we both knew it.

"Do you think you're applying for social security already or something?" she retorted.

"You know, I'm waiting on the results of my application as we speak."

Stassi snorted.

I swallowed. Was it really so wrong to want her? Stassi was beautiful and intelligent and funny -

"Fine, good night then," she bit out, and as she stood up from the couch, I grabbed her arm, pulling her towards me, crashing my lips onto hers.

Stassi gasped, falling onto my lap. I pulled her closer to me, one hand instantly in her wet hair, the other on the back of her neck to bring her closer.

Her lips were soft and warm from her shower, and her lips parted as she gasped, her minty breath mingling with mine. She kissed me back instantly, wrapping her arms around me. I kissed her hungrily, letting myself get lost in her as her scent wrapped around me. I breathed her in, pulling at her lips, sinking into her.

She leaned into me, pressing her hips against my body, her tongue licking into my mouth.

I was so hard, so fucking turned on.

I felt drunk on her.

My tongue was on hers. I had my hands in her hair, on her back.

I felt out of control.

Too out of control.

I broke away from our kiss, panting, my heart racing a thousand miles an hour. I shouldn't be doing this with her. She was my boss's niece. We were from two completely different worlds. She would regret this one day.

I got up from the couch.

"What –" Stassi had a dazed look in her eyes, her lips puffy and beautifully swollen.

"I'm sorry," I stammered. "We shouldn't –I shouldn't have done that. I'm sorry."

I went to my room and shut the door before she could say another word.

# CHAPTER TWENTY-THREE

## *Stassi*

*June 19*

*Dear Nya,*

*Fuck Connor. I hate him, and we're not going to bang, so you can officially give up on any notion or idea of us banging. I am going to live a bang free existence, and then my pussy is going to dry up like the fucking Sahara desert.*

*Besides, Connor is so fucking stuck up and stubborn I bet he would suck in bed, anyway. I bet he only fucks missionary at exactly eight o'clock at night after taking a shower and brushing his teeth. I bet he would never be rough in bed. I bet he would never just fuck me from behind or fuck my ass and treat me like a dirty little slut even if I fucking begged him to.*

There was a knock on my door before I could finish writing my angry hate letter. I threw the letter and pen down in frustration. The pen flew off my bed, rolling noisily onto the floor.

Yes, I was sexually frustrated. Sue me.

I opened the door of my bedroom to find Connor standing there.

"What do you want?" I bit out, injecting as much venom into my voice as I could.

"I'm sorry. I freaked out. I shouldn't have walked away like that," he said. He took a step into my bedroom, his eyes burning into mine.

"You're the most fucking amazing woman I've ever met in my life. You're smart and funny, and I'm so fucking attracted to you I can't think straight half the time. I just don't want you to regret anything because we've been locked up here together for over a month now. Our situation here –this isn't normal. But I don't want you just because you happen to be here. I would want you fucking anywhere, and I –"

"Just kiss me, Connor," I said, and I pulled him to me.

Our lips met again, and I shivered as I felt his hands on my back. He pushed me back into my bedroom and shut the door behind him. My thighs clenched together with anticipation.

Connor kissed me, his mouth hot and his lips soft and hard at the same time. He kissed me thoroughly, turning me around to press me up against the wall. His fingers were around my waist, gripping me as he pressed me into the wall.

He kissed me roughly, his tongue sweeping in, and I whimpered against him.

I've never had a kiss like this before in my entire life. I've never wanted to kiss someone so badly, and I've never had someone kiss me the way Connor was kissing me now.

Like he wanted to devour me.

I reached for him and grabbed his shirt, pulling it over his head. My breath caught in my lungs when I finally saw him without his shirt. He was almost exactly as I'd imagined him - an expanse of muscles on smooth olive skin, dark nipples, subtle but present abs...

*Yum.*

I smiled as Connor moved back towards me, but I pushed him backwards instead, pushing him towards my bed. Connor sat down on the edge of the bed as I took off my shorts. My camisole went next.

Connor's dark eyes drank me in. I stepped between his legs, putting my hands on his chest, feeling the hardness of his chest. My hands roamed across his body. I wanted to touch every inch of him. Connor pulled me closer to him, his hands on my ass, barely contained in black lace panties.

"You're beautiful," he husked. He pulled down the left strap of my bra, planting a kiss on my bare shoulder.

"You're kind of beautiful too," I murmured before I kissed him again.

I pushed him backwards onto the bed, and he pulled me on top of him. I ran my hands through his hair as I arched into him. Connor's hands were still on my ass as we kissed, our tongues mingling deliciously together.

I loved his tongue. I loved the smell of him so close to me. I loved the way he moved his lips. I loved –

Connor rolled onto a piece of paper on the bed. He paused, his hand leaving my ass to reach for the paper.

"What is this?"

My eyes flew open in alarm. It was my letter to Nya.

"Nothing!" I reached over to grab my unhinged, unfinished letter from him.

Connor held me back with one arm as he read the letter, muscles and veins bulging in his arm.

"Connor, wait! Don't read that!" I said quickly, trying not to get distracted by his hard, thick arm around me. I squirmed against him, my hand wriggling to snatch the letter from his grasp.

*Connor is so fucking stuck up and stubborn I bet he would suck in bed, anyway.*

Shit.

Connor finished reading, turning the piece of paper over as if to check for more content on the back. Nope. All unhinged thoughts on a single page.

*I bet he would never just fuck me from behind or fuck my ass and treat me like a dirty little slut even if I fucking begged him to.*

"Connor –" I started in a panic, trying not to wince as his arm released me.

He sat up on the bed and looked back at me.

"Okay, I wrote that when I was mad at you," I said, my face turning red. "I don't actually mean it."

"Did you write this just now?"

"Erm, is there an answer that you would prefer?" I offered, trying to laugh it off.

*Maybe I can take off my bra right now and he would forget about the letter.*

"You think I only have sex in a missionary position?" Connor's expression was completely unreadable.

Why can't I read all of his facial expressions by now? It was so hot how I couldn't read him sometimes, but it was super fucking inconvenient right now.

"Umm, no?" I said, still panicking inside. "I wrote that in a complete moment of –"

"Do you want me to fuck you like you're a dirty little slut?"

My heart raced. I felt myself getting wetter despite my nerves.

"What?" I squeaked, letting out a small, nervous laugh.

Connor dropped the letter to the floor and moved towards me on the bed. He grabbed my chin with one hand, forcing me to look up at him. His thumb swept over my bottom lip once.

Fuck, that made me so wet.

"Do you want me to fuck you like you're a dirty little slut, Stassi?" he asked again.

I swallowed, and I nodded.

"Yes," I whispered, looking into his dark hazel eyes. I couldn't see the green in them right now. It was just darkness, darkness and a little bit of unhinged, untamed wildness.

"Do you want me to be rough with you, Stassi? Is that what you want?" he said, his voice low.

I shivered and nodded.

"Then get on your hands and knees," he commanded.

I looked at him, my eyes flaring open with surprise. Was he serious? I felt so overwhelmed and so turned on at the same time. It was the strangest combination.

"You heard me. Get on your hands and knees."

I swallowed again, and I did as he asked, getting onto my hands and knees on the bed. Connor brushed my hair off my shoulder.

"You seem nervous." His voice was still hard and commanding. "Are you worried? You think I don't know how to fuck a woman properly?"

"N-no," I stammered.

Connor moved next to me on the bed, and he spread my legs wider apart. He put a finger over my panties, finding my clit through the fabric.

"You're soaked for me, Stassi," he murmured as he rubbed me with his thumb.

He pulled my panties to the side.

"Were you worried I wouldn't know how to lick you? How to make you come?"

Before I could say anything, I felt his tongue sweeping over my clit, and then his mouth was on me completely.

I gasped out loud, gripping the bedsheets. He sucked on me, and I moaned, closing my eyes at the sensation.

Holy shit.

Connor's mouth left my pussy abruptly, and as my eyes flew open, he ripped my panties apart with one swift motion. Fully apart. He tossed the soaked, shredded pieces of lace onto the pillow in front of me.

I tried to turn around, but Connor slapped my ass.

"Don't move," he ordered.

I shivered with arousal.

He unhooked my bra, and he moved me to remove the straps from my arms. His hands came around from behind me, squeezing my breasts. I was completely naked now.

"You like it when I spank you, Stassi?" he murmured as he continued to squeeze me.

"Yes," I whispered.

He spanked me again, and then he leaned down to kiss me, forcing me to look up at him. Our tongues met, wet and warm, and then Connor pulled away again.

I let out a sound of protest, needing more, needing to feel him, but Connor moved behind me. He put a finger into my pussy, inserting it slowly, and then suddenly, without warning, he pulled out and thrust his cock into me.

I cried out with surprise, squirming at the sudden fullness inside of me, feeling myself tighten at the shock of him inside of me. He held me tighter to prevent me from moving, pausing for a second, letting me adjust to his size, but it was just a second, not nearly long enough, and then he was pounding into me from behind. Connor gripped my waist as he fucked me roughly, relentlessly. I screamed with pleasure.

"You're so tight, Stassi," he gritted out.

I couldn't speak. I closed my eyes, feeling simultaneously overstimulated and overwhelmed with him and wanting more. So much more. I would die if he stopped now.

"You've been teasing me, haven't you? Wearing those tiny fucking shorts around the house."

Another spank to my bare ass as his cock continued to pound into me. I was dripping onto him. I could feel myself dripping down my thighs.

"And those goddamn shirts that you wear. Did you wear those because you wanted me to be looking at your tits? Did you want me to be looking at these every day?"

His hands slid to my breasts again, kneading them roughly together before he pinched both of my nipples. I moaned.

"Do you know how much I thought about these every fucking day for the last month? Do you know how much you turn me on?"

Connor pulled out, and I let out a scream at the sudden friction. Connor pulled me roughly from the waist, and I collapsed onto the bed. He turned me around to face him, and I tried to reach for him, to touch the length of him. I wanted to taste him.

Instead, he leaned down and sucked on my clit, both of his hands on my breasts. His tongue lapped at my juices, and he licked the sides of my thighs before plunging his tongue back into me.

*Oh, my God.*

Connor resurfaced, and then as I reached for him again, he pinned my arms down. He pushed my thighs apart and thrust back into me.

"Oh my God," I half-moaned, half-whimpered.

Connor fucked me harder, keeping my arms pinned, my breasts shaking violently with each of his thrusts.

"You like getting fucked like this, Stassi?" he growled. "You like it when I use your body like this?"

Yes, I tried to say. I couldn't get the word out. I tried to nod instead, but I couldn't do that either. It was all too much. It felt too good. I couldn't get anything out.

Connor let go of my arms, slowing down for a second only to grip my breasts again in his large hands. He leaned down and kissed me.

My whole body shook as he kissed me. And then he was thrusting faster and faster again, and when he kissed my neck, his tongue and teeth wet and hard against my pulse, I came.

I came hard, seeing stars, gripping Connor around his neck, gasping, my entire body melting with the sensation.

Connor pulled out of me as he came too, and he panted, pressing his sweaty body into me as he did.

I pulled his face down towards me and kissed him.

He kissed me back more tenderly now, still panting against me. He pulled me back on top of him, and we continued kissing. When we finally pulled apart for air, Connor smiled at me. I forgot to breathe for a second when he did. He stroked my hair and kissed me softly.

"You're so beautiful," he murmured.

"Will you stay with me tonight?" I whispered. I didn't want Connor to leave. I wanted to stay here, touching him and kissing him all night.

My heart was still racing. I felt happy and relaxed, sleepy and alert all at once.

"I'm not going anywhere," Connor said against my lips, and he leaned back in to kiss me again.

# CHAPTER TWENTY-FOUR

## *Stassi*

Connor and I were wrapped around each other in my bed. When I opened my eyes, I found Connor smiling at me. He had the most beautiful lips. I smiled just as he leaned in to kiss my mouth. I kissed him back, twisting my body towards him.

"Good morning," he said.

"Good morning," I whispered back. I couldn't stop smiling.

Connor held me close to him, drawing lazy circles around my back, his fingers the perfect consistency and pressure.

"Mmm, that feels so good." I closed my eyes.

"Better than last night?" he teased.

I pretended to think hard about it.

"Different from last night!" I squealed as he tickled me. I laughed, moving my body even closer to him as his fingers moved back to my back.

His fingers pressed into me, so warm and firm against my skin...

Which reminded me!

"I want to show you my ideas for the massage rooms for the spa."

Connor laughed. "Later," he said, trailing kisses from my lips down my neck.

"Later," I agreed, smiling as I closed my eyes. I don't think I could ever get enough of his hands on my body.

"So these massages at the spa," murmured Connor, "are they going to be...like this?"

He turned me gently over onto the bed, his hands rubbing on my shoulders.

Fuck, that felt good.

"Yes...exactly." I moved my hair to the side to give him better access to my back. Connor's hands were warm on my back, and he moved them like he knew what he was doing.

"Oh my God, that feels amazing...You know, if you wanted to change careers, you could totally be a massage therapist instead. Except normally, they do this with oils. Oh, wait!"

I sprang up, and Connor chuckled at my sudden movement.

"Where are you going?" he asked.

"I have oils! Wait here."

Connor looked at me, amused, turning in bed to watch me spring naked from the bed. Well, after last night, there wasn't much to feel self-conscious about. I ran down the hallway to the closet in search of my oils.

Maxi appeared in the hallway and yowled at me, letting me know it was time for breakfast.

"Okay, okay, but I am in the middle of something very important, buddy." I grabbed my bottles of body oils before rushing to the kitchen to pour Maxi way too much dry food before running back to my bedroom.

I shut the door behind me. Climbing into bed next to Connor, I put the bottles of body oils in his hands. I lay on my stomach.

"Okay, I'm ready," I announced.

"I guess I shouldn't be surprised you brought bottles of body oil here?"

"I am prepared for anything and everything," I said, hugging the pillow in front of me. "You should see my full shoe collection."

"I believe you. Now close your eyes and relax."

I closed my eyes, and Connor kissed my lips again. I opened my eyes, kissing him deeper, our tongues meeting.

Connor grinned at me as he pulled away, the look in his eyes pure mischief. He poured oil onto his hands, rubbing them together. Connor's warm hands slid back on my back as I smelled the citrusy scent of oranges.

I didn't just love Connor's hands all over my body. I think I was addicted to it now. Who knew all this time how good he was with his hands?

I almost moaned as he hit a spot on my back. He pressed into that spot again before his hands slid down my sides, dangerously close to my breasts. Connor moved the blankets off the bed, exposing my ass and the rest of my legs. He rubbed oil onto each of my butt cheeks, slowly, sensually, before slowly pushing my thighs apart. I felt myself getting wet at his touch.

"Well, I'm not sure they do *this* at spas," I giggled.

"No?" murmured Connor, both hands on my left leg.

He moved his hand from my ankle all the way up my thigh, his fingers grazing the edges of my entrance. I shivered, and my legs moved closer together on instinct.

"Did I say you could move?" Connor's voice low near my ear as he pried my thighs back open.

Fuck, he was so hot. I was dripping.

"Connor –" I started, but then his finger went inside of me and I gasped.

"You're still so tight, Stassi," he said, and slowly, carefully, he put another finger inside of me, "I guess I didn't work you hard enough last night."

I arched into his touch, feeling myself dripping all over him as he fucked me with his fingers. His other hand was on my ass, rubbing warm oil into it. I moaned.

I could feel myself getting close already.

So close.

Connor pulled his fingers out of me.

"Don't stop," I hissed.

"Turn around," he commanded instead, giving my ass a small spank.

I was so aroused I just wanted to push him down and ride him.

But I also wanted him to keep spanking me.

I turned around like he said, too turned on to express my thoughts. I lay on the bed and Connor moved closer to me, pouring more oil into his hands. He rubbed his hands together, his biceps bulging with the movement. I stared at him shamelessly.

"You're hot," I smiled.

Connor chuckled, looking away almost in embarrassment, which made him look even cuter.

"Hmm, you sure you don't want a massage like this at the spa?"

Connor spread the oil across the front of my shoulders. He massaged me gently, looking into my eyes as he continued to massage me down my arms. He was so good with his hands.

My nipples hardened into peaks, and I was almost certain I was still dripping onto my thighs.

"I never said that," I swallowed as his warm hands covered my breasts, "but only if you're the one doing it."

He palmed each breast gently, gliding his entire hands over them, his touch smooth and rough and hot and sensual all at once. I bit my lip to keep from crying out when his hands grazed over my nipples.

"You don't have to hold it in, baby. It's just you and me. No one will hear you if you scream," said Connor, and he pinched my nipples.

I moaned loudly.

Connor's hands roamed down my stomach and back down to my thighs. He thumbed my clit, stroking it with expert precision. I squirmed beneath his touch. I wanted more. I needed more.

I reached for him, yanking his pants down, and his hard cock sprung free. I sat up in bed, wanting to touch him, wanting to taste him. I wasn't able to last night. I had fallen asleep in his arms before I could.

Before I could touch him, his warm hands were on my breasts again, squeezing, pinching my nipples.

I gasped at his touch, and he pushed me back down on the bed before grabbing my thighs. He pushed my thighs open and thrust into me. I cried out with pleasure.

"Is this what you wanted?" he husked. "Is this what you were looking for?"

"Y-yes," I gasped. I gripped the bedsheets, my fingers digging into the fabric harder with every thrust that sent shockwaves of pleasure into my body.

"More," I demanded.

Connor fucked me harder, and I screamed.

"I want..." I started, but it was hard to talk.

"What do you want, Stassi?"

"I want to taste you," I managed, "I want you to come in my mouth."

"Fuck," groaned Connor.

He continued to thrust into me, and when he pinched my nipples again, I came, crying out his name as I did.

Ripples of pleasure spread out over me, and then Connor came too. He pulled out just in time for me to catch him with my mouth, and I felt him unload into me. He pulsed into me.

I stared up at him while I drank him in, finally tasting him on my tongue the way I wanted to, and he looked at me with a surrendering kind of awe. He looked at me with so much tenderness, more than I've ever experienced before in my life.

I swallowed, and then when I pulled away to breathe, I squeezed his cock with my hand. One last drop of cum appeared at the tip. I leaned in and licked it clean, my hand still on the smooth skin of his shaft, wanting to lick around his entire cock.

"Fuck, Stassi," breathed Connor, and he leaned into me, kissing me.

I kissed him back, wrapping my arms around him.

"That was the best massage I've ever had," I said.

Connor laughed.

We stayed in bed for another hour. It was hard to leave, but the coffee called, so we reluctantly got dressed and went into the kitchen.

I snaked my arms around Connor as he made us coffee.

He smiled, turning his head to kiss me.

I kissed him back enthusiastically. "So where do we go from here?"

"After coffee?"

"No, I mean with us," I said, and Connor opened one arm to put his arm around me. "Do we keep having sex? Do we share a bed now?"

"Do you want to keep having sex?"

"Yes."

"Do you want to share a bed?"

"Yes."

"Then we'll do both," said Connor as the coffee started to drip into the carafe. "I want to be with you, Stassi. We can have whatever relationship you want. We can go on dates, celebrate anniversaries, whatever you want. I am all in."

"Really?" I smiled, my heart fluttering like a butterfly.

"Really," smiled Connor, and he leaned in to kiss me again.

# CHAPTER TWENTY-FIVE

## *Connor*

"This works," said Valerian.

He was nodding, and I could see him on the screen, clicking through the slides of my second pitch deck.

"The Master Plan is mostly done for the north side of the resort. Elodie and I have also finished our work on the sustainability strategy," I finished listing off progress from the last three weeks.

Stassi and I met with Elodie several times at Le Robinet, and I was relieved that the initial animosity between them seemed to have faded.

"Fitzgerald, I'm impressed," said Valerian finally. "This is good. You can continue working on the Master Plan for the south side of the resort."

"Thanks."

I debated asking him about the Creative Director role. Valerian hadn't brought it back up since I arrived in Fleurmont, and I had no idea how Harrison was doing in Arizona.

I was about to ask him when Valerian spoke again. "Before I forget, can you write me a report on Stassi?"

"A report on Stassi?"

"Yeah, nothing complicated or too formal. I just want a one-pager on her progress and how she's doing as an architect."

"She's been doing great. Most of these new ideas are her ideas, actually. She deserves all the credit for her work. All the accommodation designs are hers too."

Valerian looked surprised. "That's good to hear. Still, send me that report this week."

"Sure thing."

All doubts I had about my future with Stassi had evaporated after I had gone into her bedroom that night.

I didn't care about the possibility of Valerian or the rest of her family finding out; we would deal with it.

I didn't care that she might feel differently if we ever left Fleurmont; I would fight for her.

I was hooked on Stassi Salvati. I was hooked, in way too deep, and honestly, I wasn't mad about it.

"Would you fuck me in the town square?" Stassi asked me.

"Yes."

"Would you fuck me while on a call with my uncle?"

"Yes."

"Would you eat out my ass?"

"Yes."

"Would you let me eat out your ass?"

"I'll try anything with you twice," I conceded.

Stassi laughed.

We were hiking up the mountain again, but this time, it was our first official date.

"So where are we going again?" asked Stassi.

"Aster Falls. It's a small waterfall by a lagoon."

"Mysterious."

Aster Falls was a destination that was not well known to tourists. It took a steep hike in the opposite direction of the flower fields to get there, but it was beautiful.

From our cabin in the old mining town, the hike to Aster Falls was about an hour. There was a path leading to the small lagoon, but it hadn't been maintained in years, and weeds and grass grew haphazardly across the path.

As we got closer though, purple aster flowers appeared more and more frequently, and then it was impossible to miss the sound of the waterfall rushing into the lagoon in the distance.

"This is beautiful," gasped Stassi as we made it to the edge of the lagoon.

The waterfall was just as beautiful as I remembered, spraying and misting the surrounding air.

The lagoon at Aster Falls was small. More than ten people in the lagoon at once would have made swimming in it uncomfortable. The water was a vibrant turquoise, and the area around it was all rock and purple flowers.

I put my backpack down, taking out a beach towel and spreading it over a piece of flat rock for us to sit on. Stassi took out a box of blueberries from her own backpack, feeding me blueberries while I sat down cross-legged on the towel and unpacked the rest of our things.

"I think I get it now," said Stassi between blueberries, sitting down on the towel next to me, "Why people want to live in the middle of nowhere. It's freaking beautiful up here."

"It is," I agreed, taking out the rest of the food we had packed.

"I could see myself living here," smiled Stassi.

"And here I thought you were getting cabin fever," I teased.

"I *do* feel myself getting pretty warm pretty regularly when I'm around you." She pretended to fan herself with her T-shirt.

"Maybe you're wearing too many clothes," I suggested.

"I think you're right."

Stassi stood up and took off her shorts. Her T-shirt went next, revealing her yellow bikini underneath. She took a step towards me to where I was sitting and stepped her legs on either side of me. Her bare thighs grazed mine as she sat facing me in my lap.

She touched my now hard cock through the fabric of my swim trunks before putting her arms around me.

"Much better," she sighed, smiling up at me mischievously.

I leaned in to kiss her, my hands cupping her ass, forcing her to grind against me. She kissed me, only to pull away and reach for the box of sandwiches I had taken out earlier.

"Wait. Food," she said. She opened the box of sandwiches to offer me one, smiling slyly back up at me.

"Such a tease." I was tempted to show her exactly how little teases like her should be treated.

I resisted. We had challenged ourselves –promised each other, really– to not have sex for at least half an hour after arriving.

It was our first date, and part of why it had taken us almost two weeks to have a first date was because we had spent the last two weeks mostly naked around the cabin. We alternated between having sex and working through designs and bidding documents.

More construction workers had appeared over the last week for the demolition work of the mining town. Every day from six in the morning until five o'clock in the evening, we could hear the constant rumble of machinery as the old buildings were taken down one by one.

The next step for the resort was to find the right contractors for construction. The bidding documents were a project proposal with all the design specs, our timelines, and budget. We would send this project proposal to different construction contractors, and then we would pick one after they sent us back their offers. It was exciting to see the project progress.

As my design work for the resort tapered off, I had already started to imagine what it would be like if I did get that Creative Director role. I brainstormed all the ways I would consolidate different business processes and jotted down the ideas I had for the brand.

"Tell me something then," I said as Stassi and I bit into baked brie sandwiches.

"Okay," nodded Stassi, covering her mouth as she chewed.

"How did you learn how to speak Mandarin? I've been thinking about that for months now. And French, too," I added, remembering that latest revelation at the Spring Festival.

Stassi laughed. "I can't believe that's how we met."

"You know, we almost met before that," I told her. "I saw you once before I saw you in Taipei."

"What? No way. How? And where?"

"It was October of last year. I was at the Sphinx Hotel in L.A. for my parents' wedding anniversary. I saw a very hot woman wearing a pink dress push another woman into a pool."

"Oh my God, no way!" Stassi's eyes widened with shock and delight. "You were there? Where?"

"Two floors above you. I was on the balcony of the ballroom."

"Oh, man. It was probably good you didn't meet me then. I was a little unhinged back then –okay, okay, fine, maybe I was still a little unhinged when we met," Stassi amended at my raised eyebrow, "and maybe I can still be a little unhinged at times now."

"It wouldn't be you if you weren't just a little bit unhinged."

"Well, hopefully, I'm a little less unhinged now." She smiled contently, looking out at the waterfall and then back to me.

"So why did you push her in?"

"I was defending my friend's honour," she explained simply.

"How noble of you."

"Very few people share that sentiment."

"Hmm."

"Well, I might have gone a bit overboard at times defending my friends' honours. Apparently, there's this thing called...communication? And it's supposed to be a better way to share disagreements with other people."

"I think I've heard the same thing."

"It's ironic, too, actually, because that's actually why I speak Mandarin. Well, not just Mandarin. I speak five different languages."

"You speak *five* different languages? Which ones?"

"English, Mandarin, French, Swahili, and Spanish."

"Damn," I said, impressed. I could honestly say that Stassi surprised me every single day. "How?"

"I learned Swahili when I lived in Kenya. Both my parents spoke Swahili, too. My mom was the one who told me that communication is really important. Specifically, she believed more than anything that knowing different languages was the most important social currency a person could have. She told me that once you can speak the same language as another person, no matter how different you are, you will be able to connect just a little bit better."

"She always encouraged us to learn new languages, so throughout middle school and high school, and even in college, I was learning different languages. I learned Mandarin in high school."

"Your mom sounds really incredible."

"She was," said Stassi with a sad smile. "I really miss her."

I squeezed Stassi's hand.

"How did you decide which languages to learn?"

She laughed. "Okay, don't judge me." She set the now empty sandwich box down on the towel.

"I'm not going to judge you."

"Well, English and Swahili were a given, and Spanish I learned because it's a really common second language taught in schools in the U.S."

"Okay."

"But I learned Mandarin and French because when I was younger, I was obsessed with these two shoe designers. One of them was from China and the other was from France. They were the two designers who first got me into shoes and fashion and design, and I was kind of obsessed with them. I liked watching interview clips of them talking about their design process. So I thought it could be fun to learn French and Mandarin."

"That's amazing," I laughed.

Only Stassi could learn two whole languages because of her love of shoes.

"You speak so many languages, too," she said to me, taking my hand. "What language do you dream in?"

"What language do I dream in?" I thought about it. "Probably English, if I'm being honest. We have a lot of English speakers in Fleurmont, and my mom was still just learning French when I was growing up, so we mostly spoke English at home."

"What about Mandarin?"

"My mom taught us Mandarin when we were growing up, but it was hard. There aren't a lot of learning resources in Fleurmont. She had textbooks and audiobooks shipped from Taiwan to help us learn when we were younger. I took some classes in college, too."

"What about this?" she asked, reaching for my face to touch the small scar on the left side of my face, just above my jawline. "How did you get this?"

"Oh, that," I said, embarrassed. "It's so stupid, you'll laugh."

"I won't laugh," she said, wrapping her arms around me again.

"One winter when I was fourteen, I was with my brother and a bunch of other kids, and we were hanging out by the lake. Michael and a bunch of guys were racing this short distance at the edge of the frozen lake. I was just sitting there watching them, and then someone asked me if I wanted to race. Michael laughed at me and said I would never do it. I felt like I had something to prove, so I went out onto the ice, and I raced him. Only the lake wasn't completely frozen over, and I was going so hard because I was so determined to prove myself. I stomped so hard on the ice that I just fell straight through. I cut my jaw and my face on the ice as I fell through."

And then I had to get fished out of the lake by Michael and one of his friends before getting sent to the hospital. Not my finest hour.

"Oh my God, that sounds awful," she said, taking my face in her hands. She stroked the scar on my face gently, kissing it.

"It wasn't that bad," I murmured. I liked her touching me like this. Looking at me like this.

"That water must have been freezing," she said, shivering at the thought.

"It was pretty damn cold," I nodded, remembering how my whole body had seized up at the temperature of the water.

"Do you think the water here is cold?" asked Stassi, looking towards the lagoon.

"Definitely not nearly as cold as the lake when I cut my face. Do you want to go swimming?"

"Is it going to be freezing?" She wiggled her legs in anticipation.

"One way to find out."

"Okay." Stassi got up, and then she turned back to me. She smirked. "Aren't you a little overdressed?"

I laughed, and I took off my shirt, conscious of the way she continued to look at me.

Tossing my shirt next to the one she discarded earlier, I walked over to her and took her hand. Together, we walked into the lagoon.

We walked into the lagoon on cool, mostly flat rocks. The water was surprisingly warm, and the natural staircase of rocks stopped when the water level reached just above our knees. We took one more step in, and our bodies dipped in, submerging completely before resurfacing and floating. We swam together, the water glittering turquoise around us.

"This is so nice," breathed Stassi.

She drifted over to me, her arms wrapping around my neck. I wondered if she knew just how fucking crazy I was for her, how fucking wild she drove me.

"There's one more thing I want to show you," I said to her.

Her eyes dipped to the space between us beneath the surface of the water.

"I think you've already shown me that. And for the record, I really like it," she drawled.

"Not that," I laughed, and I pulled her towards the waterfall.

We swam towards it before stopping right in front, squinting together as the water got into our eyes.

"Take a deep breath, and then we're going to swim through it to the other side."

Stassi nodded. We took a breath together, and at the same time, we dipped under the water beneath the waterfall. A second later, we were on the other side. We wiped the water from our faces, and I sat up on the rocky ledge. Stassi reached for me, and I pulled her up next to me.

"Woah," she breathed, looking around us.

Behind the waterfall was a small, flat ledge almost like a small cave. From the outside, you couldn't tell what was inside, but from the inside, you could still see out into the lagoon.

The air was more humid inside the small cave, creating almost a little steam room effect.

"This would have been a great inspiration for designing the spa," said Stassi. "How did you find out about this?"

"My friends and I used to go camping in the mountains once a year every summer. We found the lagoon during one of our camping trips, and I discovered the back of the waterfall when I came back here by myself on a hike."

"I love it," she said, and when we turned to face each other again, we kissed.

She pushed her tongue into my mouth, and my hands found her back. I unlaced the strings of her bikini top, letting her breasts fall free. Her nipples were already hardened into rosy pink pebbles. I tossed her bikini top to the side, and I took her into my mouth, sucking and licking the sensitive spots on her breasts.

Stassi moaned, and I pushed her down gently on her back, pulling down her bikini bottoms until they came all the way off.

I slipped back down into the water, finding solid footing. Slowly, taking my time, I pushed Stassi's thighs apart. She let out another soft whimper.

I pressed my mouth on the folds of her pussy, and then I devoured her.

# CHAPTER TWENTY-SIX

## Connor

"So you don't shower for like, four or five days when you go camping?" Stassi asked, looking unconvinced.

We were having a late dinner and were down to the last two pieces of the slightly burnt lasagna we had made together last week. We would have to go grocery shopping tomorrow.

"No, but usually there's swimming involved, so no one smells that bad."

"No offence, but that sounds so gross. And you have to pee in a bush?"

"No, there's a...thunderbox that you go in," I said, fighting a smile. "You know what, never mind. I don't think you'll enjoy camping."

"Ew, please don't tell me a thunderbox is what it sounds like."

"It's exactly what it sounds like."

"See, this is why our treehouses and yurts were approved by the entire marketing team for *Fleurs de L'Étang* –because we incorporated modern day plumping."

"I do appreciate modern day plumping."

My phone rang.

I looked at my phone, frowning. My brother was calling me. Why was Michael calling me?

"Is my uncle calling you this late?" Stassi frowned.

"No, it's my brother," I said to her as I accepted the phone call. "What's up?"

"Hey, sorry to interrupt whatever you're doing, but have you spoken to Mom recently?" Michael's voice sounded a little grainy and distant, like he had bad reception.

"I spoke to her a few days ago, why?"

"Mom's fine, she's okay, but I just got a call from the hospital. She was in a car accident."

"A car accident? What happened? Is she okay?"

Stassi looked at me with concerned eyes. She took my hand in hers.

"She's okay," said Michael quickly. "She's fine, but she's at the hospital with a broken leg, and she needed some stitches."

"Why didn't the hospital call me?" I asked. "I'm right here."

"I'm listed as her emergency contact. Don't worry, I talked to Mom on the phone. She's fine, just a little shaken up. And I'm on my way back."

"Back? You mean you're coming back to Fleurmont?"

"Yeah, I'm going to take care of her for the next few weeks while she's recovering."

"I can do that. You don't need to come all the way from Toronto."

"No, it's fine. I'm already on my way. Besides, I know you need to be up on Mt. Aster for work. I can work remotely. I'll work from the house, it'll be fine."

"Are you sure?"

"Yeah, I'm sure."

"I should still go see her tonight."

"Meet me at the hospital tomorrow. She just got out of surgery; she's resting."

"Which doctor is she with?"

"Connor, seriously. She's okay."

"Which doctor?" I repeated.

"Dr. Ahuja," sighed Michael. "I'll text you her number."

"Thanks."

I hung up, and Stassi squeezed my hand as I dialled Dr. Ahuja's number.

"Is your mom okay? What happened?" asked Stassi.

"Michael said she got into a car accident –"

"Hello?"

"Hi, Dr. Ahuja? It's Connor Fitzgerald."

"Oh, hi Connor. I was just on the phone with your brother," said Dr. Ahuja.

"He told me about the car accident. Is my mom okay? Can I come see her?"

"She's fine, but she's sleeping right now, so don't worry about it for tonight. She's in excellent hands. If you want, you can come in tomorrow morning," said Dr. Ahuja, repeating Michael's words.

"Alright," I sighed. "Thank you."

I hung up the phone, still feeling unsettled.

"It'll be okay," said Stassi, wrapping her arms around me. "It sounds like she's got all the care she needs. We'll go see her together tomorrow morning."

"Really?"

"Yes," said Stassi, kissing my face.

When Stassi and I got to the hospital, Michael was already in the waiting room. Only he wasn't alone.

Arden was sitting awkwardly two seats apart from him, and they both jumped when we entered, as if they had been caught doing something they shouldn't have.

"Arden?" I asked, confused why she was here.

"Oh, hey, Connor," said Arden, looking embarrassed.

She glanced at Michael, who quickly looked away from her. There was a weird energy between them.

"What are you doing here?" I asked.

"My mom...well, our moms kind of...crashed into each other," Arden winced.

"*What?*"

Our moms had been driving through town and had crashed into each other right in front of the town square. They had both been texting, and Arielle was the one who had called an ambulance for them.

We found Mom and Aunt Janie in a semi-private room together. They were both resting their eyes when we came in. When they heard us coming in, they both opened their eyes like they had been waiting for us.

They both seemed equally shocked to see the four of us coming in at the same time.

"Connor?"

"Arden?"

Dr. Ahuja stepped into the room with us.

"They're both fine," said Dr. Ahuja, who seemed to not know which mother to address first. "But they both have mild concussions, a femur fracture –that's in their right legs– and some internal bleeding. Mrs. Lee needed three stitches for her head injury, and Mrs. Lin has a fractured rib on her right side."

Mom and Aunt Janie looked horrified.

"I think this can be discussed *privately*?" hissed Mom to Dr. Ahuja.

"Sorry," said Dr. Ahuja, looking at Arden and Michael in question.

"Umm," Arden gave a helpless shrug, looking at me and Michael to see if we had an opinion.

"It's okay. I'll be back in just a few moments. We'll have the nurses check-up on both of them in the meantime," said Dr. Ahuja, and she smiled at us before leaving the room.

"Arden, close the curtain!" Aunt Janie whisper-snapped at Arden even though we could all hear her.

"Sorry," mouthed Arden, and she moved to close the curtain.

I turned my attention to Mom.

"How are you feeling, Mom?" asked Michael.

Michael and I moved to stand closer to her. Stassi hesitated by the door, and I extended my hand for her to take. She looked pleasantly surprised and didn't hesitate to reach out and hold my hand. Our fingers laced together.

Mom's eyes bugged out. Michael looked between me and Stassi and smirked.

"I'm fine," croaked Mom, still staring at where I was holding Stassi's hand.

"Do you need water or anything?" I asked her.

It looked like she was still on some IV fluids.

Mom shook her head no, and then winced as if her head hurt.

"I'm fine, really. Thank you for coming to see me," she gave us a soft smile.

"I tried calling Dad, but it went to voicemail," I said. "I'll try calling him again in a few minutes."

"No! Don't tell your dad," said Mom quickly, eyes flashing.

"What?"

"Why?"

"He's in London. Just let him enjoy his trip. He's wanted to see his brother for so long."

"He would want to know that you're injured," said Michael, shaking his head at her.

"It's fine, it's fine. I don't want him to come rushing back."

"Mom –" I started.

"Do *not* call your dad," hissed Mom sharply.

"Alright, alright," I muttered, not wanting her to strain herself.

"It's good to see you again, Stassi," said Mom instead, her eyes twinkling.

"I'm so sorry about the accident," said Stassi. "I hope you feel better soon."

"I will, I will. I'm honestly fine," said Mom, smoothing out her hospital gown.

"Says the woman with multiple broken bones," muttered Michael.

Mom glared at him.

Someone knocked on the door.

Mom rolled her eyes. "What's the point of knocking if they're going to shove us into a public space like this?"

"I can hear her!" I heard Aunt Janie say to Arden.

"Mom, it's fine, it's fine," whispered Arden.

"Okay, we're just going to do a check-up for Mrs. Lin and Mrs. Lee," said one of the nurses. "It shouldn't take too long."

"I'll stay with my mom," said Arden.

"That's fine."

"You kids head out," said Mom. "I'll be fine."

"We'll see you soon."

"I'll be back in a few minutes."

We were about to head out when Mom called out to me.

"Wait, Connor," she whispered.

I stopped and turned back towards her.

Michael and Stassi headed out of the room and into the hallway.

"Hey, Mom," I said, coming to stand next to her.

Mom looked at me and then back at the door Michael and Stassi had just exited.

"So, is Stassi your girlfriend now?" Mom's dark eyes were curious.

"She is."

"I like her," murmured Mom with a small smile. "You seem to really like her too."

"I do," I said, surprised she had pulled me aside to tell me this. "I'm really serious about her."

When it came to Stassi, I knew I didn't just like her. I had blown past 'like' a long time ago. In the less than three months she had been in my life, she had completely turned my world upside down.

"I know," said Mom. "You've always been the committed type, unlike Michael. But I still want you to be careful, Connor."

"I think I'm old enough that you don't need to give me a talk about using protection," I said quickly, remembering a particularly cringey lecture she'd given me and one of my college girlfriends.

"No, not that," said Mom. "I mean, with girls like Stassi. She's from a wealthy family, and that is a very different world from this one. Wealthy families like the Salvatis can look down on our small town life, and I know you're in the international world of work now, but where you're from and who your family is matters to these people."

"Trust me, Stassi isn't like that."

"Well, maybe not her, but her family could be. What would her family think of your relationship? Would they accept you for who you are? I know you don't want to hear this, but I just don't want to see you get hurt."

"I know," I said, "but really, I think we'll be just fine."

"Alright, alright."

"Rest up. I'll come back soon, okay, Mom?" I said as the nurse started to approach her bed.

"Alright. See you soon, honey."

I left Mom's room, trying to brush off her words and not let them fester. I found Michael and Stassi still standing in the hallway. Stassi reached for my hand as I closed the door behind me.

"Thanks for coming," I said to her.

"Of course," she murmured.

"I need coffee. Do you guys want anything?" asked Michael.

"I'm fine."

"Fine, thanks," said Stassi.

"Good to meet you, by the way," said Michael to Stassi. "I thought Connor was committed to celibacy for life. That or he was just really, really bad with women."

"You can go now," I said to him.

"It's nice to meet you too," said Stassi, looking faintly amused.

Michael grinned at us once more before heading down the hallway.

Stassi and I took a seat out in the waiting room.

"So, that was your brother," said Stassi.

"Yep. I think you've officially met the whole family."

"Why would your mom not want your dad to know that she was in a car accident?"

"I don't know...Pride? A lifetime of bad communication? It's a bit of a cultural thing with her, I think," I sighed. I thought about all of the times Mom kept things close to her chest and how much it used to drive me and Michael crazy.

Stassi nodded thoughtfully before wrapping her arms around me. "Well, I hope she gets better soon."

We spent the rest of the day in Fleurmont. I took Stassi to Chez Suyi's for lunch, trying to protect her from the town's ogling stares and Aunt Suyi's not so subtle comments about our relationship. In the afternoon, we went back to visit Mom at the hospital before heading back up to the cabin.

I was relieved that Michael was going to be in town for a while. It seemed like Arden was going to be staying in town for a while too.

It felt kind of strange, all of us except for Clara back in Fleurmont after all these years.

**Arden:** Ugh, I'm so sorry. I was so thrown off this morning I didn't even get to meet your girlfriend properly.

**Me:** Hey, no sweat. There was a lot going on.

**Arden:** Can I meet her officially sometime soon, after I figure out the deal with my mom's treatment plan?

**Me:** Yeah, of course. No rush at all. We're here till the end of August.

**Arden:** Great. When we meet, we should go axe throwing.

**Me:** You want to meet my girlfriend while throwing axes?

**Arden:** I want to meet your girlfriend. Separately, I'm going to be spending an indefinite amount of time with my mother this year. I need to throw some axes.

**Me:** Got it, got it. Alright. Axe throwing it is.

# Chapter Twenty-Seven

## *Stassi*

*July 2*

*Dearest Stassi,*

*You're in love?! What! In Canada for less than three months and you've already found love. I am jealous. Perhaps I should go to Canada, too. There are no men here in Nairobi. If there are, I am either too busy or never in the right place. I can't wait to meet this Connor Fitzgerald. Will he be at the Architect Gala in August?*

*Separately, I am SO happy to hear that you are doing design work again. I'm still waiting for you to design me the chateau we are supposed to retire in together in Switzerland, but I'll settle for a new office first. You must show me all of your designs when we are reunited.*

*I am heading to Burundu village in the west first. We'll be making our way clockwise over the next month. I may not be able to reply to your letters as quickly, as I will likely not receive them until I'm back in Nairobi, but keep sending them anyway, please. I'm living for these letters!*

*And because I won't be back in Nairobi until August...happy early 24th birthday, Stassi!!*

*All my love,*

*Nyambura*

It was almost the end of July when I finally officially met Arden Lee, Connor's childhood friend. Connor and I drove to the Charbonneau Farm, the farm belonging to the family of the man we'd met at the Honeycomb Stall during the Spring Festival.

The farm was beautiful. Like everything in Fleurmont, the backdrop was the sea of endless mountains. The first thing we saw after the mountains was the fenced paddock, a beautiful grassy area where about a dozen chickens were running around, chasing each other and pecking at the ground. Next to them, two horses grazed in the paddock, their tails flickering back and forth.

The first horse had a golden, almost caramel-coloured coat with a creamy white mane. The second was a slightly smaller grey horse with a silvery white mane. They were both so gorgeous they could easily have been show horses, their coats shining brightly in the afternoon sun. When *Fleurs de L'Étang* opened, our horses needed to be this beautiful.

I thought of alpaca yoga as Connor and I got out of the car and walked along the paddock. The Charbonneau Farm still smelled like farm animals, but for some reason, the smell wasn't so bad now. I didn't mind it at all. In fact, there was something almost heartwarming about the way the air smelled here. Maybe things were just different in Fleurmont.

Connor and I held hands as we made our way to the main barn house, our fingers intertwining. We walked past the large wooden sign for the Charbonneau Farm. There was a maple leaf and a beehive carved into the sign.

"The Charbonneaus are a maple syrup and honey farm," Connor explained to me on our drive over. "It's honey harvesting season right now, but in early spring, it's maple syrup season and they host a lot of sugar shacks."

"What's a sugar shack?"

"It's the place where they boil the sap from the maple trees and turn it into maple syrup. They'll do some demonstrations to show people the production process, and normally, it's followed by a traditional meal covered in maple syrup. We need to come back next spring so that you can try the *tire d'érable* and the maple coffee."

"Mmm, maple coffee sounds good."

Winter in Canada used to sound like the worst thing ever —months and months of endless snow with no chance of getting a tan? I remembered just a few months ago when the idea of coming here felt like a punishment. Now, this beautiful place felt more like home than any place I'd ever been.

It had only been three months, and technically, I only had a month left here...but already, I wanted to stay longer. I wanted to stay until autumn, when the leaves changed colours. I wanted to see what the mountains looked like in the winter.

The thought of what would happen after August made me uneasy. We hadn't talked about it. Neither Connor nor Uncle Valerian had brought up what would happen after August. I knew Connor would be happy if I stayed...but would Uncle Valerian want me to? Would he even let me?

I would worry about that later, I decided as Connor and I rounded the corner to the sound of metal hitting wood.

*Thunk. Thunk. Thunk!*

"Damn, you're good!" came a familiar voice with a chuckle, and we turned to see Ithier Charbonneau standing with his arms crossed over his chest as he watched Arden chuck steel axes at a wooden target.

All three of her axes had hit the bullseye at the center of the large wooden target.

Arden was in comfortable-looking clothes, her long black hair tied in a ponytail. Her face was a little pink from the heat, and she wiped the sweat from her forehead as she turned to look at us.

"Hey," said Connor.

"Hi!" Arden broke out into a large smile. She ran over to us as Ithier walked over to the wooden target to remove the axes. She hugged me first. "Stassi, it's so nice to finally meet you. Officially, that is. I'm sorry I didn't get a chance to introduce myself at the hospital."

"That's alright. It's so nice to officially meet you, too. And how's your mom doing?"

"She's good. She just got discharged a few days ago, and she's recovering."

Arden was gorgeous. I knew this because even in simple athletic wear, sweating, and wearing no makeup, she was gorgeous. Her features were dark and delicate at the same time –black hair, dark brown eyes, and a petite frame. She was objectively even more beautiful than Elodie, and I knew that she and Connor had not only grown up together but were still really close. This would normally have made me feel a sharp stab of unrelenting jealousy, but I felt...surprisingly fine.

I looked over at Connor. His eyes were right on me, a tender expression on his face. He gave my hand a quick, warm squeeze. My insides fluttered happily.

"I'm really glad to hear that," I said, turning my attention back to Arden.

Connor's mom had also recently been discharged from the hospital. We had gone to visit her a few more times before she had left the hospital, and it seemed like Michael was on top of it when it came to her home care.

"Who's up next?" said Ithier, holding up the axes in his hands.

"You guys want to try?" asked Arden. "It's super cathartic."

"Yes, it's a popular breakup activity. Are you imagining Jared's head?" asked Ithier as he mimicked throwing an axe at the target.

Connor winced as Ithier said this, but Arden didn't look too bothered.

"*No,*" she retorted with a snort. "Although I hate that even you know about Jared."

"Sorry," said Ithier sheepishly.

"Is it bad to ask who Jared is?" I asked curiously.

Okay, so I liked some good relationship gossip. But who doesn't?

"No," sighed Arden. "Jared is my ex-fiancé. We were together for four years and broke up over a year ago, although *apparently,* everyone in this town still likes to talk about it."

Ithier gave Arden a smile, crossing his arms over his chest. "Sorry, it's just that you're back in town, and Arielle was talking about it."

Arden groaned. "Okay, fuck it, can I go again?"

"Yeah, yeah, we're in no rush," said Connor.

"Ooh, yes, can you show me how to do it?" I added.

I wanted to throw some fucking axes around.

Ithier handed Arden the set of axes. Arden gave a wry smile, setting down two of the axes at her feet and keeping the third in her right hand.

"Yes, okay, well everyone has a preferred way of throwing their axes, but I personally prefer a one-handed throw. You kind of stand like this, similar to how you're throwing a dart, and then –" Arden chucked the axe at the target, her right arm swinging forward in a straight line while the rest of her body stayed locked.

*Thunk.*

The axe hit the centre of the target.

"Nice." Ithier let out a low whistle.

"Thanks," grinned Arden.

Connor nodded. "You can also do an overhand throw and use both hands. Sometimes, that can be easier in the beginning."

Arden threw another axe, just as Abel Boivin appeared from the other side of the barn.

"*Allo!*"

Arden's axe landed on the outer red circle of the target. Connor chuckled.

"Oh, shut up. I was distracted," said Arden. "Here, you go."

She handed Connor the last axe.

"Hey, Abel," greeted Ithier with a wave.

We all smiled and waved at Abel, who was carrying a massive toolbox and wearing a forest green T-shirt that read "Appelle Abel" in a large, bold font.

"It's upstairs on the second floor?" Abel asked Ithier in French.

"That's right. Bathroom on the left. Thanks, Abel."

"Alright, I'll take care of it." Abel waved at us again before heading towards the house.

"Plumbing issue," explained Ithier as Connor took the axe. He handed it out to me. "Do you want to try?"

"Okay!"

I threw the axe the way Arden had done it, but it barely hit the target, hitting the edge of the wooden frame before falling into the dirt ground.

I laughed. "Wow, that was bad."

"No, it was only your first time. Try again," said Arden encouragingly.

"You hit the target at least," agreed Connor. "You should have seen us when we first tried this. We just missed it completely."

"Once, I threw so badly I almost hit a chicken," added Arden.

Ithier laughed and ran to remove the axes from the target. "As long as you don't kill one of my chickens, you're fine."

I tried again and missed the next three times. Finally, my fifth throw stuck to the wood, just below the red centre of the target.

Arden and Ithier cheered as Connor pulled me in, kissing me deeply. I giggled, kissing him back.

"Aww, you guys are so cute and gross," said Arden.

"Do I get a kiss if I hit the target?" asked Ithier, winking at Connor.

"Fuck off," said Connor, and he pulled me back in again for another kiss.

We spent the rest of the afternoon taking turns throwing axes at the target. Axe throwing was fun. And it *was* cathartic. Part of me wondered if axe-throwing would have helped me process my emotions better two years ago. Either way, I was happy to have it now, especially with Connor next to me, kissing me every time I hit the target.

# Chapter Twenty-Eight

## *Stassi*

**Miranda:** Happy birthday, Stassi. Have a great day!
**Adrian:** Happy birthday, Stass. Hope it's a good one.
**Me:** Thanks :)

"Hey, Stassi, how's it going?" said Uncle Valerian over the phone. He had a static-y connection, and his voice was breaking out. He must be on the road somewhere.

"Not bad, not bad."

I was sitting on the couch with my sketchbook on my lap when he called. Connor was in the kitchen making a salad for us.

"I just wanted to check in with you, see how things were going up there. Fitzgerald tells me you're doing a really great job. Said a lot of great things about you in his last report."

"Did he now?" I said with another big smile as I looked at Connor, who was shamelessly eavesdropping. "Connor said I was doing a *really great* job in his last report?"

Connor stifled a laugh.

It was the end of July, and I was officially twenty-four. The craziest part was that just a few months ago I would have been excited to count down the months until I turned twenty-five and could cash out on my trust fund and disappear. But now? It seemed like the stupidest thing to care about. I was designing again. My life up here had Connor and Maxi. I've never felt happier my whole life.

"He did, and listen, I don't have much time to talk today, but I wanted to tell you that you did a great job with the accommodations designs," said Uncle Valerian.

"Thanks, Uncle Val."

"Alright, I got to go. We'll talk soon, Stass?"

"Yeah, of course," I said, ignoring the slight disappointment I felt as he hung up without wishing me a happy birthday.

It wasn't unusual in the Salvati household. Uncle Valerian had never forgotten before, but my parents had forgotten at least twice —once for my tenth birthday and once for my fourteenth. They had suddenly remembered the next day, and tried to make up for it by sending presents and sweet treats over the following week, but I knew they had forgotten. Both times.

Julian seemed to have forgotten my birthday too, though, which was a bit more surprising —he never forgot my birthday. But it was only twelve o'clock here, which meant it was nine o'clock in Los Angeles, so I ignored it for now and made my way to the backyard to find Connor.

Connor and Maxi sat on the lounge chairs in the backyard. Over the last month, Connor had finally cleared out the fallen leaves and branches from the last fall and winter, and the backyard was now speckled with tufts of green grass and little white and yellow flowers.

I walked over to Connor.

"How was your call?" he asked, taking my hands in his.

"Good. In fact, I was told that you wrote a really good report about me."

"Did you now?" Connor smiled.

"Uh huh," I nodded, and I climbed on top of him, wrapping my legs around him as I sat on his lap, "So, what did you write in your report, Mr. Fitzgerald?"

"I wrote that you are a really hard worker," said Connor, his strong arms coming around from behind me to pull me closer, "and that you're a great designer."

"Oh, yeah?" I smiled. "What else did you write?"

Connor's right hand snaked into my shorts.

"I explained how...*precise* you are," said Connor, his thumb expertly finding and stroking my clit in a single motion, "and how...flexible you are."

I arched into him, stifling a moan as the sensation over my clit overwhelmed me, my arms tightening around his neck for balance.

Connor pressed a kiss to my throat before he dragged his lips down to my chest, leaving a trail of fire along my neck and my collarbone.

"You know," I breathed as Connor put a finger inside of me, "before I got here, my uncle told me that I had to do anything you wanted me to do."

"Did he? What did he say exactly?" Connor inserted a second finger inside of me.

"His exact words were 'you will do anything Connor Fitzgerald tells you to do'."

"Anything?" Connor raised an eyebrow.

I nodded silently, biting back a scream as Connor's fingers pumped into me. My whole body shook. His thumb was still pressed on my clit, stroking and pressing into me as his fingers moved into me. I closed my eyes to savour the feeling.

"Look at me, baby," ordered Connor. "Look at me while I fuck you with my fingers."

I blinked open my eyes to look at him, my thighs trembling.

"Good girl," he praised, one hand on my chin, keeping my face levelled with his. "Don't sit. Just stay there."

I looked at Connor, trying to focus on him instead of what I was feeling to try to drag it out longer. It wasn't the best strategy.

I looked at Connor's full lips, which were slightly parted. His dark hazel eyes and jet black hair. I was so close.

"Are you going to be a good girl and come for me?"

I nodded.

Connor reached into my shirt, groping my left breast before pinching my nipple. I gasped.

"Answer me, baby. Are you going to be a good girl and come for me?"

"Y-yes," I stammered. "I'm going to come for you."

"Good."

He pinched my other nipple before stroking my clit again with his thumb, his other fingers still fucking me.

It was too much, and I shattered.

Connor kissed me, his tongue thrusting into me as I came for him, coming right there on his fingers. I struggled to breathe, feeling beautifully suffocated as I panted into him, our tongues intertwined, pulse after pulse.

"Happy birthday, Stassi," Connor whispered when he finally pulled away.

In college, Nya and I used to go out dancing every time it was one of our birthdays. We would start the day with a late brunch at Baltaire, spend the day shoe shopping, and then go out dancing with the rest of our friends at night. So when Connor asked me what I wanted to do for my birthday, I knew exactly what I wanted to do.

Before we headed out for the evening, Connor led me to the shed next to the cabin.

"One more birthday present for you before we go," he said.

"Two presents? Really?" I said, touching the necklace at my neck.

Connor had gifted me a beautiful gold necklace this morning with a purple wildflower pendant. It looked exactly like the purple wildflowers we had seen when we had gone up the mountain to watch the sunset.

"Really," smiled Connor.

He turned on the light to the shed before he opened the door.

I let out a soft gasp of surprise.

It was a cat tree. Only it wasn't just any cat tree.

Connor had created the most magnificent cat tree I had ever seen. It was made to look like a real tree. The base of the trunk was thick, sloping and winding its way up as it stretched out into different branches. At different heights of the tree, Connor had added large wooden steps, perches, and two rounded plush sleeping baskets. The baskets were a soft purple, and at the very top of the cat tree, there were two realistic, decorative branches sticking out, with clusters of beautiful purple flowers at the tips of the branches.

"You made a jacaranda cat tree," I gasped.

"Do you like it? I know it's technically for Maxi, not for you, but –"

"I *love* it," I said, feeling my eyes fill with tears.

I felt overwhelmed with emotion, and I pulled Connor closer to kiss him.

He had made me a jacaranda cat tree.

Le Robinet was crowded when we arrived. Connor and I had been a couple of times before during the day for coffee when we drove into town for groceries or when we met with Elodie. I loved the artsy, cozy vibe of the place. Connor told me it was the only place in town that occasionally had dancing. People in Fleurmont were generally a little older, so there wasn't a whole lot of clubbing going on. Dancing was usually limited to themed town events.

There was, however, a group of townspeople singing boisterously in the corner of the bar. They were likely in their fifties or sixties, drinking frosty beers and singing in French.

Connor looked at them, amused.

"Only for you," said Connor as the server brought us a tray of drinks.

Three shots of tequila for me and a shot of espresso for Connor. He was still our designated driver back to the cabin.

"You mean you don't normally sing your heart out every Friday night at Le Robinet?"

"I'm not going to lie to you. I have not once done that in my life."

Connor sipped his espresso, his free hand lingering on my thigh, tracing lazy shapes dangerously close to the hem of my dress. Feeling a strong need for him again, I pressed closer to him. I kissed his warm lips, tasting the espresso on them, and my heart warmed when Connor kissed me back enthusiastically, unbothered by the fact that we were surrounded by people.

"We could get a hotel," I drawled. "I want to drink with you."

I could not picture stoic, serious Connor drunk, at all. Then again, I didn't think stoic, serious Connor was the type to order me to crawl for him before giving him head like he had two nights ago, so I guess anything was possible. It was exhilarating to know someone so well and yet still be able to be surprised by them.

"Next time," murmured Connor, eyes twinkling. "Don't we have Maxi to get back to?"

"I guess you're right," I sighed.

Even though I knew Maxi would probably be fine for one night, I still didn't love leaving him alone for too long. He was almost four months old now, and he constantly wanted to be next to us or to play. Before we left the cabin, we'd moved his jacaranda cat tree into the living room, and he had immediately sprinted up the branches. We left him up in his new tree, chewing on a toy chicken.

Connor looked at the tequila shots in front of me. "So how does this work?"

"You've never taken a tequila shot?" I gasped.

"No."

Okay, now I had to get him drunk one day. Specifically on tequila shots.

"What did you do in college? Were you just a really good boy?"

"No, I had plenty of alcohol. Beer, wine, maple whiskey even."

"*Maple* whiskey? Are you the cutest Canadian or what?" I giggled.

Connor tickled me, and I squealed, trying to hold him off.

"We'll see if you're still laughing later tonight," he said.

His dark eyes were full of promise, and I shivered with anticipation.

"So tell me how this works," he said, taking a sip of his espresso and gesturing to the tequila shots.

"The thing to remember is to lick, shoot, and suck."

"You're kidding," said Connor flatly.

"Nope! You lick the salt rim, shoot the shot, and then you suck on the lime," I explained.

"Well, no wonder you love these. You're so good at licking and sucking."

"Connor Fitzgerald!" a scandalized voice cried from behind us.

I burst out laughing and covered my mouth as we turned to see Suyi from Chez Suyi's sitting at the booth behind us.

"Aunt Suyi," choked out Connor, his face turning beet red.

Suyi was sitting with Arielle from the Le Petit Toast, both women drinking cosmopolitans and sharing a bowl of peanuts.

"My ears are bleeding," she exclaimed as Arielle cackled a laugh.

"Sorry, sorry," said Connor. "I was just talking about tequila."

"Sure you were," said Aunt Suyi, and then turned around. "Alright, I'm going to pretend I did not hear anything."

"Jesus Christ," muttered Connor, his face still red. "Next year for your birthday, we're celebrating on a different continent."

I laughed, leaning in to kiss him before taking my first shot. I smiled into Connor's shoulder as he smiled at me, kissing me back tenderly. My heart fluttered. I was becoming dangerously addicted to Connor Fitzgerald, and the high of being with him was better than any amount of tequila or shoe shopping combined. And that was saying a lot. I *loved* shoe shopping.

By the time I had my third shot, I was ready to fuck Connor right there in Le Robinet. I played with the front buttons of his shirt, accidentally-on-purpose unbuttoning the top button. Suyi and Arielle had left, leaving the booth behind us empty.

"Oops," I whispered, batting my eyelashes at him, still trying to keep my voice low enough so that no one could hear me besides Connor, just in case.

"Stassi," Connor warned, but he had a wolfish grin on his face. "Is that what you want? You want me to fuck you right here in the bar? You want me to fuck you right here so that everyone knows that you're mine?"

"Yes," I all but moaned.

"Are you wet for me, baby?"

"I'm soaked."

"Are you sure? You don't sound sure." His fingers slid further up my thigh.

Fuck, I wanted him so badly right now.

"Do you want to check for me, then?"

"You really want me to fuck you right here? In front of all these people?"

My thighs clenched together with need. I wanted to rip his clothes off and touch him all over. I wanted to lick his abs and rub my hands all over those muscular arms...

"Let's go to the car," I said breathlessly.

"Don't you want to stay so we can dance together?" he teased, eyes glinting.

"Fuck dancing. I want you to fuck me right now."

Connor let out a low laugh. He paid our bill, and then guided me out of the bar.

We made our way out the doors, and the door barely closed behind us when I grabbed Connor, pushing him against the wall of Le Robinet. I kissed him and let out a moan as I felt his arms wrap around me tightly. His hands slipped down my back, gripping my ass. Fuck, I wanted him to spank me right here on the streets. I didn't know if I could make it all the way to the car.

"Fuck, Stassi," Connor groaned into my mouth, his tongue licking mine as we kissed.

I could feel him rock-hard against me, and I slipped my hand into his shirt to feel his abs.

"*Stassi?*" a shocked voice came from behind us.

Connor and I jumped apart almost violently, and my face turned ten degrees warmer and twenty shades redder before my brain could even fully register what I was seeing.

Uncle Valerian and Julian were standing in front of Le Robinet, identical shocked expressions on their faces. My uncles were standing in front of Le Robinet... in Fleurmont. My uncles were in Fleurmont.

"Uncle Valerian? Julian?" I choked out.

"Holy shit," I heard Connor breathe out in a barely audible whisper as he disentangled himself from me.

"Surprise, happy birthday," said Julian awkwardly with a half-laugh, glancing quickly at Uncle Valerian.

Uncle Valerian looked like he had seen a ghost.

Of course, he hadn't seen a ghost. No, he had just seen his niece making out with a man on the street, half-climbing and half-grinding him. He had just seen his niece making out with a man who was technically supposed to be her boss. You know, the man who reported directly to him.

My hair was not a mess, and my dress was not riding up my thighs. Connor's breath and scent were not all over me, and Connor's shirt was not completely crumpled. There was no hickey slowly forming on Connor's neck, nor on mine for that matter. No, not at all.

This was not what nightmares were made of. No, no, this was not awkward at all.

# CHAPTER TWENTY-NINE

## Stassi

"The coffee's good here," said Julian, adjusting the thin metal frame of his glasses as his coffee fogged up the lenses for a brief second.

Uncle Valerian and Julian and I were at Le Petit Toast for breakfast. Uncle Valerian had requested the booth all the way in the corner, furthest away from the kitchen, the front door, or the bathroom. He liked his privacy.

My uncles were both well-dressed; opposites in most ways, but also well-matched. Uncle Valerian was in cotton chino trousers and a dark linen shirt, while Julian was wearing a lighter-coloured version of the same outfit.

Last night had ended very, very awkwardly. It turned out that Uncle Valerian and Julian had not forgotten my birthday at all, and had actually flown all the way from Los Angeles to Fleurmont to surprise me.

After stammering out a string of awkward sentences, we had established that we would meet again in the morning at Le Petit

Toast while Uncle Valerian and Julian got checked into Auberge Fleurmont, the local town inn.

Connor and I had driven back up to the cabin, and I had freaked out the entire way back home. I don't know why I hadn't thought about telling my uncles about me and Connor sooner. The idea hadn't even really crossed my mind. I was so worried about having to talk to Uncle Valerian about what would happen after August that I didn't even think about telling him about me and Connor. It was so nice to be in our cozy little bubble in our cabin up in the mountains.

Finally, after a particularly sleepless night, Connor and I concluded that there was no better solution or explanation than to just share with Uncle Valerian and Julian the truth behind our relationship and see how they reacted.

"Here we go," said Arielle, eyeing both of my uncles as she placed large, hot plates in front of us. "Eggs with bacon, sausages, and homefries, french toast, and a fruit salad with a side of bacon."

I had a sneaking suspicion from the way Arielle was looking at Uncle Valerian and Julian that she would run to Suyi and Raphael to tell them about this encounter after her shift. Her blue eyes swept over every detail before she turned to look at me and threw me a familiar smile. I smiled back at her.

"Thank you," smiled Julian.

"So, how is your room at the inn?" I cleared my throat after Arielle had disappeared back into the kitchen. I pushed the fruit around in my bowl with my fork.

"It's great. We have a great view of the lake," supplied Julian as he poured maple syrup onto his french toast. "It's a really nice cozy room, isn't it, Val?"

Uncle Valerian was still looking at me, brown eyes hard and calculating, like he was doing a complicated math problem in his head. He really looked so much like Grandpa when he did that.

"Very cozy," said Uncle Valerian finally.

"That's great!" I said, trying to keep my voice sounding normal. "I hear it's really nice to go out onto the lake. They have kayaks and sailboats -"

"So what's the deal with you and Fitzgerald?" Uncle Valerian picked up his knife and fork and started cutting his sausages.

I flushed, half-wishing I had taken Connor up on his offer to come with me. I thought it would be best if I spoke with my uncles alone first because my family usually processed information better in smaller groups. Besides, I didn't want Connor to see my family lecturing me if it came to that. But with Uncle Valerian staring at me waiting for an answer, I was second-guessing that decision now.

"I...we're...in a relationship. It just...kind of happened."

Oh my God, I was doing such a terrible job of explaining this.

"What kind of relationship?"

What kind of relationship? What kind of question was that? What kinds of relationships were there?

"What do you mean?" I asked warily. My fruit salad and bacon stared back at me. Yep, I was definitely not hungry right now.

Julian cut his french toast into little pieces on his plate, dipping it into the pools of maple syrup before taking a bite.

"He's your boss. So who initiated whatever is happening between you two?"

Oh, God, does he think Connor forced me into this?

"Connor didn't force me into anything," I said defensively, my voice rising. "In fact, he spent weeks trying to dissuade me from being together, and I pushed him into it. *I* wanted this."

Julian let out a laugh. I glared at him.

He looked away, still grinning, taking another bite of his french toast. "Really good french toast. I think I like Fleurmont."

"So you're telling me *you* forced him into this?" Uncle Valerian raised an eyebrow.

"No!" I flushed again. "It was mutual...I –does it really matter?"

"Well, when you're both supposed to be working for the company and I catch you two copulating on the streets, yeah, it kinda matters."

"We weren't *copulating* on the streets –" I stopped, seeing the expression on Uncle Valerian's face.

Was he...*smiling?*

"Julian, didn't it look like they were copulating on the streets?"

"Yes, it did look like they were copulating on the streets."

"Okay, can we please stop saying the word 'copulating'?" I huffed, exasperated.

"You're the one who was copulating...copulator," said Julian, eyes suddenly boring into mine with a forced, neutral expression.

Uncle Valerian burst out laughing, a low, guttural laugh reverberating through him. Julian laughed with him, and I glared at my uncles.

"Stop it," I whined, wanting to chuck a grape at both of them. I let out a reluctant laugh.

"Alright, well, you're both adults. I don't care what you're doing, as long as it's consensual and all."

Julian was still shaking with laughter. "We wanted to surprise you for your birthday, but I think the biggest surprise yesterday was for us."

"Anyway," chuckled Uncle Valerian, "I wanted to talk to you about this project you've been working on here. I know you weren't too thrilled about coming up here at first."

"No, but I actually really like it up here. And not just because of Connor," I added quickly. "I really like the design work that I've been doing."

"Good, and I know we sort of talked on the phone yesterday, but...you did a great job with the accommodations designs. I –"

"What he means to say is he loves you and he's proud of you," Julian cut in.

"*Anyway*," said Uncle Valerian, nudging Julian away, "before I was so rudely interrupted –I *am* really proud of you, Stass. I'm sorry if I was harsh on you before. You're very talented, and I just wanted to see you do well."

"I know," I said, my heart warming a little.

I knew he wanted what was best for me, and I knew he came from a place of love, even if we both had a hard time expressing our feelings.

"I know we said you'd spend four months up here, and I know you're supposed to have another month left, but I was wondering if you would actually want to come back with us this weekend."

"Do you mean go back with you to L. A.?" I said, surprised.

"Yes, exactly."

"I actually like being here. I like this project, and it's been cool to see the site transform these past few weeks."

The demolition team had completely excavated the old mining town to prepare for construction. Only the ugly ass swamp remained more or less the same, but, honestly? I kind of liked that ugly ass swamp now, too. It was where I had found Maxi.

"I'm glad to hear that, but I also don't mean to keep you trapped in one place. I know you like to travel. My intention was never to keep you prisoner."

"You mean keep me prisoner for too long? Maybe just keep me prisoner for four months or so?" I said, but I was mostly joking.

He was right back in April; I had needed this, and the most incredible thing had come out of it. Was it too much to tell him that I also wanted to stay because I didn't want to be away from Connor? I don't think he realized how much Connor meant to me.

"Alright, perhaps that's what I meant. You have to admit, Stass, you were going a little crazy for a moment there."

"Fine, maybe just a little," I conceded, "but you know, I'm actually fine here."

"We were actually hoping you'd come back with us because of your grandfather's birthday next week," said Julian.

Oh, that's right. Grandpa was turning seventy-five.

"We thought we would surprise him with a family dinner. We checked in with Miranda and Adrian, and they're both going to fly in."

"Oh, that's great," I said, but I felt my heart sink a little. Did that mean I had to leave Fleurmont tomorrow? That was way too soon.

"After that, you can stay in L.A. if you want. You can still work with Fitzgerald on this project if you want to, but we have people working from all over the world, so you don't need to be in a specific place, at least not all the time."

I didn't know what to say. I looked at Julian, who was observing me again. He smiled at me kindly.

"The most exciting update I have for you though," Uncle Valerian continued, glancing at Julian, looking pleased with himself. "I have a job for you in Paris if you want it."

"What?" I gasped.

"That's right. I mean it when I say I'm impressed with your work. I sent your portfolio to the head architect in our Paris office, along with the report Fitzgerald wrote about your work here, and she was impressed. There's an architect position opening in September, so the position is yours if you want it. I know you've always talked about living in Europe, and I know how much you love Paris."

It was what I had asked for in April. I've always talked about how much I loved Europe, and of course I loved Paris. Miranda lived in Paris, too.

The idea of moving to Paris made me feel an almost painful sadness and hollowness in my chest. No more wildflower fields. No more maple syrup and axe throwing. No more waking up next to Connor every day. I know it had only been three months of me being here, and technically Connor and I had only been together for six weeks...but it had been an intense three months. I had seen him every single day for the last three months...and now I couldn't help but feel an intense feeling of loss.

"Think about it," said Uncle Valerian, studying my face curiously, probably wondering why I wasn't jumping up and down or calling Nya to organize a shoe shopping marathon for the first week of September. "You don't need to decide immediately."

"Thanks, Uncle Val. I really appreciate this."

"Of course." Uncle Valerian's pleased smile returned.

After brunch, Uncle Valerian and I walked along the lake. Julian had some work to catch up on and stayed behind in their room at the inn, but I wondered if it was also to give us some additional time to catch up.

I was still processing everything he'd shared at brunch as we walked along the lakeshore. It was sunny out, and the lake was a beautiful, glittering bright blue today. We walked along the shoreline along a semi-defined path.

"You know, your dad would have loved this place," said Uncle Valerian, looking out at the lake.

"Really?" I was surprised. Uncle Valerian rarely talked about my dad.

"Really. He used to talk about wanting to retire somewhere by the water, and specifically by a lake."

I didn't know that about my dad. Then again, there was so much I didn't know about him that this was hardly a surprise.

"Do you know why?"

"He said it felt peaceful. We stayed at a cottage by the lake for a few summers in Vermont, and he used to go out on the water every morning for a swim or to go canoeing."

"Did you ever go with him?"

"No," Uncle Valerian smiled sadly. "He was eight years older than me, and I'm sure he thought I'd be too much of a burden. To tell you the truth, we weren't all that close growing up."

I looked at Uncle Valerian, wondering if he felt about my dad the way I felt about Adrian and Miranda. He gave me a sad smile.

"We became a little closer as adults, but I will always wish that I had more time with him. He was a good person."

I nodded, blinking a little. We watched as a flock of Canadian geese landed noisily on the lake, splashing each other with their landing. A family of ducks swam away from them, and the largest of the geese ducked its head into the lake.

"He would be proud of you though, Stassi. I hope you know that."

"Thanks."

I hoped he would have been proud of me, or at least not too disappointed in me. Neither of my parents would have been proud of who I was just three months ago, but now that I was designing again, now that I'd been in Fleurmont for three months…it felt like I had found a little piece of myself again. For the first time, I felt like I was becoming someone I could really be proud of.

Was it bad that I felt like I couldn't have found myself without Connor? More importantly, what should I do now? Should I come back to Fleurmont in September, or take that job in Paris? If I took that job in Paris, what would that mean for me and Connor?

# Chapter Thirty

## *Stassi*

**Connor:** How's the flight?

**Me:** Okay. Uncle Val and Julian are drinking and bickering.

**Me:** I miss you.

**Connor:** I miss you, too. Let me know when you land.

"We have a belated birthday surprise for you," said Julian as we entered the penthouse apartment.

We were back in Los Angeles after almost a full day of travel. My heart was already aching from missing Connor.

"What is it?" I set Maxi's cat carrier down in the hall and opened the little metal door. Maxi took a tentative step out, sniffing cautiously as he explored his new space. I had thought about leaving him in Fleurmont with Connor...but I was too conflicted. What if I didn't go back to Fleurmont?

My stomach knotted as I remembered the look on Connor's face when I told him about the job offer in Paris and that I was taking Maxi with me. We both knew it meant there was a chance I wasn't coming back.

"It sounds like a great opportunity for you. You should take your time to think about it," Connor had said.

The fact that he was so supportive only made this decision seem even more impossible.

"Go check in the guest room," smiled Uncle Valerian. He set down his two suitcases at the front entrance.

Raising an eyebrow suspiciously at them, I smiled and walked to the guest bedroom.

I opened the bedroom door, only to find Nya sitting on the bed, a huge grin on her face.

"*Nya?*"

"Stassi!"

We flung ourselves into each other's arms, and I enveloped her in a tight hug.

"I thought you were still travelling all over Kenya!" I cried when I finally released her.

Nya was wearing shorts and a thick sweater, her hair kept natural in a short, cropped afro. Her lips were painted a muted red, and she was wearing big, hooped beaded earrings.

"I was. I got back to Nairobi the day before your birthday, actually. Then, I thought to myself, why don't I just go to L.A. early? So I called your uncle, and we came up with a plan."

"This is amazing. I'm so glad you're here!"

"I want to hear everything," said Nya. "And I want to see photos of –oh my goodness, hello."

We both looked up as Maxi appeared at the doorway, still sniffing furiously around him, looking up at the high ceilings.

"Maxi, come here." I reached into my purse for his little bag of cat treats.

I shook the bag, and Maxi came trotting over, his tail shooting straight up and shaking with excitement.

"Aww, can I feed him?" cooed Nya.

"Of course. He's been waiting to meet his Auntie Nya," I said, handing her the bag of cat treats.

Maxi jumped onto the bag, bumping his black and white head against Nya's fingers at the bag of treats.

"Oh, he's so soft," gushed Nya as she petted him, and placed the treats in her hand. "What a beautiful boy you are, Maximus."

I beamed with pride.

We petted Maxi until he had twice as many treats as he should probably have in a day. Finally, we put the bag of treats away, and Maxi settled down on a silk pillow at the head of the bed.

"Now I want to hear all about your time in Canada," said Nya and then held up a hand. "Actually, wait."

Nya hopped off the bed and walked over to her handbag, taking out a bag of Trader Joe's snacks. She sat back down on the bed and smiled at me.

"There," she said. "I have my snack. I'm ready to hear about your snack. And by your snack, I mean your man."

She grinned as she opened her bag of peanut butter popcorn.

I laughed, rolling my eyes. "Fine, okay, but then I want to hear about your time in the villages."

"In a bit. Tell me about the sex. Was it amazing?"

We spent the rest of the day catching up in my room. I told Nya about my relationship with Connor, about every little moment that had led up to the last six weeks. I told her about the project I was working on in Fleurmont and how much I loved it. Nya looked through my designs for her office and the designs I'd created for the treehouses, the yurts, and the spa.

We covered everything, including the job offer in Paris and how much I hated being physically separated from Connor. Everything had happened so suddenly and so quickly that we didn't really have time to talk about us and what it would mean for us if I took the job in Paris.

"Now I don't know what to do," I sighed, still sitting cross-legged on the bed. "Should I take that job in Paris?"

"Do you want to take that job in Paris?"

"I don't know. I feel like I should, like it's what I'm supposed to do?"

"Why?"

"Maybe because it's an actual job, with a job description, and what I have right now is just an internship? I mean, it doesn't *feel* like an internship. I've been doing so much more than I've ever done before, but I don't even know if I could keep working in Fleurmont if I wanted to. Most of the design work is done for *Fleurs de L'Étang*. Connor's been waiting to see if he gets the Creative Director role, and I don't even know what it means for his future projects, or what it would mean for me if I wanted to keep working with him."

"Have you asked Connor or your uncle about it?"

"Not yet...I just... I didn't want Uncle Val to think I just wanted to stay for Connor. He's finally proud of me for the work I'm doing –*I'm* finally proud of me for the work I'm doing, and I don't want him to think I'm just throwing away my career for a man."

"It doesn't really sound like you're throwing away your career. Didn't this project help you design again?"

"Yeah, definitely..." I bit my lip anxiously. Maybe I should just have a conversation with Connor again. But I was afraid that the second I spoke to Connor about it, I would just melt and cave and do anything I could to continue being able to work with him and live with him.

"It doesn't sound like you really want to go to Paris," said Nya.

I groaned. I should want to go to Paris. Who wouldn't want to live in Paris if they had the opportunity? And what if I moved to Paris and I actually got to connect with my sister? I shouldn't make a career decision based on a man. Even if that man was the kindest, most creative and most patient man I had ever met. The kind of man with whom I had mind-blowing sex and who made me jacaranda cat trees.

I loved Connor, I realized. I was really in love with him, and that's why this decision was so hard.

"Let's talk about you now," I said, feeling too confused. "Tell me about your work."

"Fine," sighed Nya. "But it was a shit show, so this is going to be a long story."

Grandpa's seventy-fifth birthday was a small but fancy affair. I wore a simple dress and paired it with a pair of purple and gold heels that complimenting the necklace Connor had given me for my birthday. I missed Connor so much. It had only been five days, but already, I hated long distance.

I'd spent the day with Nya finalizing her outfit for the Architect Gala, and when I got back to the penthouse, Miranda and Adrian were already in the parlour, sitting on opposite armchairs.

They looked exactly the same as I remembered. Honestly, despite their three-year age difference, they looked like they could be twins. All three of us had our mother's blue eyes, but Miranda looked the most like our mom. Miranda's features were softer than mine. Her hair was light brown. Her eyebrows were shaped in an almost straight line, her nose just a little daintier, and even the shape of her face was softer. She looked as lovely as ever in a two-piece floral outfit, complete with stunning silver heels.

Adrian looked similar, except he was a few inches taller than her, and his nose and jawline were more masculine than dainty. He wore a simple suit and was nursing a glass of wine in one hand.

"Hey, Stassi, good to see you," said Adrian, standing up to give me an awkward hug.

I hugged him back awkwardly and then turned to give my sister a hug too.

"Hi," I said to her.

"Hi," she smiled. "You look nice."

"You too. I like your outfit today."

"I like your necklace."

"Thanks."

"Looking good, Salvatis," came Uncle Valerian's loud voice from the entrance of the parlour, and we turned to see Uncle Valerian, Julian, and Grandpa standing at the entrance.

"Happy birthday!" we chimed, sounding shockingly coordinated for three people who never spent any time together.

"Thank you, thank you," said Grandpa, giving us a small smile. He looked as serious as ever, but he was wearing his burgundy suit today –his celebration suit.

We filed into the dining room for a meal, and it was, in typical Salvati fashion, an extravagant affair. Uncle Valerian or Julian

–probably Julian– had arranged for a private chef to create a five-course meal. We started with two amuse bouches in tiny ceramic dishes, followed by plates of pear and arugula salads. The first main course was seabass in some kind of buttery, lemon and white wine sauce, and the second main course was lamb chops –Grandpa's favourite, served with a bottle of Barolo. For dessert, there were gold-leaf covered tiramisus. We sang happy birthday, and Grandpa blew out his single candle.

I wished Connor were here. He would have loved the tiramisu. I took a quick picture and sent it to him as a text. He texted me back almost immediately, sending me a photo of a fresh bag of coffee beans he'd bought from Marché Fortin. I smiled.

Dinner had gone surprisingly well. Still a little boring, because all Salvati dinners meant talking about the business for at least half of the meal, but I remembered Salvati dinners being more dramatic than this one had been. Grandpa or Uncle Valerian were usually disappointed by something or someone.

We had drinks in the parlour after dinner, and everyone seemed to be in a good mood.

"How long are you in Los Angeles for?" I asked Miranda and Adrian. "Are you guys free for lunch tomorrow?"

"Unfortunately, I have an early flight tomorrow," said Adrian, looking disappointed.

"I'm free for lunch," said Miranda, looking surprised.

I'd never asked them to spend time with me before, and maybe it was a total cliché to say I felt like a new person, but I kind of *did* feel like a new person. I wanted to get to know my siblings better. I didn't want to live in the bitterness of the past and feel cheated of time. For the first time, I just wanted to move forward and be happy.

"I'm here for three more days," smiled Miranda. "This is actually my first time taking a holiday in over a year."

"I'm glad you're taking a full two weeks off," said Uncle Valerian. "You deserve it."

"Thanks. I'm really excited."

"Where are you going after L. A.?"

"Guillaume and I are going to Italy for nine days."

"Who's Guillaume?" I asked.

"Guillaume de Brissac?" Grandpa clarified, pouring himself a glass of bourbon.

"De Brissac, so fancy," said Julian. He shot me a goofy look, and I bit back a laugh.

"Yes, Guillaume de Brissac," said Miranda. "He's my boyfriend. I think you've probably met him a few times when you were younger. We met at boarding school years ago and reconnected recently."

"Good family," said Grandpa approvingly.

"Is that the family who are mostly in banking?" asked Uncle Valerian.

"Yes," Grandpa answered. "You don't remember meeting François de Brissac two years ago when we were in Paris?"

"Two years ago in Paris?" Uncle Valerian seemed to blank, looking at Julian to help him fill the gaps.

"We were at the annual Louvre Gala Dinner..." Julian said.

Uncle Valerian looked at him, still looking confused.

"We had that really magnificent bottle of wine right before..."

"Oh, that's right!" Uncle Valerian turned pink, looking away from Grandpa. "Yes, of course I remember François de Brissac."

Adrian and I both let out a laugh, and Grandpa looked away, apparently choosing to let this one go.

"Anyway, what about you? Are you dating anyone?" Miranda asked me.

"Oh, me?" I said stupidly.

I wished we could have saved this for our lunch tomorrow. I wanted to gush about Connor, but I didn't really want Grandpa and Uncle Valerian listening to me gushing about Connor.

"I am. His name's Connor," I said, feeling my cheeks warm at the thought of him.

I wished I could teleport him into my bedroom tonight. I missed lying next to him at night. I missed the way his hands always knew exactly where to...

"Fitzgerald?" cut in Grandpa, his voice suddenly sharper.

"Yes, Connor Fitzgerald."

"Valerian told me about that," said Grandpa, his voice disapproving.

Shit.

I looked at Uncle Valerian, but he shrugged, like why was that a big deal?

"Who's Connor Fitzgerald?" asked Adrian.

"He's the head architect for our resort development project in Canada," explained Uncle Valerian.

"The one you're interning for?" asked Adrian, raising an eyebrow.

"Yes, but it's not really an internship. And Connor's amazing. I think you'd really like him," I said to Adrian and Miranda.

"Well, I can't wait to meet him one day, then," said Miranda easily.

"Stassi, you can't be serious," said Grandpa. He looked at me with stoney, cold eyes.

The fire crackling behind him in the parlour suddenly looked a lot more ominous now. I had never actually talked about anyone I was dating before, and I'm sure the alarms were going off in his head. So much for a non-dramatic, non-judgemental Salvati dinner.

"I am serious about Connor," I said firmly, feeling my body tense.

I saw Uncle Valerian and Julian exchange a quick look.

"You shouldn't waste your time with someone like that."

"Someone like what?" I asked sharply, readying myself for a fight in case Grandpa said any racist bullshit because Connor was Asian.

"Salvatis don't date...architects," said Grandpa coldly.

"I am an architect," I snapped back.

Grandpa shook his head in distaste. "You're different. You shouldn't be wasting time with someone like that."

"Someone like what? Someone who's incredibly intelligent and kind, and is one of the best people I've ever met?" I felt my anger rising.

"Perhaps this is not the time to discuss something like this," said Uncle Valerian, giving me a pointed look.

Why am *I* getting looks?

"Very well," said Grandpa tightly.

"Fine," I said hotly.

Julian gestured to a maid. Shortly after, someone brought out little plates of macarons and placed them on the tables in front of us.

Miranda gave me a kind smile and gave my hand a quick squeeze before taking a pink macaron.

Grandpa and I didn't speak to each other for the rest of the dinner. We all made it through dinner, though I'm pretty sure my glares burned a hole right through Uncle Valerian and Julian's parlour rugs.

Grandpa, Adrian, and Miranda left shortly after, and it was only then that Julian found me in the guest room.

"Are you okay?" he asked me gently.

"Yes, I just don't know why Grandpa was being such a snob about my dating Connor."

"I didn't realize you felt so strongly about him."

"Well, I do."

"Then I'm happy for you."

"Thanks," I murmured.

Julian gave me a soft smile. "Val only mentioned it to him in passing, and for what it's worth, I think your grandfather just wants to see you do well. He's thrilled that you're excited about your work, and he wants you to take that job in Paris. I think he's just worried that you'll choose Connor over your career."

"That's not what he made it sound like when he was dissing my career as an architect."

"I think the Salvati men have trouble expressing their emotions properly."

"Aren't you a Salvati man?"

"I kept my last name."

"Smart."

I sighed. "Why am I somehow always the problematic one? Isn't it Adrian or Miranda's turn?"

Julian laughed. "You're the most interesting one."

He gave me a wink, and I let out a reluctant laugh, rolling my eyes.

"Get some rest. Don't overthink it. We're all proud of you, Stassi. Me, especially."

I hugged Julian tightly.

# CHAPTER THIRTY-ONE

## Connor

Michael dropped me off at the train station just as the train started boarding.

"Thanks again for driving me."

"Anything for Fleurmont's Romeo Montague," smirked Michael.

I rolled my eyes at him.

"You're back from L.A. on Monday?" asked Michael.

"Back Sunday night."

"Have a good trip."

Construction for *Fleurs de L'Étang* was officially going to start the Monday after I got back from L. A., and I had to be in Fleurmont for the first month of construction at minimum. That is, if I was still going to be working at the Salvati Group by then.

When Stassi left with her uncles, it had all happened so quickly. One second we were laughing together at Le Robinet and talking about going back to the lagoon before the end of

August, and the next, all of her things were gone from the cabin and she was in another country. The whiplash hit hard...but I wanted to be supportive.

The job in Paris was objectively a great opportunity for her, and I wanted to give her the space to be with her family and think through her decision. The last thing I wanted was to try to convince her of anything and have her regret her decision.  Despite that, I could feel us dancing around the subject every time we spoke on the phone, waiting for her to decide whether she was going to move to Paris.

"How was seeing Nya again in person?"

"It was amazing. It was so good to catch up with her and talk."

"Did you guys do anything fun together?"

"We mostly just talked about everything. I told her a lot about you."

"Oh yeah?"

"Yeah...So...did you go to the diner today?"

But then, a couple of nights ago, it hit me. The answer couldn't have been clearer to me. I loved Stassi. I would do anything for her, even if it meant following her to Paris. Even if it meant not working for the Salvati Group anymore and giving up not just this head architect position but the possibility of becoming the next Creative Director.

It seemed counterintuitive, maybe even fucking crazy, but the truth was, I'd never been happier than I'd been the last four months I'd had Stassi in my life.

Being back in Fleurmont reminded me of the person I wanted to be, and more specifically, the kind of person I didn't want to be –Sebastien Fitzgerald. I didn't want to be like my father. I didn't want to be the kind of person who chose work over everything else in life.

I didn't want to give up on my career, either. But I felt more sure of myself now. The imposter syndrome had finally eased up, and working on *Fleurs de L'Étang* was a big part of it. I had led the design of a whole luxury resort. I was proud of the concept I'd come up with, and of every building and every feature I'd worked on.

It would suck not to work on this project. It would suck to have to give up everything I'd been working towards here at the Salvati Group, but I also knew I would figure it out. I could do it again. There would be more projects in the future, other great opportunities. My connection with Stassi was special, and she was worth it, a thousand times over.

Now, I couldn't wait to see her in L.A. and tell her in person.

The train started to move as I dropped my suitcase on the luggage rack before finding my seat.

It was hot and humid on the train, so I took off my jacket and placed it in the overhead compartment. The air conditioning must be broken.

As the train picked up speed, the conductor announced the next station and apologized for the broken AC. I cracked open the window next to me to let the air flow through. I was about to sit down again when my phone started to ring.

"Hey, Connor," came Dad's voice on the other end. "How's it going?"

"Hey, Dad," I said, sitting down in my seat. "Doing alright. I'm on the train on my way back to L.A."

"Oh, already? I thought that wasn't for another couple of days. Well, I'm glad I caught you then. Listen, I wanted to buy your mother a gift while I'm here," he said, and I could hear the sounds of other people in the background. "I'm at this perfume store, and I know what your mother normally wears, but these scents are all weird. Do you think she'd prefer a salted pistachio and leather bloom scent, or a joyful blackcurrant and plum scent?"

"Err..."

"What's a joyful blackcurrant, anyhow?" chuckled Dad. "I supposed they wouldn't want a sorrowful blackcurrant, though, eh? That wouldn't be a top seller."

The next thirty minutes were spent trying to help my dad distinguish between different perfume scents, though I knew absolutely nothing about it. Stassi would probably know exactly what the difference between a salted pistachio and a joyful blackcurrant scent was, and which scent to pick.

I felt guilty while on the phone with Dad, trying to avoid mentioning the fact that Mom had recently been in a pretty bad car accident. He sounded so happy that I debated texting Michael to get him to convince Mom to fess up.

A baby across the aisle from me started to cry, saving me from having to worry about that problem again.

"Sorry, Dad, I think I need to go."

"No problem. I've been keeping you. Alright, I'm going to go for the Coveted Duchess Rose perfume," said Dad.

"Good choice. I'm sure she'll love it."

"Alright, have a safe flight. Let me know when you land."

"I will. Love you, Dad."

"I love you too, son."

As I hung up, the train stopped.

*"Sorry, folks, we're just waiting for another train to pass us. It shouldn't be too long,"* came the conductor's voice over the speakers.

I looked at the time on my phone. I was already going to be cutting it pretty close. The trains going to Montreal only ran twice a day, and I was barely going to have an hour at the airport before my flight took off.

Twenty minutes of not moving later, I wished I had taken the train yesterday and stayed in Montreal overnight instead.

*"Sorry, folks. Little hold up on the tracks, we should be moving shortly. Thank you for your patience."*

Fifteen minutes later, the train finally started to move again. I checked the time on my phone a little obsessively, knowing there wasn't much I could do. My phone rang.

"What is it?" I asked Michael.

"Why do you have a giant purple tree in your living room?"

"That's Maxi's cat –wait, why are you at the cabin?" The thought of Maxi made my insides ache. I missed that furball.

"I'm watching the place for you. Watering your plants, checking the mail, all that good stuff."

"I don't have any plants, and we don't get mail up there. What the hell are you doing up there?"

"Nothing, I was just wondering where you kept –oh, never mind, found it," he said cheerily.

"Found what? Stop touching my stuff and get the fuck out of my apartment."

"Baby brother, relax. Alright, I should go. Have a good flight."

"Wait! Michael!"

The bastard hung up on me. I was about to call him back when I saw my phone had less than 10% battery left.

Fuck.

The train pulled into Montreal forty minutes late, and I rushed to the airport. I was still running hot from being on an overheated train and then running, so I shoved my jacket into my suitcase before checking in my bag. I ran to the security clearance line.

I made it to my gate just as I heard my name being called over the speakers.

"Paging passenger Connor Fitzgerald. Connor Fitzgerald, please come to Gate 73."

I rushed over to the counter, handing over my boarding pass and passport. "My name was called?"

"Yes, Connor Fitzgerald?" said the gate attendant, taking a look at my passport and boarding pass.

I nodded.

"I'm so sorry, but this flight is full. We're going to do our best to put you on the next flight."

Well, so much for trying to make it in time to see Stassi before the Architect Gala.

# Chapter Thirty-Two

## *Connor*

"Connor! You finally made it!" came Dustin's cheerful voice. He clapped me on the back, and I hugged him quickly.

"Hey, good to see you," I said distractedly, glancing around the crowded venue.

I ended up arriving in Los Angeles just barely in time to make it to the Architect Gala. Stassi and her friend Nya were getting ready together before the gala, so we agreed to meet directly at the gala instead. I was itching to see her.

"How've you been? How's it going up in Quebec?" asked Dustin.

"Yeah, it's been great," I said, still looking around.

The Architect Gala was held at a fancy hotel in downtown L.A. We were in the largest venue space, a series of adjacent rooms separated by stained glass doors.

Dustin and I were in the reception area, a carpeted banquet room with round tables covered in long, white tablecloths. Each table had large floral centerpieces, which partially obscured my view of the room. Loud, lively jazz spilled through the space, loud enough that I suspected a live band was playing somewhere in the venue.

The room on our right was the exhibition room. There were architectural art installations that celebrated architectural history in addition to some models of notable buildings that had been constructed over the last year. The room to our left was the dining room for the meal service, far enough away that I couldn't see into it.

I was still waiting for Stassi to appear.

"Have you heard more about who is going to get the Creative Director role?"

I forced myself to stop looking for Stassi and pay attention to Dustin instead. "No, but I'm supposed to meet with Valerian tomorrow to discuss it."

"I think you have a good shot," said Dustin, his voice a little lower as he nodded over to the table across the room.

I looked to where Dustin was looking, and there he was. William Harrison. Dressed in an expensive-looking blue tuxedo, William was holding a glass of wine in one hand and looking straight at me. I met his gaze with an impassive stare of my own. If I was being honest, I didn't care about William Harrison anymore. A few months ago, I would have been pissed about seeing him again, but now? He seemed wildly unimportant and insignificant.

"Rumour has it Salvati wasn't too happy with how he's been handling the project in Arizona."

"How do you know that?"

"I ran into an old friend who works in marketing for the Salvati Group now. She told me Harrison and Salvati have been clashing a lot. They've had a lot of creative differences. Oh, shit, I think he's coming over here."

I looked up again, and sure enough, William Harrison was making his way over to us.

William nodded at Dustin. "Dustin."

"Wiliam."

"Fitzy." He turned his attention to me mockingly. "Good to see you."

"Wish I could say the same." He was unimportant, but I still didn't enjoy having to talk to him.

"Why so bitter? Are you jealous Valerian gave me the head architect position in Arizona?"

"We have the same job," I said blandly.

"Sure, if that makes you feel better. I guess a job in Canada still counts as a job, even if it's in some village no one's heard of."

"Don't you have some overused design concept to recycle and parade around?"

"Shit talk. I'm terrified, Fitzy," said William, feigning shock with a hand to his chest. "Don't worry. When you're older, you'll understand the difference between designing with the Grand Canyon as the backdrop, versus whatever hill you're designing for up in Canada."

I tried to keep my cool as William drained his wine and set his empty glass down on the table. Dustin looked between us uncertainly.

"Things must be headed south for the Salvati Group if they're letting fresh-faced rookies design their resorts. Makes you wonder if they're falling short on their charity pledges for the year, or if Valerian Salvati just likes your pretty face."

Anger rippled through me, and I was about to snap back a retort when someone beat me to it.

"Harrison," came a crisp voice from behind us, and the three of us turned to see Valerian and Julian making their way over to us.

"Oh, shit," muttered Dustin, his eyes widening.

William's face turned a deep shade of red, no doubt understanding that Valerian must have overheard him.

"Fitzgerald," Valerian acknowledged me, and I nodded at him and Julian.

"Valerian, I –" William swallowed.

"I was going to tell you tomorrow, but since we're all here," Valerian interrupted him, that cold, hard look still in his eyes. "I'm letting you go. Fitzgerald is going to be the new Creative Director of the Salvati Group."

I looked at Valerian in surprise.

William sputtered, his face turning an even deeper shade of red. He seemed lost for words, and I took a moment to revel in this. I was still willing to walk away from this, for Stassi, but I had to admit it felt pretty damn good to watch Valerian Salvati put this bastard in his place. I resisted the urge to look at Dustin to see his facial expression.

"I –very well," said William coolly, and to my surprise, he didn't argue or say anything else. "Good luck, Fitzgerald."

William walked away, and Valerian waited until William had disappeared into the exhibition room before he turned to me again.

"Congratulations," he said to me with a small smile, the corner of his lips just barely upturned. "We can go through the details in our meeting tomorrow."

"Thank you," I said, stunned.

"It's well deserved," said Valerian matter-of-factly.

"Congratulations," said Julian, and I smiled back at him.

Valerian's attention drifted away from me just then, spotting Mara Moretti, another architect.

"Excuse me, Fitzgerald, I should say hi to Mara," he said, stepping aside. "We'll talk more tomorrow."

"Of course, thank you. See you later."

"See you soon," said Julian.

I watched them make their way to Mara Moretti, and then I turned to see the look of disbelief on Dustin's face.

"Holy shit," Dustin whispered to me.

I nodded at him and was about to say something else when someone said my name again.

"Fitzgerald."

Dustin and I turned to see Anton Salvati standing close to us.

"Mr. Salvati."

"Will you excuse us for a moment? I need to speak with Fitzgerald," Anton said to Dustin.

"Yes, of course. See you later," Dustin said to me.

I nodded to him.

"It's good to see you, Mr. Salvati."

Anton Salvati put his drink on the small table between us as Dustin walked away. I could see his expensive leather and gold watch poking out from the sleeve of his suit. Both his beard and facial expression were as severe as ever.

"Valerian has been keeping me informed about the project in Fleurmont. He's impressed with your work."

"Thank you. It's been an incredible experience so far."

"I understand construction is starting on Monday?"

"Yes. Everything is on track so far."

"Good." He paused for a moment, taking a sip of his drink and looking into the crowd around us. "I also heard you found a way to get through to my granddaughter."

I swallowed. Stassi and I had been texting and talking enough for me to know that he wasn't our biggest fan.

"Stassi deserves every credit for her work. She's an excellent designer."

"Hmm."

Anton Salvati took another long pause, and I took a sip of my drink.

Finally, he spoke again. "I know you've been waiting to hear from my son about the Creative Director position."

"I actually just ran into Valerian –"

"Well, I'm prepared to offer you an even better job. How would you feel about being Vice President of Design and Development for the Salvati Group?"

Vice President of Design and Development? I looked at him in surprise, and he looked back at me with unblinking eyes.

"That sounds incredible," I said slowly.

I waited for the catch. Judging from the look on Anton's face, there was definitely a catch.

"It would be a role based in East Asia. We have an office in Singapore, and I know you've done a project there. You would oversee the architectural vision and engineering execution for large-scale commercial and residential developments."

"That sounds like a great opportunity."

"Of course," continued Anton, "the work is limited to work in East Asia, so it would make sense for you to move there. We would pay for your expenses and, of course, pay for an apartment for you in Singapore."

Anton took a sip of his drink.

"Does Valerian know about this? He seemed to think…"

"My son will be on board with whatever I suggest. It's the best move for the company, and the job is yours. If you agree to stay away from Stassi starting today."

And there it was –the catch. Here I thought this kind of thing only happened in movies. Anton Salvati looked at me, stone-faced and as serious as a heart attack.

"Are you asking me to break up with Stassi?" I asked in disbelief.

"Stassi is young and impulsive. She doesn't need distractions right now when she's finally focused on her career."

"I care a lot about Stassi. I want to see her do well, and to see her achieve her full potential as an architect –"

"Good. Then you will stay away from her, and you will be the new Vice President of Design and Development for the Salvati Group in East Asia."

"Respectfully, I'm not breaking up with your granddaughter."

A look of irritation flashed across Anton's face. "Don't be a fool. I know what I'm offering you is an opportunity of a lifetime. Don't throw your career away for a woman."

"She's not just any woman to me."

I was in love with Stassi, not that I was about to say that out loud for the first time to her grandfather, who hated me.

"I'll say this just once," said Anton, his voice low. "You are not good enough to be with someone like my granddaughter. You may be a talented architect, but there are a lot of talented architects. You are not worthy of being with a Salvati."

Anton finished his drink, setting it down harshly on the table, the remaining ice cubes clanging noisily against the sides of the glass.

"Think about it and let me know. Otherwise, I'll assume you're no longer interested in a career at the Salvati Group at all."

He walked away from me, and I was left standing there, trying to process what had just happened.

Anton Salvati had just threatened to have me fired if I didn't break up with Stassi.

Well, fuck that. I wasn't going to break up with her. I had made my decision before speaking with either Valerian or Anton, and I wasn't about to change my mind now. Stassi was more important to me than that, and if I had to start over somewhere else for her, I would.

It wasn't even a question at this point.

# CHAPTER THIRTY-THREE

## *Stassi*

"The job is yours if you agree to stay away from Stassi starting today," came Grandpa's voice.

"Are you asking me to break up with Stassi?" said Connor.

I stopped just behind a group of people when I heard them talking. Nya and I had just finished touring the exhibition room, and I'd been eager to find Connor.

Nya left me to find Connor, telling me she'd meet me back in the dining room for dinner, and I watched her walk away in her bright yellow dress. Her dress was made from a kitenge fabric, a combination of floral and geometric shapes that zigzagged in bright blues, oranges, and traces of green. I loved how much she celebrated her culture in her personal style.

After watching Nya walk into the adjacent room, I'd walked right into the reception area, past groups of people in tuxedos and ball gowns. I heard my name and stopped before they could see me.

"Stassi is young and impulsive. She doesn't need distractions right now when she's finally focused on her career."

Rage fueled me as I tried to stay calm.

"I care a lot about Stassi. I want to see her do well, and to see her achieve her full potential as an architect –"

"Good. Then you will stay away from her, and you will be the new Vice President of Design and Development for the Salvati Group in East Asia."

"Respectfully, I'm not breaking up with your granddaughter."

I held my breath as I waited for my grandfather's reply.

"Don't be a fool. I know what I'm offering you is an opportunity of a lifetime. Don't throw your career away for a woman."

"She's not just any woman to me."

"I'll say this just once. You are not good enough to be with someone like my granddaughter. You may be a talented architect, but there are a lot of talented architects. You are not worthy of being with a Salvati. Think about it and let me know. Otherwise, I'll assume you're no longer interested in a career at the Salvati Group at all."

I watched Grandpa walk away from Connor. His steps were slow, unrushed, his suit dark and severe around him, and I don't think I've ever been angrier with him in my entire life.

Jazz music continued to play, almost disconcertingly upbeat around us as I rushed over to Connor. He saw me, and a look of surprise flashed across his face before his eyes swept over the dress I was wearing. I could barely register how handsome he looked in his suit before I threw my arms around him.

"Stassi –"

I kissed him on the mouth.

"I love you," I rushed out.

Connor's eyes softened. "I love you, too."

His fingers touched the side of my face softly, and he looked at me with so much tenderness in his eyes. "I wanted to be the first to tell you that. I should have told you I loved you sooner. I think I fell in love with you the day we were up in the wildflower fields."

"When we were waiting for sunset?" I murmured.

Connor nodded, and he put his arms around my waist. "Listen, I don't know how much you heard –"

"Enough," I seethed. "I'm so sorry he talked to you like that. That's so fucked up. I'm going to talk to him right now. I just wanted to see you first."

"It's alright," said Connor, shaking his head. "Really."

"It's not alright. I can't believe he said that to you. The *nerve* –" I could feel my anger rising again.

"Stassi, Stassi, wait. I mean it. It doesn't matter. That's what I wanted to tell you, too. I don't care about the Creative Director position, or the Vice President position, or whatever other position. I care about you. I love you, and I'll go wherever you go. I meant what I said a few months ago. I am all in, so if you want to take that job in Paris, you should. Don't let us –assuming you want there to be an us–"

"Of course I do," I couldn't help but interject.

"Then you should take the job in Paris if that's what you want. Don't let us be a factor, because I will go wherever you go."

"But what about everything you've worked for?"

"You're more important," he shrugged almost matter-of-factly. "I think I've finally worked long enough now to know my worth and to know what I value. And what I care the most about is you, Stassi. I know it's only been, what? Four months of us knowing each other, but..." Hazel green eyes burned into mine.

"It feels like longer," I finished for him, because that's exactly what I'd been thinking and grappling with over the last few weeks.

He nodded.

I took a deep breath as Connor and I laced our hands together. "It means so much to me that you're saying all this, but...I'm not taking the job in Paris."

Connor looked at me in surprise.

"I've thought about it a lot over the last month. I don't want to just take a job in Paris because that's what people want me to do. It took me so long to figure out how to really feel like myself again. I finally feel like myself again, and...I want to be happy. I want to feel excited and inspired, and I've never been happier than when we were up in Fleurmont with Maxi obsessing over designs together. I want our life together, even if everyone else thinks it's too soon after just four months of being together. I want to keep designing for *Fleurs de L'Étang,* and see that project through until it opens. And if we can work together on the project in Colorado, I want that, too."

"Are you sure? You could have equally if not more exciting projects in Paris."

"I want to work with you. I have *fun* working with you."

"I don't know if you heard, but there's a good chance I get fired after today."

I snorted at my grandfather's ridiculousness. "Then we'll start our own architecture firm together. We'll go rogue."

Connor grinned at me, a huge smile on his face. "Are you one hundred percent sure about this?"

"Yes, silly!" I laughed, and I kissed him again.

Connor put his arms around me, pulling me in at the waist. He kissed me back, and I wanted to melt into his kiss. I forced myself to pull away from him.

"I love you," I said to him again. "And there's something I need to do right now."

Connor must have noticed the fire burning in my eyes because he took my hand.

"Let me come with you," he said.

I shook my head. "No, I need to do this myself. I'll be right back."

Connor nodded, letting me go, and I marched out of the reception hall to look for my grandfather.

I found Grandpa closer to the entrance of the venue. He was talking to Uncle Valerian, who raised an eyebrow when I came marching towards them. It was good that they weren't with anyone else, because I could barely contain my anger. Grandpa looked at me warily as I approached them. He set his drink down on a tray with a passing waiter, sighing.

"Grandpa, I need to talk to you," I fumed.

"Hello to you too," said Uncle Valerian.

"I need to talk to Grandpa now."

"Stassi, if this is about Fitzgerald –"

"You mean when I overheard you *bribing* Connor to break up with me?"

Uncle Valerian groaned. "Oh, come on, Dad. Are you serious right now?"

"This has nothing to do with you. Stay out of it," snapped Grandpa.

"You offered to send Connor off to East Asia!"

"Will you keep your voice down, Stassi?" Grandpa glared at me.

Another server that was passing by with a platter full of hors d'oeuvres heard us, carefully U-turning back around to avoid us.

Uncle Valerian looked at Grandpa in disbelief. "I think it is my business if you're going around manipulating my employees."

"Oh, for fuck's sake –"

"He offered him a Vice President of Design and Development role based in Singapore," I told Uncle Valerian.

Uncle Valerian made a sound that sounded somewhere between a snort and a scoff.

"Stassi, this is hardly the time or the place to discuss something like this," said Grandpa angrily, his voice low, and I saw the angry tick of his jaw.

Well, too fucking bad.

"Vice President of…that's not even a real –what the hell were you thinking?"

Grandpa glared at Uncle Valerian before turning to me again. "I know you're angry right now, but it's for your own good. You're twenty-four years old. You don't need to be bogged down by a relationship or be making life decisions around a relationship."

"And you would say that no matter who I was dating?" I challenged. "You're not just saying this because I'm dating *someone like him?*"

"Yes," said Grandpa firmly, unwaveringly.

"Well, it doesn't matter, because I've decided not to take the job in Paris. I'm going back to Fleurmont with Connor."

Grandpa's nostrils flared. "You will do no such thing. Why would you not take the job in Paris?"

"You were the one who sent me to Fleurmont in the first place. I'm not just some puppet you can throw around wherever you want. I like the work that I've been doing in Fleurmont. I'm proud of the work I've been doing in Fleurmont."

"You're just saying that because you want to be with that - that -"

"No, I'm not! I'm doing this for myself. This is what I want."

"Stassi, don't be ridiculous. I refuse to let you get derailed yet again –"

"Connor is the one who helped me get unblocked. I couldn't design anything for months, and he helped me. Not only that, but he's someone I love, and you just treated him like crap."

"You are as stubborn as your father was," snapped Grandpa. "And just like him, you'll be making a huge mistake if you go through with this."

I looked at Grandpa in shock.

It was the first time he had ever compared me to my dad. It was the first time anyone had ever compared me to my dad...My dad, who had fallen in love with an English teacher and gotten married young...My dad, who ended up caring for Sylvia for most of his adult life. Is that what this is about? He was worried I would end up like my father?

"Ladies and gentlemen, if you will now join us in the dining area," came a voice over the crowds. "Professor Fournier from MIT will now give the Opening Remarks."

"We should go," said Uncle Valerian.

"I'm not changing my mind," I said to Grandpa. "I hope you can respect my decision."

I didn't want to work in Paris. I knew that for sure now. If I couldn't work with Connor in Fleurmont or in Colorado, then I'd rather apply to be an architect somewhere else. I could build a career at another firm, and who knows? Maybe Connor and I really could start an architecture firm together. Or maybe one day I could have my own firm, or build a name for myself and work freelance.

The future was uncertain, full of unknowns, but for the first time in a long time, I felt hopeful about the future. For the first time in a long time, I was letting myself truly be happy.

Connor and I made it through the gala dinner before we headed back to Connor's hotel room. Connor and Nya finally met, and we had fun, exchanging stories while I ignored the looks coming from the table two down from us where the rest of my family was. I didn't need to look to know how stoney Grandpa's expression must have been.

By the time the next round of speeches came around, Connor and I said goodbye to Nya and slipped out the door.

Connor had already ended the lease of his former L.A. apartment and was staying at the same hotel where the gala was being held, so it didn't take us long to reach his room on the fifth floor. I felt giddy with anticipation. We hadn't slept next to each other in so many nights. I hadn't touched him the way I wanted to in so long.

Connor tapped his key card against the door, and I pushed the door open, stepping inside.

Connor's things were all over the hotel room –his laptop, that knit sweater he always wore, his blue jacket... I smiled at the two empty coffee cups on the desk.

Connor came in behind me, and I shut the door behind him, locking it quickly.

"So eager," Connor murmured, his breath hot against the shell of my ear. He wrapped his arms around my waist as he leaned in to kiss my neck.

I shivered.

"Help me get out of my dress?" I asked him innocently.

"Still such a fucking tease."

Connor unhooked the back of my long red dress. Slowly, I felt him unzipping it. His knuckle grazed along my spine.

"You look fucking beautiful in this. Have I told you that yet?"

Kisses trailed along my back. Connor's warm hands came around me, smoothing the fabric over my stomach. Heat followed where he touched me, and then his hands glided down towards my thighs as he wrapped his body around me.

I shook my head no as I turned my head to look back at him. His lips found mine, and he kissed me softly, his hands still roaming over my body, over my dress.

"I don't think I was prepared for how beautiful you looked tonight. How beautiful you look right now."

I turned towards him fully, letting my dress fall to the floor in a twist of crimson fabric.

Connor took a step back to look at me, a hungry look in his eyes. I stepped out of my dress, careful not to catch the long heel of my shoe on the dress.

"Alright, that's it," said Connor. He took off his tuxedo and tossed it to the side before stepping back towards me. In a single motion, he lifted me up into his arms.

"Connor!" I squealed, grabbing on to his neck as he carried me towards the bed.

"I love it when you say my name like that," he growled, kicking off his shoes.

Still carrying me with one hand, he carefully took off each of my heels. He set each shoe down carefully on the nightstand next to the bed.

Connor tossed me onto the bed, and before I could say anything else, he was between my legs, ripping my panties apart. I *loved* it when he did that.

I moaned at the sudden feel of his mouth sucking on my clit.

I ran my fingers through his hair as he continued to suck on me, and then his tongue was deep inside of me. I moaned, closing my eyes, letting the sensation spread out over my entire body.

"You taste so fucking good."

I moaned, savouring the sensation.

Connor came up to me, and my eyes flew open as he kissed me roughly. His tongue swept in, and I tasted myself on him. I put my hands against his chest, trying to breathe, but Connor didn't stop. He gripped my breasts in his hands, flicking my nipples with his thumbs as he leaned down and kissed my neck.

"Oh, fuck," I rasped.

I let out a string of expletives as Connor pushed my legs open and thrust into me. I screamed his name as he pounded into me, hard and fast.

My hands flew up to the headboard, trying to grip onto anything as Connor rammed his cock into me. The headboard was all smooth fabric, so I gripped Connor's arms instead.

"I missed this," he growled, pressing his weight further into me.

I felt every inch of him inside of me. Connor put his thumb over my clit, rubbing circles. He knew my body too well, and it brought me over the edge.

My vision blurred as I came for the first time that night. I savoured every second of release as I closed my eyes, panting even as I wanted to keep going. Connor slowed his thrusts, leaning down to kiss me tenderly before he pulled out. My eyes fluttered open, and I leaned in to kiss him back. I looked at his still-hard cock.

"Let me touch you," I panted, reaching for him, but he leaned away just out of reach. He flashed me a grin, leaning back against the headboard.

"Now who's being a tease," I laughed breathlessly, and I turned around, getting on my hands and knees before crawling over to him.

His eyes heated as he watched me, stroking my arm as I climbed on top of him.

I sat down on his cock, feeling myself squeeze around him. Connor grunted, his eyes glazing over a little, and I put my hands on his shoulders to steady myself as I rode him.

"You look so pretty when you're bouncing on my cock," he murmured, and he cupped my breasts in his hands as they bounced for him.

My thighs were drenched. I could hear the wet sounds of our bodies coming together as I continued to ride his cock.

Connor groaned, and I could tell that he was close. I could see it in those dark, intense eyes of his.

"I missed this." I leaned in and kissed him, licking his tongue.

Connor gripped my ass as he came. He groaned, his breath hot on my neck, and I breathed in his earthy, pine-like smell.

We caught our breaths together, holding on to each other, and I sank back into his arms. Connor pulled me close.

"I love you," I whispered to him.

"I love you, too."

Connor held me in his arms. He kissed me and drew circles on my back. I fell asleep with the feel of him wrapped around me.

# CHAPTER THIRTY-FOUR

## *Connor*

The next morning, Stassi and I woke up together later than we planned. In a rush, she headed out to meet Nya, and I headed out to meet Dustin. We hadn't really been able to catch up during the gala, so we met at his favourite local restaurant, and we caught up, talking over steak and potatoes just like we used to when we were still working together.

After lunch with Dustin, I headed to Valerian's home office, not too sure what to expect.

"Take a seat," said Valerian. He gestured to the armchair in his office.

I took a seat, and he took the seat opposite me.

"So, I heard about the drama with my father last night," said Valerian with a wry smile. He let out a loud exhale. "I apologize on behalf of my family."

"It's alright."

I genuinely liked Valerian Salvati. He was a hardass when it came to work, but he was a good man, and someone I'd come to really respect.

"I spoke with him again, and I'm sure I'll need to speak with him again about this, but for now, ignore him." Valerian sighed. "He's an old bastard who likes to control everything. Believe it or not, I think he has his reasons, which have nothing to do with you. He doesn't like feeling out of control, and well, Stassi is Stassi. In the best way of course, but it will be a while until they figure it out."

I nodded slowly. "I see."

"Anyway, I meant what I said yesterday. Putting my father's...issues aside, I want you to be the Creative Director for the Salvati Group, so...congratulations, Fitzgerald."

"Thank you," I said, surprised I wasn't getting fired.

I took the hand he held out to me and shook it. Valerian grinned, his mood shifting a little, his body loosening just a little.

"It's well-deserved. I've been very impressed with your work over the last four months. The whole team has given me really positive feedback, and I know you're the right person for this job."

Valerian sat back down and handed me a stack of papers.

"Here is your official contract. Take some time to look it over. If you accept, I'll announce it at the next company meeting."

I picked up the thick stack of papers, flipping through it.

"I'll be in Fleurmont next month," continued Valerian. "I want to spend some time workshopping with you the creative direction and vision for the brand. And then, of course, I want you to lead the design work on the Colorado project."

"And Arizona?"

"Another architect will take over the project in Arizona. Starting next week, assuming you take up my offer, that architect will report to you, so I expect you to be overseeing the Arizona project to some extent as well."

"And is the plan still for the Salvati Group's real estate projects to be global instead of regional by continent?" I asked, unsure if any of what Anton had said the previous night was true.

"Exactly. I've been speaking with all of our global CEOs on the direction of real estate projects, and we've agreed to turn it global. This is still confidential, but we're restructuring, and I'll be the CEO of all the Salvati Group's real estate development projects. It will be global, and I'll be letting go of my role in the energy space, and that's going to the current CEO in East Asia. You can ignore whatever bullshit my father spun up yesterday about a role in East Asia," Valerian added.

"I see. And just to be clear, you don't care that I have no intention of breaking up with Stassi?"

"No, that is your business and Stassi's business, as far as I'm concerned. You are a talented individual, and I'm not wrong about people. You are the right person for this job."

"What about Stassi? Can she stay on the Fleurmont project?"

Valerian nodded. "Yes. I don't think she should report to you anymore, at least not officially, but it doesn't mean the two of you can't work together. We can figure out the details later."

I let Valerian's words sink in for a moment. This was it. Part of me couldn't believe this was real. I'd been so prepared to let this go, and somehow, everything had fallen into place. This was what I'd been working towards, only it was even better than I could have imagined. Infinitely better.

"So, are you in?" asked Valerian.

I didn't hesitate to answer him.

# CHAPTER THIRTY-FIVE

## Stassi

I finally enjoyed the authentic winter experience of Fleurmont in January, about five months after the Architect Gala. Connor and Maxi and I had gone back to Fleurmont for the first month of construction. Uncle Valerian and Julian had made it out again as well so that Uncle Valerian and Connor could brainstorm the next phase of the Salvati Group's real estate endeavours. Uncle Valerian was also officially my boss now, which kind of worked out perfectly. We spoke more and bickered more, and Connor and I took turns complaining about him but also secretly admiring him.

In October, Connor and Maxi and I moved out to Colorado. We stayed there for the next three months while we worked on the concept and initial designs, going back to Los Angeles only for Christmas.

Grandpa had not entirely come around to the idea of me and Connor, but we were getting there slowly. Very slowly. Through some talking, Uncle Valerian and Julian and I concluded that maybe Grandpa really was just…afraid. He was afraid that he would lose me the way he lost my dad. As irrational as it was, as different as our situations were, I felt a little less angry with him knowing that.

At Christmas, Grandpa seemed relieved that I was still doing design work, and that it was going well. And it really was.

Colorado was so different from Fleurmont, and with Connor leading so many of the Salvati Group's projects and taking on a whole new role, I'd taken on an even bigger design role for Colorado.

Now, we were back in Fleurmont for the winter months, both for Connor's birthday, but also to stay long enough to celebrate Lunar New Year with his family.

"Hot chocolate?" Connor offered me as Maxi hopped onto my lap, cold but determined to be with the rest of the family. He snuggled up against me, curling up into the soft blanket on my lap.

We were sitting on our lounge chairs in the backyard, and Connor had placed a metal fire pit right in the centre of the backyard. He'd placed large logs of wood in the pit, gathering twigs from around the cabin to create kindling before lighting it up. The fire crackled between us now in the semi-darkness. I loved the smell of campfire. Other than the smell of pine, it was probably one of my favourite smells in the world.

"Thanks," I smiled at Connor, taking the mug of hot chocolate from him.

I laughed when I saw that he had picked out a mug with a moose print.

"I wanted you to have the full Canadian experience," he teased.

"Where's the maple syrup then?" I asked. I took a sip of the hot chocolate and shivered with pleasure when I tasted sweet, molten chocolate on my tongue.

Connor took out a can of maple syrup from his jacket and set it on the empty lounge chair.

"There, maple syrup can keep us company now," he said.

I laughed.

"Tomorrow, we can go to the Charbonneau's farm for a real sugar shack meal, but today, I thought we could roast some marshmallows."

"Ooh, yes! I want to roast a marshmallow," I said, sitting up straighter in my seat, so excited I almost spilled hot chocolate everywhere.

Maxi chirruped at me in surprise, hopping out of my lap and looking up expectantly at Connor.

"Alright, buddy, here you go," Connor folded another soft blanket he had brought out and placed it on the empty lounge chair. He created a makeshift cat bed, set the maple syrup on the floor, and lifted Maxi into his new bed.

Maxi purred loudly in satisfaction, making biscuits into his new hangout spot.

I pulled Connor closer to me so that we could sit next to each other. He kissed me quickly.

"Mmm," he said, tasting the chocolate on my lips.

I kissed him deeper, and when we pulled away, identical clouds of breath puffed out into the night sky.

It was truly beautiful here in Quebec. Every branch was covered in a thick blanket of snow, and up here on the mountain, the night sky was so clear, so blue. We could see so many stars from here in the backyard we didn't even need a stargazing lodge. I loved watching my breath travel and dissipate around us. Where the firelight and the light from the cabin hit the snow, the snow glittered like fairy dust. It was almost as mesmerisingly beautiful as the wildflower fields. Almost.

"Here you go," said Connor, handing me one of the long sticks we had carefully picked out together on our walk earlier. He handed me a bag of large marshmallows, and I smiled, excitedly stabbing my stick into a squishy marshmallow.

"I'm so excited!" I squealed, setting my mug down on the ground. "I'm going to make the best roasted marshmallow you've ever seen."

Connor laughed, stabbing his own marshmallow with his stick and holding it out over the fire.

"Why do people complain about winters here? It's so beautiful," I murmured, looking back out at the glittering snow piled high next to the cabin window.

Maybe Connor and I could build a snowcat tomorrow.

"In people's defense, we've only been here for two weeks. Tell me if you're still this excited about winter two months from now."

I smiled, turning to look back at my marshmallow just in time to see it catch fire.

I let out a shriek, and Connor laughed. He took my marshmallow stick from me and blew it out.

"Oh, no!" I cried, looking at the black lump that was formerly my perfect marshmallow.

"Have mine," said Connor, handing me his marshmallow stick.

Of course, his marshmallow was roasted to perfection. The marshmallow was puffed up and a perfect, golden brown with crispy, toasty, caramelized edges.

I pouted, but then couldn't resist. I took the marshmallow stick from Connor.

"Is it going to be really hot?" I asked, bringing it closer to my mouth.

Connor touched the edge of the marshmallow.

"Maybe. Be careful around the middle."

I popped the marshmallow into my mouth, gently taking it off of the stick...and then I moaned. The center was all soft and gooey and sweet.

"The inside of this marshmallow is how I feel about you," I said to him, my mouth still full, moaning again.

"You mean you like taking me in your mouth?"

I laughed, nodding. "That too."

I handed Connor back his marshmallow stick. "Okay, I want to try again."

Connor handed me another marshmallow. We sat out in the backyard roasting marshmallows. We sat outside until I had roasted three perfect marshmallows. Then we stayed there, wrapped in a single blanket under the stars, listening to the sound of crackling fire.

I'd never felt more at home.

# Epilogue: Stassi



"Do you think we should get Maxi a sibling?" I asked Connor, not for the first time.

We were at *Fleurs de L'Étang*, and finally, finally, after almost two years of construction, the resort was opening for the first time this weekend for its soft opening.

Friends and family from Fleurmont and the Salvati Group alike would be gathered here over the weekend to experience *Fleurs de L'Étang* for the first time.

Everything was exactly as I had imagined it would look. It had all come together so beautifully.

Connor and I had spent the last year and a half travelling all over the world. We mainly split our time between Fleurmont, Los Angeles, and Colorado for different design projects, but we had also made the time to travel to Kenya and to Taiwan.

In Kenya, we stayed with Nya and I showed Connor the jacaranda trees I loved so much. In Taiwan, we made it a point to take the same elevator we had met in.

Every time we came back to *Fleurs de L'Étang,* it was like watching a kitten or a baby grow –so much changed so drastically between visits even just weeks or months apart, and now suddenly, everything was ready.

It was May 1st, exactly two years since the day I had first arrived in Fleurmont.

Connor and I were staying at the cabin we had stayed at –Uncle Valerian had let us keep it, and it was Maxi's favourite place to stay by far. He still had his jacaranda cat tree in the living room of the cabin, and that's where he was curled up as Connor and I completed our walkthrough of the resort grounds.

"Human sibling or cat sibling?" Connor grinned, giving me a sly look.

I blushed. "Cat sibling."

We had talked about *that* too. The idea of a smaller, tinier version of Connor sounded extremely appealing to me, but eventually. Not right away, and not right now.

In fact, I was still impatiently waiting for a certain other thing to happen first. Like a massive diamond ring, perhaps? My nails have been perfectly manicured for six months straight. I was so convinced it was going to happen in Taipei when we were in *the* elevator we had met in and the elevator stopped. But then, ten seconds later we were moving again, and it didn't happen.

"It might be easier if we didn't travel so much. I think we got really lucky with Maxi being such a good traveller."

"He is a good boy," I agreed.

Dozens of trips and only one vomiting incident -and that was because he had a hairball.

"Besides, I think he kind of likes being an only child for now."

"That's true," I agreed.

Connor smiled as we reached our final destination, and I looked up in surprise.

"Wow, the swamp!" I said excitedly.

I hadn't been to the swamp in over a year. We drove by it on our way to the cabin, but I was always too distracted by the beautiful welcome lodge and the Panorama Express ride that systematically looped around the east side of the mountains.

The swamp was beautiful now. The water was clear and blue, surrounded by beautiful willow trees and flowers. There were little art installations in the pond, and they glowed with strings of LED lights.

The pond sat at the edge of the mountain, and between the willow trees, you could see the mountains in the distance that hugged all around Fleurmont.

It was golden hour, and everything glowed an orangey yellow light.

"You know it's a pond, right?" Connor clarified as we walked along the little stone path towards the wooden bridge at the center of the swamp pond.

"I know, I know. It's more of a nickname, because I will never forget how *horrified* I felt when I first saw it. And also because this is where I found Maxi," I said affectionately, smiling as we stepped onto the wooden bridge.

I looked towards the bushes where Maxi had first emerged. They were still there, exactly as before. I'm glad they had kept most of the natural landscaping.

I loved this place now. It was hard to imagine why I had hated the idea of coming here two years ago.

"So what do you think of how it turned out?" asked Connor, his arms coming around from behind me as we leaned against the railing of the bridge, now looking out into the mountains in the distance.

"I love it. You know, I really thought the spa or the stables would be my favourite since I was the brilliant person who came up with it all, but there's something really special about this place."

I whipped around suddenly as an idea came to me. I tried to turn around to face Connor with some difficulty, his arms still around me.

"Oh! You know what this place would be great for?"

"What?" he smiled, giving me a quick kiss on my nose, opening his arms wide enough for me to turn around but still keeping me caged in.

"A *proposal*," I huffed emphatically. "I mean, not to totally do the work for you, but this would be such a great place for a proposal. I mean, you've got everything. There are the mountains and the water and the flowers. There's even a bridge that looks like it came straight out of a fairytale, and –oh my God, are you ever going to ask me to marry you?"

Connor burst out laughing, shaking his head.

"Oh my God, Stassi," he said, letting me go.

"Connor! It's not funny!" I huffed again, crossing my arms over my chest irritably.

"Stassi, turn around," said Connor, putting his hands on my shoulders to get me to face the view of the mountains.

"Connor, I'm serious –"

"Stassi, please just turn around. Turn around," he said, his voice quieter now, and then I turned.

I turned, looking down at the pond at first, not seeing anything out of the ordinary.

But then I looked up.

I looked up, and my breath caught in my lungs.

The lights from the art installations had been turned off.

Instead, there was a string of lights hanging against a massive tree, and it spelled out the words 'Stassi, will you marry me?'

I gasped, turning around to face Connor, only I had to look down because Connor was now on one knee, a glittering diamond ring in his hand.

"Oh, my God." I clapped my hands over my mouth.

I felt my heart pounding like a drum in my chest.

"I love you, Stassi," said Connor, the ghost of his laugh from earlier still in his eyes, but his voice was almost gruff. "You have completely changed my life. From the moment I first saw you, I knew you would be different. And from the moment you entered my life, you have made my life all the more exciting and chaotic and amazing. And even though it's so damn hard to surprise you, it also would not be you if you had not just demanded that I propose to you right before I proposed to you."

I let out a watery laugh, suddenly feeling overwhelmed with emotion.

"I wouldn't have it any other way. I love you, every part of you. You have brought so much love and happiness to me in my life, and if you'll let me, I want to spend the rest of my life trying to make you feel as happy and loved as I feel with you. So...Stassi Salvati, will you marry me?"

Connor swallowed, blinking up at me nervously, like he was afraid the answer could be anything but what it's been since the moment we first kissed. Like I could possibly not be madly in love with this man who was my rock, my best friend, my partner in everything that life had to throw our way.

"Yes, yes, of course I'll marry you," I said. I leaned down and kissed him passionately, throwing my arms around his neck, feeling tears escape from my eyes.

Connor kissed me back, his lips warm against mine.

"Wait, wait...here," he said, pulling back to take my hand.

"Oh, that's right," I giggled, holding out my left hand.

Connor laughed too, his dark hazel eyes swimming with mirrored emotion as he slipped the ring onto my finger.

It fit perfectly.

"It's so beautiful," I whispered, watching it glitter in the waning orange sunlight.

"You promise you like it? Because if not –"

"It's *perfect*."

Connor kissed me again, and in that moment, everything really was perfect.

# Bonus Chapter




Read the first chapter of *Almost Mine,* the next book in the
Fleurmont series!

# Chapter 1

ARDEN

The canvases were heavy. With some difficulty, I dragged it over to the display area. The foam corner protectors squeaked against the wood floor, and I cringed, stopping to make sure I wasn't damaging the pieces.

The glassine paper was still perfectly in place. The paintings were semi-abstract pieces, loosely inspired by different Montreal neighbourhoods. They were painted with acrylic, but the epoxy resin gave each piece a high-gloss finish, making the colours pop.

"Hello, hello!"

I turned to see Layla, Bizarre's store manager, entering the store, taking off her sunglasses and tucking them into the front of her shirt.

"Good morning!"

"Ooh, the canvases are here."

"Yeah, Seynabou just dropped them off here last night," I smiled.

"Need a hand?" offered Layla.

"Yes, please."

"Oh, my God," grunted Layla as we lifted the canvases together. "Whoever buys these will need wall anchors for sure."

Layla and I hung up the pieces as customers started to come in. July was the middle of tourist season in Montreal, and we usually had customers coming in from the moment the store opened.

"*Bonjour!*" I called out cheerfully to a group of women coming in.

They smiled politely back at us as they browsed the store. Bizarre was an artisanal goods store that mostly carried lifestyle goods from local artisans across Quebec. Located in the Mile End in Montreal, most of the artisans whose products we featured were from Montreal.

"That looks amazing," said Layla, taking a step back to admire our exhibition corner. "Best Local Artist Spotlight ever. This is going on our social media immediately."

"The loveseat is kind of perfect for it, too," I said, admiring the space.

We had a blue loveseat in the small gallery space, which often drew people in. Seynabou Torou's art was mostly a vibrant electric blue, and it complemented the blue loveseat perfectly. Layla and I both snapped pictures on our phones, and I sent mine directly to Seynabou, knowing she'd appreciate it.

My phone rang just as I sent off the text, and I quickly stepped into the staircase leading to the basement to take the call.

"Hey, hey!" came Dom's singsong voice over the phone.

"Hi! What's up?"

"I just wanted to check to see if you were coming tonight," said Dom, and I could hear the wheels of his swivel chair rolling across the wood floor of his apartment.

"Coming to what?" I asked blankly.

"The event at Luxe? Drag show and mai tais?"

"Oh, that's right," I said, even though I had completely forgotten.

Luxe was a popular gay club in the Village, and one of Dom's favourite spots. When Dom and I used to bartend together, it was the number one place we would hit up.

"I think I'll pass tonight, but you guys have fun," I said.

"What? No, come with us! Come on, we can dance all our troubles away. It'll be great."

"I don't know...I'm kind of tired. I was up pretty early today." Besides, my apartment's big cozy armchair was calling my name.

"But you have to come out!" whined Dom. "I got tickets for all six of us."

"I...will think about it," I said, and looked at my phone to check the time. "Ooh, okay, I have to go. I'll talk to you soon?"

"Where are you going? I thought you were at work."

"I am, but it's Donut Day, so I need to go buy donuts for the team."

"Oh, my God, what a good boss," teased Dom. "Can I come by and get one?"

"Uh, no. Donut Day is for Bizarre employees only," I smiled.

"Don't I count as an honorary former employee? Former Catoux bartenders have to count, right?"

"Yeah, yeah. Alright, talk to you later." I hung up, heading back up to the first floor.

"I'll be back soon!" I called to Layla, who was behind the cash register now.

Her eyes widened. "Ooh, is it finally Donut Day?"

"That's right!"

Okay, so maybe I was getting donuts because I've had three people whining at me for weeks about how we should have a donut day. But whatever.

"Oh my God, you're the best. Ooh, can you get a maple cream one? Oh no, wait. Can you get an Earl Grey one?"

"You'll get what you get, you hooligan," I said over my shoulder, and headed back out the door.

The donut place was just a few blocks down the street from Bizarre.

I loved Montreal. Like Fleurmont, the small town three hours away from Montreal I had grown up in, Montreal was walkable. But in Fleurmont, everyone knew your business. In Montreal, you could walk down every street, enjoy the sunshine and a coffee from Olimpico and not run into a former teacher or classmate every other block.

When I arrived at the donut place, it was already crowded. It was only ten in the morning, yet somehow, it was packed. I stood in line, debating how many donuts six people could eat. Yasmine and Ella weren't working today, but the donuts would still be good tomorrow. Dom probably would make an appearance this afternoon. He worked from his apartment, which was only a few blocks away in the other direction.

My phone buzzed, and I pulled it out of my dress pocket.

**Dom:** Please come out tonight. I wanna drink with youuu

**Me:** We drank together yesterday.

**Dom:** Lol, apéro doesn't count as drinking. And come on, it's been so long.

I sighed. The end of my engagement thirteen months ago meant I hadn't been the most fun friend over the last year, and my post-breakup strategy mostly involved staying at home moping and overworking. Overworking, I discovered, worked really well for me, so much so that it was hard to stop overworking.

"*Prochain*, next!" called the cashier.

I placed my order, opting for a dozen donuts of various flavours. I mean, okay, there were only six of us –seven, if you counted Dom– but I didn't want to be stingy after almost experiencing a mutiny. What kind of pushover of a manager would I be if I didn't –

"Arden?" a too-familiar voice said from behind me.

Speak. Of. The. Devil.

I would recognize that voice anywhere. For one wild second, I seriously contemplated whether I could somehow hide behind the donut box I was now holding and sprint out of there.

Reluctantly, I turned to look at the source of the voice.

He was exactly as I remembered him. Five foot eight, with short black hair –lightly gelled, of course. Signature navy blue polo shirt.

Jared. My ex-fiancé.

"Jared, hi!" I said too brightly, and then I saw that he wasn't alone. "Sharon, hi!"

"Hi, Arden," said Sharon awkwardly, glancing at Jared quickly and then shifting on the spot.

They were holding hands.

That would have been a shock to my system had I not been stalking them on social media over the last six months. Sometimes, stalking your ex was a good thing. Even if it meant confirming his relationship with a woman you always suspected he was into for most of your relationship. A woman who had been the source of an uncounted number of arguments. A woman you were not sure whether he cheated on you with.

"It's good to see you, Arden," said Jared, glancing at my massive box of donuts.

Oh God, I hoped he didn't think they were all for me.

"They're for work," I said.

"Oh, that's right. I forgot you worked in the area."

I felt a flicker of irritation at the blatant lie. I had worked in the exact same building every day for the past ten years –and we were together for four of those years.

"*Prochain*, next!" said the cashier again.

Sharon pointed to the cash register and gave me a small smile as she excused herself, and that's when I noticed what was on her hand. Her left hand. Fourth finger.

Jared registered that I had seen it.

"Oh, congrats on the engagement," I said, my mouth feeling dry, every muscle in my face working overtime to form what was hopefully a smile.

Pity and guilt flashed across his expression. I kind of wanted to slap him.

"Thanks," he mumbled, and then, "Arden –"

"I should really head back now," I said quickly, and to my horror, I felt the physical beginnings of tears forming in the twitch of my cheeks and the lump in my throat. "It was good to see you guys."

I made a rush out the door, except I turned too quickly, almost bumping into someone, and stumbled. Catching myself before I could fall completely, my sweaty fingers clamped around the donut box, and my face radiated heat. I tried to laugh it off as I continued to exit the shop, and then I was speed walking so fast down the street I was sure I could break records.

That did not just happen.

But it did. Okay, breathe, breathe. I sucked in air through my teeth and nose, my cheeks pulsing, forcing myself to keep my eyes open to watch where I was going.

I went through my mental checklist of how bad running into my ex-fiancé had gone.

The exit was bad. I get a negative one for my grace of exit.

Did I have a hot boyfriend with me while running into him? Not so much.

The hair situation... It was okay. My hair was in a ponytail. It was not my best look, but at least I showered this morning.

Makeup situation? My makeup was good.

Outfit situation? I was wearing a denim overall dress and a T-shirt. Cute, but not sexy.

It could have been worse. This whole thing could have been a lot worse. I mean, yes, did I want the next time I saw Jared to be when I had Victoria Secret model-level hair while wearing something ridiculously sexy that I would never actually wear to work, and have some hunky Brazilian stud on my arm? Sure, yes. I mean, I guess he didn't have to be Brazilian. But definitely super hunky.

But it could have been worse. Yes, it totally could have been worse. I could have fallen on my face and broken my nose. I could have been not wearing makeup at all and been wearing my at-home workout clothes. I could have been eating a jelly-stuffed donut and gotten it all over my shirt.

Oh my God, that was so fucking awkward. The way I ran out of there, Jared probably thought I still wasn't over him or something, which is so stupid because I *was* over him. I just really didn't do well with surprise encounters. But it's not like I can run back there and yell, "Just to clarify, I am over you! I just didn't expect to see you in my city, because Montreal is my safe haven."

Oh, God. Someone just kill me now.

I burst back into the store, my heart thumping like a hummingbird's.

"Donuts!" cried Maxime and Charlie in unison. They must have both arrived recently.

"Did you, like, sprint back here? Why is your face all red?" asked Layla.

"I'm fine, just excited about donuts." I handed the box over to Maxime, who set it down behind the counter.

"Ooh, yes, Earl Grey!"

"Save some for Yasmine and Ella, please." I took out my phone.

> **Me:** I changed my mind. I'm coming tonight.
> **Dom:** Yes! Okay, you are coming to my place before and we're going to get ready together.
> **Me:** Sounds like a plan.

I forced another smile at some customers who were looking at me curiously, probably wondering why I looked so crazy. I said to no one in particular, "I'm going to go downstairs and check my emails."

The basement was our informal staff area and our storage space.

"Arden, hold on!"

I turned around at the bottom of the staircase to see Layla holding out a squishy blue penis. It was a penis stress ball, a new product I'd come across at a crafts show. When I saw them, I knew I needed to have them at Bizarre.

Layla tossed me the penis stress ball. "We're almost completely sold out! This is our last one. Can you believe it?"

"What? No way. What about the boobs?" The stress balls also came in the form of different-shaped boobs.

"All sold out! There have been a lot of bachelor slash bachelorette parties."

"That's amazing. I'll order more," I smiled at her.

Layla flashed me a smile and headed back upstairs. She disappeared, and the door shut behind her. Instead of going to my laptop, I sank into the armchair we had in our kitchenette.

Jared and I had a messy breakup. We met in college. We were part of the same friend group, which included Sharon. Then, I dropped out of college, and we'd drifted apart. We didn't start dating until later. A few months after we got engaged, he'd gone on a trip with his friends and lied about running into Sharon and spending time with her. A few days later, he felt bad enough about the lie to confess it to me. He denied having cheated on me, but I just couldn't be sure. We broke up six months later. After our breakup, Jared had moved to Ottawa and gotten together with Sharon.

I let out an exhale, taking out my phone to text the first person who always came to mind for me when weird relationship stuff came up.

> **Me:** I just ran into Jared.
> **Connor:** Holy shit, where?
> **Me:** At a donut shop.
> **Connor:** He's in Montreal?
> **Me:** Yes, and he came with Sharon.
> **Connor:** No way. Fuck that guy.
> **Me:** They're engaged.
> **Connor:** What the fuck? Haven't they only been together for like eight months?

Connor was my childhood friend, and we had grown up together in Fleurmont. While I loved my friends here, I knew they were sick of me talking about Jared. They had been around in the months when our relationship was falling apart, and I didn't want to continue to burden them with it over a year later. Connor, on the other hand, was infinitely patient, especially over text. He was back in Fleurmont designing a luxury resort, and I was half-tempted to drive back up to Fleurmont on my day off just so I could complain to him in person.

Except that would mean having to see Mom, and I didn't want to see Mom right now.

I groaned out loud, grabbing the penis stress ball and squeezing both balls as hard as I could.

I needed to get hammered tonight.

# Connect with Cat Morgan

**Website:** catmorgan.ca
**Instagram:** instagram.com/authorcatmorgan
**TikTok:** tiktok.com/@authorcatmorgan